Aftermath

The Unforeseen Series Book Two

Keith McArdle

National Library of Australia Cataloguing-in-Publication data:

McArdle, Keith, 1978- author.
  Aftermath / Keith McArdle ; Terri King Editing Service ; Cohesion Editing.
  Unforeseen duology ; v. 2.
  978 0 9925657 3 2 (pbk.)
  1. Alternative histories (Fiction). 2. Australian. 3. War stories, Australian. 4. Australia--Invasions--Fiction.
A823.3

Cover design by Christian Bentulan, Covers by Christian
Printed and bound in Australia by IngramSpark on 50lb white paper

Connect with Keith online:

Facebook: https://www.facebook.com/KeithAuthor
Twitter: https://twitter.com/KeithAuthor
Website: http://www.keithmcardle.com

ACKNOWLEDGMENTS

To my wife, Simone, thanks for your tireless support, no matter the circumstances (and giving me a kick in the pants when I needed it). You are my rock.

Mal you old bugger, without your ceaseless nagging, smart arse comments and an abrupt deadline for which to aim, *Aftermath* would have taken far longer to produce. You'll probably never know how much you helped motivate me.

Stewart Mundell for teaching me how to speak (and write) bootneck style.

To my editors Geoff Brown from Cohesion Author Services and Terri King from Terri King Editing Service, thanks for being thorough and giving me some tough love. If writing has taught me one thing, it's thick skin is imperative!

To the men and women who are serving or have served as a member of the Australian Defence Force, thanks for ensuring we remain a free country. You are too often overlooked or forgotten.

Chapter 1

"Reports suggest 40 Commando supported by the Royal Navy have driven Indonesian invaders away from the coast in Queensland. The war in Australia is all but won." – *Yorkshire Post (UK)*

The half-rotten corpse that had once been an Indonesian soldier lay prone, riddled with maggots. SGT Craig Linacre knelt slowly beside the stinking mess, rifle cradled across his chest. The large exit wound at the back of its skull showed the fatal wound. Craig could see what was left of the decomposing brain beyond. But what interested him more was the soldier's webbing. The pouches appeared full and might hold valuable information. Wary of booby-traps, Craig tied a rope to its belt buckle and moved back, feeding the rope out as he went.

Taking cover behind a nearby boulder, the special-forces soldier looked across at Matty in the near distance and nodded. CPL Matty Nasution gave thumbs up, before returning his attention down the barrel of his weapon, giving cover. Taking a breath, Craig pulled hard on the rope. He felt the weight at the other end shift and knew the corpse had rolled over. Good, no booby-traps so far. Bringing the rifle into his shoulder, Craig was stepping out from behind the boulder when the corpse exploded. He was thrown to the ground, winded. In a few seconds he climbed back to his feet, dazed, yet instinctively scuttling behind the boulder. The charge had obviously been rigged with some kind of delayed detonator.

Shaking the fogginess from his brain, Craig peered around the boulder and saw a pair of half rotten legs – from the knees down – lying beside a crater. Nothing else remained of the corpse. Gaining Matty's attention, he signalled they were moving out. The explosion would have been heard from kilometres around, and if there were any Indonesian soldiers still in the area, they would be moving towards the explosion.

As the pair of SAS soldiers slowly made their way through the brown, dry, waist-high grass, several dull thumps could be heard in the distance. The men paused, taking a knee to listen.

Silence.

Soft wind teased the surface of the grass for acres in every direction. Then a high-pitched shriek, growing in volume, shattered the peaceful deathly quiet.

"Cover!" roared Craig, diving to the ground as artillery rounds exploded nearby.

An Indonesian artillery battery had zeroed its guns in on the corpse, waiting for the booby trap to be triggered. If they fired fast enough, they'd be able to take out an entire platoon. Maybe more.

Pushing himself into a crouch, Craig was deafened by a ringing screech in his ears. He looked across at Matty, who was shouting something. No sound reached Craig.

"Go!" Matty's lips formed the word. "Go!"

As the ringing in his ears began to dissipate, he heard more thumps in the distance.

"Go!" he heard Matty screaming loud and clear. "Go!"

Sprinting through the grass, the pair heard a familiar high-pitched shriek as artillery rounds streaked down onto their position. The rounds slammed into the ground exploding between the two men with devastating effect.

* * * * *

Pain wracked Craig's body. It felt like he'd been in a cage fight. Groaning, he pushed himself off the ground, spitting dirt from his mouth as he moved into a crouch. Patting down his arms and legs, he checked for injury, but nothing seemed broken or bleeding. Spotting his M-4 nearby, he reached for it, checked it over before cradling it across his chest.

Matty lay prone nearby, motionless. With a grunt, Craig moved to him, squatted beside him and checked for a carotid pulse. With relief he felt a strong pulse and patted Matty's cheek.

"Hey mate," Craig muttered. Patting the skin of Matty's face Craig spoke again. "Oi! Matty, time to move mate."

There was no response.

"For fuck sake," Craig said, knowing time was of the essence. He was strong enough to drag Matty perhaps five hundred metres before being forced to rest and find concealment. That distance was not enough to clear the current area which would more than likely be crawling with Indonesian soldiers within the next hour.

Craig slapped Matty's face hard. "Oi, dickhead!"

This time there was a groan and slight movement in one leg.

Unceremoniously rolling Matty over, Craig slapped him again. "Wakey wakey," Craig said, casting a glance over Matty's body checking for obvious injury or haemorrhage.

More dull thumps reverberated in the distance.

"You're fuck'n joking!" snarled Craig.

Picking up Matty's weapon, he tucked the rifle into the unconscious man's chest webbing. Grabbing Matty under the arms, he dragged him as far as possible before the distant shriek indicated artillery rounds were inbound. Dumping Matty, Craig dived to ground, buried his face into the dirt and hoped for the best. The barrage fell slightly short of their position, exploding on and around where the Indonesian corpse had been.

When the last shell exploded, Craig slowly climbed to his feet, body still aching. Keeping as low a profile as possible, he dragged Matty away from the area. Three more artillery barrages hit, some close, others not so much, showing the enemy gunners were making small elevation changes to ensure maximum coverage. By the time night began to fall, Craig, now exhausted, had dragged Matty close to a kilometre out of the area and had found a small depression in the ground where he had chosen to lay low for the night.

Setting up a Claymore anti-personnel mine facing towards the most likely enemy approach, he kept the clacker, the device used to detonate the explosive, tied to his right hand. Inadvertent detonation was near impossible, as the clacker had a safety catch of sorts. The safety catch was easy enough to disengage with a single hand, meaning the mine could be fired within two seconds. Filled with seven hundred steel ball bearings embedded in composition explosive, the weapon was designed to injure and maim rather than kill. One wounded man required two others to carry him, effectively taking three soldiers out of the fight.

Should enemy stumble upon their position, seven hundred ball bearings would whistle through their ranks at knee height, before Craig opened fire. If the Indonesians did find his position, more than likely, Craig would be overrun and killed along with the unconscious

Matty. But at least it would be a bittersweet victory for the Indonesians.

Eventually the artillery fire stopped. Before long, the sun slid below the horizon and dusk arrived, the light beginning to fade. Craig checked Matty every five minutes. He felt for a pulse, listened for breath sounds and while light remained, continued checking for any obvious sign of blood seeping through his clothes. He placed Matty in a lateral position so that if he vomited, at least it wouldn't compromise his airway.

He slung Matty's weapon across his back and shoved the unconscious man's spare ammunition into his own half full pouches, so that if a fire fight started, at least he'd have plenty of ammunition. Craig was conscious of the fact that he and Matty had been inserted on the understanding that they were to patrol out of the area themselves. No friendlies were looking for them. The Australian Blackhawks were no longer operational. They had been decimated within the opening weeks of the invasion. The Royal Marine choppers that had inserted the SASR patrol would be busy on other taskings, infilling, exfilling, resupplying or providing air support for Royal Marine Commandos or Special Boat Service (SBS) soldiers on the ground.

Craig found the first few hours easy to remain alert. The majority of the time, he stared through the night vision goggles, ever watchful for enemy movement. Every fifteen minutes he pushed the goggles up, away from his eyes, allowing a minute or two for his vision to rest, before lowering them back into place. Apart from the chirping crickets, the night was silent. A far cry from what Craig expected. No Indonesian soldiers had arrived to investigate.

Slowly crawling to the opposite side of the small depression, Craig watched. Every hour he changed position, moving between the four compass points around the circular depression in the ground. It was past midnight when he began rubber necking, exhaustion attempting to claim him. He had not experienced a decent night's sleep in more than three weeks. Craig lost the fight, cheek resting on his weapon, breathing softly as sleep embraced him. He did not hear the vehicles approach. Did not see the headlights in the near distance. It was the slamming of the car doors that broke Craig's slumber. He was immediately alert, adrenalin responsible for his fast response. He pushed the night vision goggles up and away from his eyes, instead using the night vision capability of his weapon mounted scope. He watched the Indonesian soldiers exiting a number of four wheel drives to swarm the area where the booby trapped corpse had been lying earlier in the day. No problem, he was close to one kilometre away, and at night it would be near impossible for them to track him.

His heart sank a second later when he heard dogs. A series of aggressive barks broke the still night. *German Shepherd,* he thought. *A goddamn military dog.*

"Fuck," he muttered to himself.

He hoped his track had gone cold by now and the dog was incapable of finding his scent, but anything was possible. Flicking the night vision goggles away from his eyes, Craig stared down the infrared scope of his weapon and settled the target reticule over the dog's body.

For close to ten minutes, he watched the animal seeking his scent without success. Happy that the dog was no longer a threat, Craig slowly swept the weapon's infrared scope across the gathering of Indonesian soldiers. They were all armed with military grade automatic weapons; most with their native SS1, which was the standard assault rifle of the Indonesian Army. Some, however, held the Steyr, used by the Australian Army. No doubt taken from dead Australian soldiers. A wave of anger warmed Craig. He counted the vehicles, seven in total, all four wheel drives, one of them a Land Rover. Thirty enemy soldiers in total, and one clueless dog. Craig smiled, allowing the target reticule to settle over the animal once more. It was not particularly well-trained. Over such a short distance, and regardless of the hours which had passed, any tracking dog worth its salt would have found his scent, faint as it may have been, and worked towards him .

The scent of a human was given by dead skin cells drifting from the body, and a good scent trail in perfect conditions with little wind, rain or snow, could remain in place for more than a week. If tracked by dogs, the most secure place was on high ground, particularly on the peak of a mountain, where the wind was more likely to change directions easily, move in obscure patterns and scatter a person's scent in random, un-trackable arrangements.

Craig had no such luxury. If the animal were testament to any true formal training, it would have made a bee-line straight to him.

Thankfully, although it had obviously been given some informal instruction, the German Shepherd still had a long way to go before it would join the ranks of the true tracking dogs.

Sweeping the infrared scope across the Indonesians once more, Craig settled the target reticule over the chest of a man wearing a bandana and holding an SS1 across his chest, with a pistol holstered on his hip. He was the only man with a pistol, and was also the only soldier talking and gesticulating angrily at the others gathered around him in a half moon. The leader; the leader of any group of soldiers, whether it be a corporal or a general, was always discouraged from advertising their status, particularly out-bush, as they would always become the first target of a sniper team or a deliberate ambush.

There was a loud groan beside Craig and Matty rolled over.

"Fuck me dead," Matty said, holding his head.

Craig shot a glance at the soldier, "Welcome back, now shut the fuck up," he hissed.

Matty crawled up beside Craig. "What's goin' on?" he asked, still nursing his head.

Craig did not answer, instead returning his attention to the night vision scope attached to the top of his weapon. Staring down the scope he saw that the Indonesians, to a man, were all staring in his direction. The dog was barking and carrying on like it had rabies. Then a torch was turned on, and several enemy soldiers began walking towards them.

"Shit," whispered Craig. "It's on, mate."

It was at that point he realised Matty had slid down onto his back, holding his head and groaning.

"You right, mate?" Craig whispered, tapping Matty's shoulder.

"Yeah," he managed between groans. "Gotta killer headache."

Returning his attention to the weapon's night vision scope, Craig saw that the enemy had halted whilst the dog handler took a knee, wrestled with the barking animal for a moment and then released it from the leash.

The German Shepherd now had no need of scent trails. The dog was intelligent enough to marry up the sound of Matty's voice with the scent trail it was unable to find so recently. It zeroed in on the Australians' position, sprinting towards them.

Ignoring Matty as he rolled around groaning and muttering meaningless phrases, Craig settled the weapon's target reticule upon the dog's chest. The sooner he killed the animal, the greater the area the Indonesians would have to search in order to find the Australians. He knew from previous reconnaissance that none of the enemy were using night vision goggles, and if they had them, were probably now out of usable batteries.

Lying silent, continuing to ignore Matty, Craig waited and watched as the German Shepherd sprinted towards them. He willed the animal to veer away, to become confused and return to its master. He tried to avoid killing dogs where possible. But the animal made a bee-line straight towards him. Tongue lolling from the side of its mouth, the animal began barking in a staccato of noise, which was Craig's cue to fire the shot. There was no squeal or howl of pain. The dog simply dropped to the ground like a used doll. The dog's barking had hidden Craig's silenced weapon, and with the animal now dead, the Indonesians still had no idea exactly where their enemy lay.

Craig had no idea what the Indonesians were shouting, and thought better of asking Matty, who was now lying prone, still holding his head and snoring softly. Something was wrong, Craig knew instinctively. He had worked with Matty through operations in Kosovo, East Timor, The Sudan, Iraq and Afghanistan. Never had he seen him act like this.

The Indonesians retreated to the vehicle as more orders were shouted. A mortar tube and base plate were unloaded from the rear tray of the vehicle and setup within a matter of minutes. Then a mortar round was fired with a dull thunk, heading almost vertical. A loud pop was followed by daylight in a square kilometre area as the illumination round activated. Craig pushed his head closer to the ground and clenched his right eye firmly closed. If the night vision from his master eye was destroyed, he would be unable to use the night vision scope attached to his weapon.

"Happy new year!" roared Matty, now lying on his back, arms splayed out beside him. "What a light show! Give me a beer ya jack prick!"

Craig dived on top of him and pushed his hand over Matty's mouth.

"Shut the fuck up!" snarled Craig. "You wanna get us bloody killed?"

Matty muttered something, but the noise was rendered into a slurred mash of sound beneath the palm of Craig's hand.

Within minutes, Matty had rolled onto his side and deteriorated back into sleep, snoring softly. Craig knew something was very wrong. Ensuring the Indonesians were still confused as to their exact location, Craig took the time to send a text burst transmission via the PRC-112, a radio slightly larger than the size of a man's hand, requesting an immediate medical evac and air support. Almost three minutes passed before a secure text appeared on the radio's LCD display:

"Exfil your loc 5 mikes."

Five minutes until exfiltration. Craig silently berated himself for not requesting exfil hours before. However, in his defence, he had been told the British choppers were flying to the limit in support of Royal Marines and SBS troops on the ground in the area. Any requests, he had been instructed, would either be refused flatly or could take up to two hours to fulfil.

Five minutes to exfil. It did not sound long, but in current circumstances it would feel like an eternity. Craig still clamped his master eye shut against the bright illumination round fired by the mortar. He remained silent and still, praying that Matty continued to sleep. Now with the dog neutralised, apart from the faint splutter of the flare as it drifted towards earth, there was silence. One sound, one word uttered too loud would alert the Indonesians to their whereabouts.

He could hear them muttering amongst themselves. Peering through the blades of grass into which he had buried his face, Craig saw the Indonesians looking in all directions, still oblivious to his whereabouts. The dog handler was distraught, he noticed, feeling sorry for the soldier. Craig loved dogs, and hated killing them. Tonight had been the second time in his career he was forced to kill a dog in order to protect his patrol. The illumination round slowly faded out, the dark night once again closing in around them.

Matty was now lying supine, breathing loudly. Craig moved to him.

"Wake up, mate." He patted the man's face. "Matty, wake the fuck up!"

"You got that beer bro?" asked Matty, his speech slurred.

"No, mate, no beer," whispered Craig. "We're in the shit, we've been compromised. Air support and exfil are inbound. They're a few minutes out. How you feeling?"

"Exfil?" Matty roared with laughter." What the fuck? What, are we playing Call of Duty? Wanker!" He laughed again. "Bring me a bloody beer!" he shouted.

The Indonesians were hissing amongst themselves and looking in Craig's direction. He left Matty giggling and muttering to himself on the far side of the depression. Lying prone and staring down the night vision scope attached to his weapon, Craig watched the enemy soldiers push out into extended line and advance toward his position. In the background, he saw the mortar team, consisting of two soldiers, preparing another round, more than likely a second illumination round. Now they knew the general direction in which the Australians were hidden, a second illumination round would kill all hope for Craig and Matty. They would be found and overrun in less than a minute.

Two dull thumps from Craig's silenced weapon and the two man mortar team were no more. The Indonesians, apart from three, went to ground and returned fire. Bullets hissed and cracked less than a metre above Craig's head. Ignoring the return fire, he settled the target reticule over the chest of the first of the three men still standing, firing un-aimed shots from the hip. Squeezing the trigger, Craig watched the man fall from sight. With the number of organs and vital arteries in the chest and upper abdomen, one bullet in or around the chest area could do so much damage. The second man dropped as fast as the first. The third soldier dived to the ground before Craig took a sight picture, although he released several shots into the long grass where he thought the soldier had landed.

Rounds slashed through thigh-length grass metres from Craig, or snapped above their position. He remained prone, holding his fire, allowing the enemy to deplete their ammunition. One Indonesian stood and ran forward. Reacting in less than a second, Craig took a sight picture and fired, the bullet passing through the man's intestines and exited his back in a bloody swath. He fell to the ground howling in agony.

Feeling the PRC-112 buzz in his trouser pocket, Craig pulled the device out and read the infrared screen.

The AC-130, or affectionately known as the Spectre gunship, was a heavily modified C-130 Hercules, a heavy-lift aircraft operated by the United States Air Force. Along the left side of the aircraft were two 20mm cannons, one 40mm cannon and one 105mm Howitzer artillery gun. The pilot wanted Craig's position marked so that his crew would not inadvertently fire upon him.

Opening a pouch and keeping his head down as enemy fire continued to rip through the air metres above him, Craig pulled out an infrared strobe, activated it and tied it to the back of his webbing. Thus, lying prone, the strobe would be facing skyward, flashing an infrared pulse twice per second.

A moment later, the infrared LCD of the PRC-112 displayed the pilot's response, which consisted of two words. Two words which brought relief to any patrol in the middle of nowhere, outnumbered and in the shit:

Although the enemy fire was loud, Craig still heard the soft rumble of the Spectre gunship high above him. The pilot would begin a left pylon turn, bringing all the aircraft's guns to bear upon the Indonesian position.

Trace seemed to streak out of thin air 5,000ft above him, followed closely by the roar of the 40mm cannon, sounding like the deep howl of some enraged dinosaur. The rounds hammered into the Indonesians. Craig felt the thump of massive bullets smashing into the ground.

"What a bloody light show!" Matty roared with laughter, splayed out on his back again, watching another long stream of trace rounds pouring from the AC-130 towards the enemy position below.

The Indonesian fire had mostly stopped, although some must still have been alive as the Spectre gunship continued its destruction. A bright flash from the sky destroyed Craig's night vision. The boom of the 105mm gun followed a second later but was quickly overshadowed by the ever increasing screech as the artillery round descended towards earth, on target for the enemy position. Exploding with deadly efficiency, chunks of earth rained down around the Australians.

Apart from the distant hum of the AC-130 high above them, the area was silent. Craig ensured the infrared strobe was still securely fastened to his back before crawling forward. Staring through his weapon's night vision scope, all he saw was the empty enemy vehicles parked several hundred metres away. Knowing that their engines would now be cool, he was not sure the gun crew of the AC-130 would be able to see the four wheel drives.

Attached to the barrel of Craig's weapon was a small rectangular infrared laser pointer. The device was used for indicating an enemy position to close air support assets that may have overlooked a particular area.

Lying still, he lased the middle vehicle and waited. Close to ten seconds later, the mighty 40mm gun spoke again, explosive rounds hammering through the vehicle and turning it into a piece of scrap metal. Flicking the laser off, Craig allowed his night vision to recover. Minutes later, he stared down the scope. Two vehicles were destroyed completely; the remaining pair seemed relatively unscathed. Lasing the furthest vehicle, Craig waited half as long before the 40mm opened up again, rounds slamming through the remaining vehicles with violent ferocity, rendering them useless.

Matty was breathing noisily, although not quite snoring. It sounded more like his tongue had relaxed back in his throat. Craig moved to him and rolled him onto his side, which seemed to help. Something was wrong and the more time passed, the greater confidence he felt calling for a medivac was the correct decision. Craig crawled back to the rim of the depression in the ground and stared down the night vision scope towards the former enemy position. Nothing moved. The vehicles were decimated; one of them was alight, the hiss and pop of melting paint, upholstery and rubber echoed gently out over the silent plain.

His concentration was so deep that Craig barely heard the helicopter approach until it was slowing and descending less than twenty metres from his position. Even before the chopper touched the ground, a medic and two soldiers were running towards him carrying a stretcher between them. Noise, time and situation precluded any thorough questioning as to the events which had occurred. Matty was simply lifted onto the stretcher, the medic tapped Craig's shoulder and then they were running back towards the helicopter.

"Fuck me!" shouted Craig as he climbed aboard, the scream of the chopper's engine deafening him.

A headset was pushed into his hand. Taking off his combat helmet, he promptly placed the headset over his ears, inhaling a breath of relief as the noise was dampened. With the helicopter on strict blackout, Craig used his weapon's night vision scope to look for, find and ensure that Matty too was wearing a headset. He was. Unconscious or not, the last thing he needed was permanent hearing damage. The stretcher was strapped to the floor of the helicopter with Matty buckled to the stretcher.

Noticing a cord attached to the headset, Craig followed it with his fingers until he found a communication plug. All he needed to find was the comms jack into which to plug it. A firm hand grasped his shoulder, probably one of the loadmasters, who had night vision goggles attached to their helmets. The load master grabbed the jack out of Craig's hand and following a half second burst of high pitched sound, he was listening to the crew's conversation.

"—I hear you, just not sure," said the American voice. "That dude got comms yet?"

"Roger that," said another voice. "Hey pal," said the same voice. A hand tapped Craig's shoulder. "Pal, you gonna need to fold the boom mic down in front of your mouth. "

Craig found the mic and pulled it down to his lips. Following the comms cord with one hand, he found the small box. Pressing the transmit button, Craig said, "Thanks for the exfil."

"You're welcome, guy," the broad American voice said, which was probably the aircraft captain. "I'm in contact with the Spectre. They've spotted an artillery battery off to the west. That one of yours?"

"No, mate, not ours," replied Craig. "They're the fuckers responsible for this whole mess!"

"Roger," said the pilot.

Feeling the seat straps dig into his shoulders and belly, the chopper banked hard away from the exfiltration area. In the far distance, Craig saw the faint, flickering outline of the AC-130 Spectre gunship as every gun on board opened fire upon the Indonesian artillery battery below. The Indonesians had no chance of survival. They had nowhere to run and nowhere to hide. He almost felt sorry for them. Almost.

"How's Matty doin'?" he asked.

"Is that his name, hun?" it was a woman's voice.

"Yeah."

"Matty's not in a good way," she sounded distracted or busy and probably was, he realised.

"Okay," Craig replied, trying to sound calm. "Will he be alright?"

There was no reply. Craig felt anger and fear welling in his chest, although he remained silent. The chopper descended violently and turned hard to the left, before levelling out. Craig brought his weapon to bear and looked through the night vision scope to see treetops whipping by close beneath them.

Christ, don't hit a power line, he thought.

"Will he be alright or not?" Craig asked.

"Look hun, I don't know. He's got a dilated right pupil and weak grips on his left hand. He has diminished consciousness. I'm suspecting he's haemorrhaging on the right side of his brain. He'll need a CT scan and possibly burr holes drilled into his skull. I won't lie to you. He can survive this, but it's gonna be a close call."

Craig didn't say anything. He knew it had the potential of being serious, but he now realised the situation was critical. He might lose a brother tonight. He felt numb, unaware of the seat belts digging into his body as the chopper turned. He was oblivious to the door gunners calling out fast approaching structures, trees or power lines over the intercom and was clueless as those same obstacles whipped by only metres beneath them. Everything seemed to be a blur.

The dull impact as the chopper touched down upon the deck of USS *Ronald Reagan* brought Craig out of his reverie. To the east, the sky glowed a faint gunmetal grey, silhouetting the mighty aircraft carrier. Before the pilot began the shutdown procedure, the medics had carried Matty's stretcher clear of the aircraft and were running. Unstrapping, Craig unplugged his headset, pushed himself clear of the chopper and sprinted after them. One of the door gunners tried to stop him, but he broke free of the grip.

Chapter 2

"USS Ronald Reagan continues to unleash merciless air raids upon enemy positions. Indonesian Army decimated!" – *The New York Times (US)*

Soft hues of pink crept upon the eastern sky. Dawn was not far away and a murder of crows seemed to agree as they cackled and called in the distance. Mick yawned softly, sat up and stretched. He felt more rested than he had in a long time. Yawning again, he threw the sheet from the bed and stood, wooden floor boards creaking gently under his weight.

Dressing, he padded quietly into the living room and out onto the veranda, where he could watch the sun rise. He loved this time of day. Utter and complete peace. Leaning his forearms on the rail of the veranda, he became lost in thought as the recent past whirled through his mind. When their group left the homestead after it came under Indonesian attack, Mick had been afraid the enemy would burn his home to the ground. Luckily, they had not, instead using it as their own base.

His home was completely off the electricity grid, the home appliances relying upon solar-fed battery supply. Although more than half the meat from his freezer had been consumed by the Indonesians during their stay, they had left the home relatively clean. However, one of the bastards had decided taking a shit on the living room carpet seemed to be a good idea.

"Filthy little bastard," muttered Mick, remembering the hours it had taken him to clean the stain, not to mention the smell, from the carpet. Ben thought it was highly amusing. Mick smiled at the memory. He knew the young man was good for his daughter. He was bright, willing to learn, and not afraid to fight or even to kill to protect those he loved. Unfortunately, that had been necessary during the months prior.

With Australia under successful Indonesian occupation and the Australian Defence Force disintegrated as a cohesive force, normal Australians were left to submit, hide, die or fight to survive. Often submission and death went hand in hand. One could only hide for so long, so the only real, long term option had been to fight, and yes, kill.

Mick knew if it were between them and his family, it would be them every time, unless he was killed himself, of course. Watching a lizard scuttle between the dry leaf litter, he shook the thoughts free of his mind and tried to enjoy the sunrise. Blazes of orange streaked across the sky, heralding the imminent arrival of the sun.

Taking a deep breath, he could taste the cool, fresh air. Enjoying the silence, he relaxed, watching a flock of geese high above, gliding across the sky in a 'V' formation, occasionally honking to one another. Craning his neck, he watched them fly into the distance, eventually disappearing behind a mighty eucalyptus towering on the eastern side of the farm.

Kookaburras laughed in the distance, a flock of cockatoos squawked and bickered amongst themselves as they landed in the many branches of the eucalypt. One by one, the crickets that had kept their constant, perfect chorus throughout the night faded into silence as the sun broke the horizon.

It was strange how peaceful early morning could be. With only the most fanatical Indonesian soldiers left on Australian soil one could be excused for forgetting there were still starving Australians out there, recently liberated from death camps and slowly, patiently, being weaned back onto nutritious food. Impossible to imagine, as the silent, golden orb rose in the east, that somewhere, as Mick relaxed, there was a fearsome firefight raging as another pocket of staunch Indonesian soldiers were discovered in the Australian forests.

* * * * *

"Get that fuck'n gun up!" roared CPL Lee Flahavin, the section commander. Most of his soldiers referred to him as Flaps.

"Stoppage!" shrieked the gunner, panic beginning to envelope him.

"I don't give a fuck'n monkeys!" screamed Flaps, "get the gun up! That's not a fuck'n invitation, get the gun going now, you twat. Now!"

The Minimi, a 5.56mm light machine gun, had fallen silent, and the gunner was struggling to rectify a stoppage, probably a damaged or dirty bullet caught in the working parts.

Without suppressive fire from the light machine gun, their assault would bog down, and the Indonesians may well gain the initiative.

Pulling the assault rifle tight into his shoulder, Finn fired several shots at an enemy sprinting towards him in the near distance. The man dropped from sight and Finn was not sure whether he hit him or not.

The loud, incessant report of gunfire echoed across the Australian bush. Already one Marine was dead and three more were wounded; one critically. The Close Combat Section of 40 Royal Marine Commando was committed to the fight. Without air support and no indication of resupply, they needed to win the battle. Failure meant death, and death was not an option. Not for the Marines, anyway.

The gun remained silent as the Marine struggled with the weapon. Finally, a nearby soldier ripped the weapon off him and cleared the stoppage. Re-cocking the working parts, he pulled the machinegun into his shoulder, prepared to fire and died as a bullet shattered his skull, splattering grey matter upon the leaf litter around him.

Barely fifty metres from the Royal Marines' axis of advance, the Indonesians charged, bayonets fixed, in a mad dash, screaming curses in their foreign language.

Time stood still for Royal Marine Finn Cutajar. He breathed calmly, and relaxed, as he had been taught on the almost impossible thirty-two week Royal Marine Commando training course.

"Compose yourself!" his recruit instructor had told him, dragging him clear, spluttering and coughing, from the fifty metre muddy, water-filled pipe he had swum down as part of the five-kilometre bayonet assault course; lungs burning, aching to inhale. Finn had calmed his breathing, enjoying the fresh air.

"Good lad," said the instructor, grabbing a fistful of his shirt and pushing him onward, "get going!"

With his instructor's words echoing in his memory, Finn relaxed, firing shot after shot, well-aimed bullets leaving a host of enemy corpses falling to the forest floor before him. But it was not enough. It was nowhere near enough.

Outnumbered almost ten to one, the Close Combat Section of 40 Royal Marine Commando was overrun and destroyed.

*****

"I want bacon and eggs for breaky, Grandad!" Jade appeared from her bedroom, rubbing sleep from her eyes.

Mick smiled and looked back out towards the quiet forest held captive by the dawn's gentle light.

"I want never gets," he replied.

"Sorry," said Jade, standing beside him now and tugging on his shirt. "Can I have bacon and eggs for breakfast, *please*?" She grinned up at him.

"You had that yesterday, sweetheart," Mick said.

"I know," she looked down at the deck beneath her feet, then back up at him. "But I *really* like bacon and eggs!"

Mick winced as he knelt before his granddaughter, taking her shoulders in his hands. "Look," he said. "I'll make you a deal, ok?"

Jade's eyes widened in excitement and she nodded emphatically.

"How 'bout we have cornflakes today, and tomorrow I'll cook you bacon and eggs?"

The excitement left the girl's eyes and she nodded in resignation. "Ok," she said, looking at her feet.

Mick ruffled her hair. "It's not the end of the world sweetheart."

"I guess," Jade mumbled, straightening her hair before looking up at Mick. "We could be getting shot at, couldn't we, granddad?"

The old man burst out laughing. "Yes!" he agreed. "It could always be worse."

"Where's that little munchkin?" a voice said. "I can hear her!"

"Ben!" Shrieked Jade, sprinting inside and into Ben's arms.

The young man lifted her and held her close.

"Did you sleep well?" Ben asked, kissing her cheek.

Jade nodded. "I did, I dreamed of Craig and Matty, they were both running away from a group of nasty men."

"Oh?" Ben said, putting Jade back down. "Did they get caught?"

"Nope!" She shook her head, locks of hair flying around either side of her face. "They hid in a big tree and then ran the other way. The nasty men had no idea!"

"Wow! Craig and Matty did well, didn't they?"

"Yup!" said Jade, folding her arms as if to prove the point.

"Morning," said Katie, her voice still husky from recent sleep.

"Mummy!" Jade flew into her mother's arms.

Katie smiled and drew her daughter close, kissing her hair and rubbing her back.

"Bacon and eggs it is!" shouted Mick from the kitchen.

"Yes!" exclaimed Jade, squirming free of Katie's grip and running into the kitchen.

"We're all out of milk, sweetheart," said Mick. "I forgot about that."

Mick would have to use canned sweetened condensed milk for the coffees. With Australia still struggling to climb back to her feet, none of the supermarkets had re-opened. In the city, fresh food was scarce. The United Nations, now agreeing to help in the aftermath of the invasion, were flying in water, shelters and pre-packed rations to help feed, water and shelter millions of displaced Australians.

It would take the better part of three months for the Australian farmers to make a start on producing food once again, and at least nine months before fresh produce was beginning to become available on store shelves.

"It could always be worse," said Mick quietly, stooping down to pull the frying pan out of a kitchen cupboard.

* * * * *

The cold, powerful fingers of fear gripped Finn. He was pinned to the ground by the dead body of another Royal Marine. It seemed to be Orms, the gunner, but in the fading light he couldn't be sure. The Indonesian soldiers were all around him, walking haphazardly, kicking away weapons, or stooping to raid the pouches of dead Marines. It was easier, not to mention safer, to hide beneath Orms' body.

Finn closed his eyes, remained still and hoped the enemy would soon depart. But they did not. Long after the sun sank and night fell, the Indonesians were still chattering in their native tongue all around him, occasionally laughing at some shared jest. A group of them sat in a circle nearby, cooking up some foul smelling scran over a small butane stove.

Finn held his breath as he felt the body of above him move. An Indonesian soldier was stooped over him, going through the Marine's pouches and pockets. Pulling out a lighter, he tested it, the bright orange flame illuminating the enemy's face. Finn immediately clamped his eyes shut to protect his night vision. When he heard the soft click to indicate the enemy had extinguished the flame, he opened them again.

With a few more tugs and pulls, Orms' corpse finally settled back on top of Finn. As he breathed out a silent sigh of relief, Orms' body was rolled off him and dragged away. Seconds later rough hands grabbed Finn. He held his breath, closed his eyes and fighting his brain, which was pumping adrenaline through his body and convincing him to resist, relaxed his muscles, letting himself go limp. His rifle, ripped from his hands, was thrown away, landing with a clatter nearby.

Remaining relaxed as the enemy soldier went through his webbing, Finn tried to stay calm. Eventually, minus his water bottles and what little food he had stored in his webbing, Finn was left alone and the Indonesian walked away, grunting something in his native language to another soldier standing close by.

Trying to remain still as possible, Finn slowly looked over and spotted his weapon, an SA-80, the standard assault rifle of the British military. It was lying metres from him, but outside his reach. He knew he had to stay silent and still. Even if he could reach the weapon, he was ridiculously outnumbered and would be killed in seconds if they found him.

Staring up through the canopy of the forest at the stars beyond, Finn recalled the firefight. The Royal Marine Commandos were notoriously fierce warriors, a fact known to foreign military as much as it was to the UK defence force. No matter how often he played the fight over in his mind, he knew that his section could never have prevailed. Outnumbered an estimated ten to one, it was only a matter of time before pure numbers whittled down the Royal Marine Commandos. At least Finn held no doubt he and his section had punched far in excess of their weight, killing perhaps five or six enemy per man.

As the faint, sickly, sweet scent of death began to settle upon the immediate vicinity, Finn remained silent and still, surrounded by dead comrades and chatting, laughing enemy soldiers. He would be lucky to see dawn.

* * * * *

With breakfast finished, Mick and Ben walked out to the shed. Many of Mick's cattle had been killed by the Indonesians for food. Some had escaped through damaged fences. Others had died as a result of poorly aimed, non-lethal bullet wounds fired from Indonesian weapons. These particular beasts were able to flee the area. But over time their wounds had become infected, causing them to eventually die in agony, some with starving calves standing nearby.

Today, Mick and Ben were responsible for rounding up what was left of Mick's herd and mustering them into the paddock closest to the house. One would be killed and slaughtered for meat, but the others would be fed and protected. If Australia was to rebuild, then Mick would need something to work with in order to restore the industry he once owned. That, in itself, would take several years.

"So you've ridden a quad bike before?" Mick asked, pulling open the large roller door.

"As a kid I did."

"Yeah, right, well this ain't no 50cc toy, it's a 600cc work horse, so treat her with a bit of respect, or she'll kill ya," Mick said, walking over to the motorbike and patting the seat.

"Well, you ride it then mate, I'll take the horse," said Ben, shrugging.

Mick laughed. "No, you're safer on the quad, Ben, trust me. The quad doesn't have a brain." Mick gestured towards the distant mare, grazing in a large paddock nearby. "That bitch does, and she'll buck you off sooner than you can open a coldie."

"Right, I'll take the quad then," smiled Ben.

Mick spent quarter of an hour explaining to Ben how to start the four-wheeled motorbike, the location of the throttle, brakes, how the gears worked, how to turn it off, what to do in the event of a roll over. Ben tried several times to cut the older man off and tell him there was nothing to worry about. But Mick gestured him to silence and continued, giving every last little detail about the motorbike.

"What year and month was it made?" asked Ben as Mick walked away, saddle and bridle over his shoulder.

"What?" Mick asked, turning.

Ben repeated the question.

"I've no idea. Why?"

"Well, you know every other bloody thing about it." The young man grinned.

"Careful, mate." Mick smiled, turning away and continuing to walk towards the distant mare. "Careful."

Making sure the motorbike was in neutral, Ben tried starting the engine. The motor sputtered and coughed, but failed to ignite. Checking the petrol, Ben saw the tank was full. Given the length of time the quad bike had been sitting in the shed, it was possible water had built up at the bottom of the tank. Mick had already caught and saddled the horse by the time the quad eventually sparked into life, although the engine wasn't happy, soon filled the shed with thick smoke.

Within a couple of minutes, the engine had sputtered the foulness out of its system and was running smoothly. With a mouthful of fumes, Ben shifted into first gear, released the clutch and revved the engine. The quad bike surged forward, the front wheels leaving the ground and the young man finding himself at a forty-five degree angle, holding on for dear life.

"Holy shit!" he shouted, inadvertently pushing the accelerator further.

The engine roared in response and the quad bike managed to angle itself such that the rear mudflaps were scraping the ground. Ben was using all his strength to remain in the seat and shouting in abject fear.

Finally, he released the throttle, engaged the brake and the motorbike slammed back onto the ground, sliding to a halt, the engine idling innocently. Mick, sitting upon the mare nearby, simply shook his head. He probably muttered expletives beneath his breath as well, Ben was sure, but he was too far away to be certain.

Turning the horse away, Mick gestured for him to follow. Gently, Ben throttled up, allowing the quad bike to roll forward slowly. He would leave his application for Crusty Demons for another day. Changing into second gear, he carefully accelerated, allowing the quad to build up speed before changing into third. Passing through the large, open paddock gate, he followed Mick as the older man cantered away into the distance. As the revs increased, Ben changed smoothly into fourth, and now with a healthy respect for the motorbike, he began enjoying the feel of the wind on his face and the blur of the ground as it swept beneath his feet.

That was until Mick and the mare upon which he sat disappeared from sight down a steep creek bank. As the dangerous descent rapidly approached, Ben clenched the brake and almost ended up being thrown over the handle bars. The bike slid down the embankment onto the dry creek bed below. Neglecting to change down gears, and as the engine was about to stall, Ben applied the clutch, quickly moved back into first gear and accelerated towards the opposite bank. The quad bike made good progress, until half way up the creek bank, the front wheels left the ground and the bike began tipping backwards. Instinctively, Ben stood up out of the seat and leaned forward, adrenalin pumping, staving off the cold touch of fear that began sweeping his body.

With the centre of gravity altered, the front wheels slammed back down to earth and the bike growled up the steep slope eventually finding level ground again.

"Thank Christ," Ben muttered, accelerating towards Mick's distant figure as he cantered into the distance, disappearing behind the wide girth of an ironbark tree.

Changing up through the gears, Ben attempted to close the distance and was partially successful. However, Mick's riding skill was something to behold, at least to Ben. Mick and his horse seemed to work as one, each knowing what the other wanted or expected. Tentative as he felt, Ben pushed the quad bike hard across flat sections of ground, enjoying dodging between trees and thick areas of shrub. Although he found it difficult, Ben finally closed the distance between himself and the older man.

Almost half an hour passed before they found the first herd of cattle. The animals were few in number, perhaps twenty head, but bunched close together for protection or reassurance. Several bloated bodies lay scattered in the near distance. Many of the carcasses had been partially eaten by scavengers. Upon closer inspection, it was found that poorly aimed gunshot wounds had caused the animals' eventual deaths.

"Not necessarily bad shots, though," muttered Mick, looking down at one corpse.

Ben glanced at him quizzically.

"Many of the Indonesians are Muslim, and need a Halal kill before they will cook or eat the beef. They may have been trying to wound the cattle so they could get closer and perform a Halal kill. But wounded, angry beasts can run pretty hard. Well, for a time at least."

Ben shrugged. "Makes sense I s'pose."

Mick nodded slowly, still looking at the decaying body. "Come on Ben, let's go mate," he said eventually.

The younger man detected a touch of sadness in the veteran's voice.

Shifting himself into a more comfortable position on the seat of the quad bike, Ben accelerated, slowly catching up to Mick, who was pushing the mare into a fast canter. Passing the herd, Mick ignored them, carrying on towards the next paddock about one kilometre away.

Ben thought of asking what he was doing, but decided to bite his tongue instead. Within five minutes, he knew why. The next paddock held almost a hundred cattle grazing quietly, although their heads came up to watch the pair advance towards them. Mick dropped back so that he was cantering slowly beside Ben.

"Right, we'll circle round the far side and push them back the way we came. Then we can pick up what's left of the smaller herd and herd them all towards the house paddock."

"Sounds easy!"

Mick grinned. "Yeah, it does. It won't be though, you'll need to be on your toes," warned the older man. "Stay back and be ready to accelerate hard and chase any strays that try to break away."

"Will do!" called Ben. He was enjoying the experience.

The muster started without hassle. The cattle ambled calmly towards the distant paddock gate. Mick walked the mare behind the herd and Ben stayed further back, ensuring the sound of the quad's engine did not spook the animals. One of the cows stopped, bellowing loudly, her call sounding distressed. Hesitantly, she followed her companions.

"She's full of milk," Mick called back to Ben in explanation, "and she ain't got no calf near her either. She's probably calling for her calf, which is long dead more than likely. Probably killed by dingos, wild dogs or Indos."

Ben nodded, but did not reply. *Poor bloody thing,* he thought.

A calf ran clear of the herd, kicking and bucking. Ben reacted like lightning, accelerating hard, the front wheels leaving the ground before slamming back down as he changed into second gear.

"Wait!" roared Mick, but Ben was committed. He had a job to do and he would do it well. Steering wide of the calf, which was still carrying on, Ben brought the bike around, the rear wheels sliding. For a moment, he almost lost control. Fear and adrenalin coursed through him resulting in a loud whoop and wide grin.

"Stop!" shouted Mick, trying to gain Ben's attention to no avail.

Quickly closed the gap between himself and the calf, Ben realised what was about to happen and watched as the herd spooked at the fast approaching machine. They scattered in all directions. Mick was able to round up a small section, which he managed to control. However, the majority of the herd galloped clear of the men, eventually meeting up in a group around the area where the muster had commenced. Some began grazing, but many did not. They were intently watching the men, some flicking ears or tails as flies assaulted them. The smaller group tried to break clear of Mick in order to re-join their herd, but he contained them skilfully, his horse moving like lightning.

"The calf was just muck'n about!" shouted Mick. "Forget the calves, mate, concentrate on the adults." The older man was angry, but he held his temper in check. "Sorry Ben, should have told you that."

"Righto," Ben replied, feeling sheepish.

"I'll hold this mob here, you circle back around and see if you can drive that group back towards me, okay?"

"Yup, I'll try."

"Good man," said Mick, pushing the mare on with his legs and steering her to cut off two cows trying to make a mad dash.

Ben circled wide of the main herd and positioned himself almost exactly at his starting point. The quad bike's throttle was located on the right handle bar and was a small lever controlled by the thumb. He pushed the throttle gently, making sure not to over rev the engine and further spook the herd. As he travelled closer, the cattle slowly began moving away from him, a few of them throwing furtive glances towards the quad bike.

With great patience, Ben guided the animals towards Mick, who was still holding at bay the small group of animals in front of him. As the main herd approached, the smaller group grew less irritable, making Mick's task much easier. Keeping the bike at a constant speed and in low gear to ensure the engine remained as quiet as possible, Ben felt proud of himself.

Prior to the two herds merging, Mick gently eased the mare forward, pushing her clear of the cattle, before eventually encouraging her into a canter and circling around in a wide arc to link up with Ben at the rear of the herd.

"Good job, mate," grinned Mick. "Now forget the bloody calves, those cheeky buggers are prone to carry on. It doesn't mean they're breaking clear of the group."

"Right," nodded Ben. "Won't happen again."

"Better bloody not," growled Mick with a mock stern expression.

"One's breaking away!" shouted Ben, pointing, "I'm going after it!"

Mick's head whirled around to see a calf kicking and bucking beside its mother. Snapping his head back to Ben, he saw the younger man chuckling.

"Just jok'n old fella!"

Mick shook his head, smiling. "Smart arse," he muttered.

Within five minutes, they had managed to muster the herd through the gate into the next paddock. Mick lingered behind, closing and latching the gate, so that if for some reason the herd was again separated, they were at least contained to a single paddock, and had no way of fleeing further afield.

* * * * *

With the foreign chatter further away, Finn risked moving. He sat up slowly. As he thought, the majority of Indonesian soldiers were sat around a large camp fire in the near distance. Several were laughing amongst themselves, but the majority were silent as they listened to one soldier who was on his feet, on the far side of the fire, talking in a loud voice and gesturing with purpose towards a mud map on the ground by his feet.

Finn noticed one enemy soldier closer to him than the rest. The Indonesian was sitting in the darkness, well away from the fire, his back to Finn, eating noisily from a ration pack recently stolen from a Royal Marine. The Indonesian was scooping the contents of a can into his mouth. Even though he was demolishing the food with sucking, grunting and burping noises of which Stephen King would be proud, the soldier was still close enough that he would hear Finn moving. If Finn was to withdraw safely from the area, the enemy soldier needed to die.

Finn's weapon was too far away. In order to reach his rifle, he would need to cross ten metres of dry leaf litter strewn with dead branches. Even if he could reach his weapon without attracting the attention of the closest enemy, the sound of a gunshot would bring the entire Indonesian host down upon him. He unsheathed his bayonet.

Slurping on the cold meal, the Indonesian soldier was oblivious to the looming danger that approached from behind. Clenching the sharp bayonet in one hand, Finn slowly and silently gathered his legs beneath him so that he was in a squatting position. Upending the can, the enemy soldier began scraping the last remnants of food into his mouth. After he finished eating, he may well move back to the camp fire and re-join his comrades, in which case Finn could withdraw safely. However, he might also decide he needed to take a piss and head towards Finn.

It was not worth waiting to find out. Finn leapt in the air landing in the leaf litter directly behind the Indonesian soldier. As the enemy dropped the can of food and began to turn, Finn clamped one hand around the man's mouth and stabbed the bayonet into his throat beneath the ear. With a powerful sawing action, Finn slid the blade through the front of the man's neck in an explosion of hot, bright red arterial blood.

Finn had practised the move many times in training, but now faced with the strong, acrid aroma of salty blood, the dying strength of the victim trying to break free and the blast of wind escaping the terrible wound in the man's throat as he tried to scream or shout, Finn feel sick.

Holding the Indonesian soldier until all blood and life eventually departed, Finn gently lowered the corpse to the wet, sticky leaf litter. The Indonesian soldiers gathered around the fire in the near distance were none the wiser. Quietly gathering his weapon, Finn, his face and uniform stained with blood, silently left the area.

Chapter 3

"Sir, you cannot go in there," said the American sailor in a Southern drawl, placing a hand on Craig's chest.

"Yeah? Who says?" Craig asked, trying to push past the man to the emergency theatre room where Matty had been carried.

"Me!" insisted the sailor. "I'm gonna have to ask you to step back, sir," the sailor pushed Craig back with one hand, whilst the other dropped to curl around the pistol grip of the sidearm holstered on his belt.

Craig glanced at the sidearm and knew he could disarm and subdue the man before the sailor had time to draw the pistol. But common sense took over and he stepped back. Even if he was able to move past the guard, he would have been arrested and locked up inside ten minutes.

"Ok," Craig said, stepping back, holding up his hands. "Ok".

"I'm real sorry, sir," allowed the sailor. "I know that's your friend in there, but I can't allow-"

"Yeah righto, I get it, mate," Craig cut the sailor off mid-sentence.

Slinging his assault rifle behind his back, Craig sighed and began pacing back and forth in front of the sailor. To the sailor's credit, the American remained silent, hands once more clasped together behind him, alert eyes staring forward. Craig glanced at the young man as he paced, and knew instinctively the sailor had seen action. It was always the eyes that gave it away. It was a loss of innocence, a glint of hardened experience that only a small percentage of people would ever experience. The hiss, whizz, crack or explosion of incoming enemy fire can never be heard by others who were not there. But it can always be seen in the eyes of those who have experienced it. Always.

"How long you been in?" asked Craig stopping in front of the sailor.

"Sir?"

"In the Navy, how long you been in the Navy?"

"Six years."

Craig nodded. "Where you been?"

"Gulf War Two, sir, two tours of duty. But before that I was assigned to a destroyer in the Indian Ocean near Somalia, hunting pirates for eight months."

"Yeah? How'd that go for you?"

"Sir, it was eight fucking months too long, excuse my language."

Craig grinned. "Sounds like you had a ball, mate."

"Don't get me wrong, sir, we caught hundreds of pirates, a bunch of boats and some mother ships. But that's not why I joined up."

"Oh yeah? And why'd you join up?" asked Craig.

"Sir, I joined up to serve my country in war."

Craig nodded. "Yeah well, what you did in the Indian ocean is part of a trade war, so to speak. Think of it as protecting assets important to the USA, like cargo, oil, food and so on. You helped protect those cargo ships against piracy."

The sailor remained silent, but nodded in acknowledgement. Obviously, he had not viewed the deployment aboard the destroyer in quite that light.

"I need to see my mate," said Craig stopping in front of the sailor.

"Sir, I cannot allow you access," he replied.

"That's my brother in there," said Craig, gesturing at the doorway behind the sailor. "I just want to know that they're helping him."

"I'm sorry, sir," said the sailor.

Craig stood in front of the man. He stood close, very close. "You really think you can draw that weapon on me, mate?" the Australian gestured at the holstered sidearm.

"Sir, yes I do," the sailor replied, although his voice wavered with uncertainty.

"I could kill you before you drew that weapon," Craig said softly, taking a step forward so he was looking directly into the sailor's eyes.

The man's hand dropped and curled around the pistol grip of the sidearm.

"You're gonna need to be quick, mate," Craig said quietly. "You can either let me in there to see Matty, or I'm gonna go through you. And let me tell you, ya won't be getting up in a hurry."

"Sir," the sailor spoke, and was contemplating on finishing the sentence, but after opening and closing his mouth several times, fell silent instead.

"Let me in there," said Craig.

Silence.

"Mate, I don't want to hurt you, just let me in there to check on Matty," Craig said. It was the sailor's last chance. His next move would be to slam the sailor's hand away from the pistol grip, followed by a stiff jab of the palm that would crush the cartilage of his throat. Craig realised just in time what he was about to do and took a deep breath, a step back and lifted his open palms, nodding.

"Sir, you know I can't do that."

The door to the theatre opened, forcing the sailor to step aside as a woman appeared. She was dressed in US Marine camouflage, and her weapon, an M4, was slung in front of her, her hand naturally clasping the pistol grip of the assault rifle.

"What in hell's goin' on out here?" she asked, the doors slamming closed behind her.

"What's going on in there?" asked Craig, pointing at the door behind her.

"Hun, he's in good hands," she said, reassuringly, disarming him by placing a hand on his chest. "He's fine."

Craig nodded, although he was not convinced.

"I'm SGT Tanya Harris," she said, "who are you?" she asked in a bid to diffuse the situation.

"Craig," the Australian replied, shaking her hand. "Is Matty gonna be ok?"

"They're operating on him as I speak," said the woman. "He'll be fine."

"Just let me see him," said Craig.

"Sir," began the sailor standing behind Tanya.

"You fuck'n call me sir one more time, mate, and I'll kill ya. No offence, I know you're doing your job, but my name's Craig, and I fuck'n work for a liv'n. Don't call me sir. Yeah?"

"Yes…Craig," the man said awkwardly.

"Come on," said Tanya, grabbing Craig's arm. "I'll show you."

She pushed back through the doors, leading Craig into the room. He found himself standing in a large viewing room, into which he could see the sealed theatre room beyond. The staff operating on Matty were gowned, masked and gloved.

"We can't go in there," said Tanya.

"Yeah, I understand," replied Craig. "I just wanted to know he was being treated."

"I know, hun," said Tanya, smiling. "Like I said, he's in good hands."

Craig remained silent. *You can do it, mate, you can pull through this.*

"Come on," Tanya was about to steer Craig out of the room, but paused as the pager attached to her belt began beeping. She pulled the pager out and read the screen.

"Gotta go, another rescue's come up."

"Where?" asked Craig.

"Not sure exactly, but it doesn't sound pretty. We got three critically wounded and one dead. Troops are still in contact."

"I'll come with you," said Craig.

"No, you wait here for your friend."

"I'm coming with you." The mission would give him something else upon which to concentrate. He felt useless standing around doing nothing while Australia was still under threat.

"Alright," Tanya said, pushing the theatre door open.

Within two minutes of brisk walking, and negotiating several steep, narrow sets of steel stairs, they were enveloped by the cool, salt-soaked air. Although they were walking on the exterior of the ship, looking out over the ocean below them, they were still one deck below the flight line, where another mission was outbound. Every thirty seconds the deep, powerful thump sounded as the catapult launched another aircraft outbound. Occasionally, the aroma of jet fuel swept over them, a smell Craig had always liked. It was either the smell of safety, as he sprinted through the dust, towards the barely visible silhouette of a helicopter, or the smell of adrenalin as the aircraft flew towards target, ready to deploy him and his men into danger.

✳ ✳ ✳ ✳ ✳

Tanya pulled the helmet down over her head. With inbuilt hearing protection, the helmet muffled the sounds of the aircraft above as they began ascending the final flight of stairs towards the upper deck.

Craig donned his combat helmet, but with no such luxury, he used disposable earplugs. Unslinging his rifle, he jogged up the steps, following Tanya as she ran out towards the Seahawk helicopter. With rotor blades already slapping the air, and dark exhaust fumes blasting out behind the powerful engines, it was obvious the pilot was ready to depart.

Jumping in, the pair had hardly buckled themselves in before the helicopter was airborne, turning and accelerating simultaneously.

Indicating to a headset in a pocket next to the seat on which Craig sat, Tanya gestured to plug it in. Pulling free the Velcro strap, Craig lifted the headset out.

"Five mikes to target," he heard a voice say.

Now that he was settled, Craig raked his eyes around the aircraft, taking in the others on board. There were three apart from Tanya, himself and the door gunners. Two of them looked shit scared. Craig could almost smell the fear emanating from them. The third was a well-built man who was glaring out to sea. His posture spoke of experience, relaxed against the back wall of the chopper, one hand curled around the pistol grip of his M-4, the other on his thigh. It was obvious the man had done this many times before. *Good.*

"Four mikes to target."

Craig noticed a Chinook banking in hard from the east, closely followed by an Apache gunship. Both aircraft accelerated to match speed with the Seahawk. Flying low, the seemingly endless ocean suddenly gave way to beach, which streaked beneath the three helicopters, closely followed by sparse forest.

"Welcome to the party," offered the voice of the Seahawk's captain.

"Roger, happy to join in," chuckled a new voice.

Watching the gunship slowly accelerating ahead of them, Craig noticed the massive thirty-millimetre chain gun sweeping from side to side, searching for threats.

"Three mikes to target."

Tanya sat silently, watching the ever-thickening forest zip by below. She looked relaxed. For the first time, he noticed her as a woman, rather than just another soldier. She was attractive, he thought, even though the helmet enveloped most of her head. She wore a United States Air Force patch on her arm, suggesting, more than likely, she was a Pararescue Jumper, or PJ. Highly-trained medics, these air men and, more recently, women were often parachuted onto or flown in to hostile environments to stabilise critically wounded patients. Well-armed, they were just as capable with a weapon as they were with a bandage or tourniquet. Noticing Tanya was watching him, Craig smiled. She smiled back, winked and looked away.

"Two mikes to target."

The soldier sitting on the back seat had not moved. He was still looking out over the forest slipping by beneath them. He wore no insignia, no patch, not even a flag. Coupled with beard and unkempt shoulder-length hair, much like Craig, it suggested the man was a soldier of a more unconventional nature than a stock standard infantryman. The remaining two men were in the same state as they were previously, in fact, probably more anxious, noticed Craig.

"One mike to target."

Only then did the man on the rear seat look around to take in his immediate surrounds. Glancing at the two soldiers huddled close together, abject terror emanating from them as if it were a disease. The man let his eyes slide past the pair until his fierce gaze rested upon Craig. He nodded, recognising a fellow warrior. Whether it was a nod of greeting, or one of good luck, it was hard to decipher. However, given the current circumstances, that was hardly relevant. Craig let one hand drop to the seat buckle at his waist, ready to unclip and exit the aircraft at short notice.

"Be advised, hot extraction," warned the pilot.

Grunting, Craig suddenly found himself staring at a cloud-riddled sky as the chopper banked violently to the left. A burst of flares exploded from the chopper's flanks, and Craig instinctively knew they were taking ground and possibly anti-aircraft fire. The hollow thud, almost indistinguishable over the engine's roar, confirmed it, as a round struck the chopper. Another struck the flank of the helicopter with as much noise as a double A battery being firmly tapped on a piece of wood. Nothing more.

As the chopper banked fiercely in the opposite direction, Craig caught the firefight below. The allied soldiers were in all-round defence and surrounded by a superior enemy closing in from all sides. The Apache came into view for a moment, its massive chain gun opening fire, engaging targets below. But the scene was soon replaced by thick forest whipping by below. Seat belts digging into his shoulders, Craig held his weapon tightly as the helicopter broke contact and pulled away from the fight.

Within thirty seconds, they banked back towards the fight and Craig could see the sheer devastation the Apache had wreaked within that short period of time. Even from one kilometre away, the dull click of the Apache's main gun could be heard over the scream of the helicopter's engine. Craig watched as two missiles were fired from the attack chopper, finding targets within the forest below, starting a small grass fire. Another long burst from the main gun and the remaining two missiles fired within seconds of one another, found separate targets one hundred metres from one another. With each explosion, at least one section of enemy troops were killed.

The Apache had been able to create a corridor for the allied soldiers, allowing them to rapidly withdraw. Craig watched them in the distance, the size of ants, bugging out from the fight, providing covering fire for each other as they made for an open area nearby. While the Apache provided suppressing fire from its main gun, the Chinook descended, sending up gouts of dust mixed with eucalyptus leaves, grass and small branches. Then the chopper disappeared from sight beneath the brownout.

Within a minute, the chinook was airborne again, clawing its way clear of the brownout, its starboard minigun bursting into life, sending three thousand rounds per minute towards the enemy. Banking hard away from the enemy and firing a string of flares, the Chinook departed at speed, barely above tree top level.

"Be advised, no wounded friendlies, those previously injured are now KIA," said the pilot, his voice, although clinical, was also respectful.

The wounded soldiers have bled out, was Craig's immediate thought. Glancing across at Tanya, he noticed she was looking down at the floor of the chopper, her jaw clenched.

"Oh fuck!" yelled the pilot.

Snapping his head up, Craig watched the smoke trail as the rocket, fired from the ground, spiralled towards the Apache. The gunship released a string of flares and turned away hard, but not fast enough. Hitting the rear rotor, the rocket exploded in blot of thick, black smoke interspersed with flame and shattered rotor blade. Spinning out of control, the Apache descended towards the ground.

"We're goin' in!" shouted the Apache pilot. "Goin' in hard!"

As little as Craig knew about flight, he could see how relentless the pilot was struggling to keep the chopper upright. Hitting the ground upright was paramount to survival. If they crashed on their side, both pilot and co-pilot would be killed instantly. Dark smoke was now spewing from the exhausts.

"Get us on the ground," spoke the American voice calmly.

Craig noticed it was the soldier sitting nearby who had spoken into his headset. He was hanging onto a strap above his head with one hand, clasping his weapon with the other and watching the worsening progress of the Apache intently.

"Say again," said the pilot.

"Get us on the ground," repeated the soldier. "Get us on the ground now," he said gently, although it was spoken with authority.

The gunship slammed onto the forest floor hard, before rolling onto its side, the main rotor slapping against the ground before splintering into small pieces which ripped through the forest canopy, landing hundreds of metres away in all directions.

"Can you land us near the Apache?" asked Craig.

"Can do, but not advisable," came the reply.

Craig exchanged a glance with the American.

"Put us on the ground, mate," said Craig.

Although not yet ablaze, thick smoke suggested the Apache was not far from being consumed by fire or an explosion, or both. Craig quietly watched the enemy, specks in the distance, racing towards the downed Apache. He hated to think what the Indonesians would do to the American pilots when they got their hands on them. The pilot rapidly brought the starboard side of the aircraft to bear upon the enemy below and began descending towards the stricken gunship. The starboard mini-gun opened up with ruthless efficiency, its rain of bullets impacting in and around the advancing group, knocking life from several, their limp forms falling to the leaf-littered ground. The majority scattered and went to ground seeking cover behind trees or dead ground.

"Gun Jam! Gun Jam!" shouted the door gunner.

Immediately, while continuing to descend, the pilot turned the helicopter one eighty degrees, allowing the port side mini-gun to open up. Dust, leaves and twigs rose up to meet them, blotting their view of the ground beneath. The mini-gun ceased fire as he too lost view of the enemy rapidly approaching the area.

Craig ripped the headset from his face and allowed it to drop to the floor. Unclipping his seat belt, he sat down on the edge of the doorway, squinting his eyes against the onslaught of dust whipped up by the powerful rotor blades. Jump out too soon and he could fall thirty metres. Instantaneous death. Keeping one hand firmly clamped on the chopper, and the other on his weapon, Craig continued to search for even the slightest hint of the ground below.

Like some chasm opening up, he saw cold, hard earth beneath him. Clean as a newborn, all leaves and twigs whipped away leaving only bare topsoil, hardly visible against the brownout. He guessed there was still six feet to descend, but that was close enough. He jumped, landed heavily, but rolled to disperse the impact. Coming up on his feet, Craig sprinted forward, going to ground behind the closest tree, the butt of his rifle pulled firmly into his shoulder.

Seconds later and the chopper was departing, the screaming whine of its engine and deafening slap of rotor blades beginning to fade. Within minutes, the noise had almost dispersed but for the distant beat of the rotor blades. As the dust began to settle, Craig saw the dark silhouette of the crashed Apache slowly emerge. Pushing himself to his feet, he ran towards the aircraft, closely followed by the American soldier. With each stride, the gunship came clearer into view.

Moments later, he was at the chopper, climbing onto its nose to help one pilot out of the cockpit. Flames were spreading forward from the engines. The pilot looked to be unconscious, still strapped in to his seat. Wrapping an arm around his shoulder, Craig helped the gunner down from the Apache and guided him away from the crashed helicopter, sitting him against the farthest side of the trunk of a tree. Should the chopper explode, the trunk would provide some protection against the blast, at least.

"Stay here, mate, you'll be right," Craig offered, before sprinting back towards the downed gunship. The American was already waist deep in the cockpit, and with several powerful kicks managed to force part of the windscreen clear of the airframe. Enough to drag the unconscious pilot out. Craig reached through the opening, unbuckled the pilot and clasped the man beneath the armpits. Gravity had different ideas, and the man's dead weight, now unhindered by the seat belts, slumped sideways, his head thumping against the far edge of the cockpit. Blood was dribbling from the corner of his mouth, one eye, half open, stared sightlessly over Craig's shoulder. With a grunt, and placing a foot against the chopper's mainframe for leverage, Craig pulled the pilot clear.

A hand pushed him out of the way and Tanya, who until now had remained with the Seahawk, knelt over the unconscious pilot. Needing no second invitation, Craig sprinted out taking cover in the distance, facing toward the advancing Indo troops.

* * * * *

Shrugging off the med pack and laying the assault rifle on the ground beside her, Tanya checked for a carotid pulse. Nothing. Bright red blood was oozing from the corner of the pilot's mouth. Reaching down, she ripped open the Velcro holding his body armour on. Pulling it clear, she threw the armour aside carelessly, placed her hands over the centre of the man's chest and began chest compressions. With each compression, bright red blood was expelled from the man's mouth in a mini-fountain, splattering both cheeks and running into his eyes.

"Craig!" Tanya called. "Craig, I need your help!"

As she was about to call again, she noticed Craig was suddenly beside her, pushing her aside as he took over chest compressions. Tanya ripped open her med pack and pulled clear a small, manual suction pump. Forcing the pilot's mouth open, she pushed a tube into his mouth and began squeezing the suction bell with her other hand. The blood was rapidly pumped out of the man's mouth, clearing his airway. When his mouth was clear, Tanya pulled the suction pump clear and carefully placed a tube down his throat. On the end of the tube was a large reservoir which she pushed towards Craig.

"Take that, squeeze it twice after every thirty compressions."

"Got it," Craig said.

Tanya busied herself preparing a tourniquet, which she pulled tight around the pilot's arm in preparation for placing a cannula into a vein, allowing her access to inject medication straight into his blood system.

Craig continued chest compressions, watching Tanya as she worked with fast, fluid precision. The pilot began making a loud gargling sound with each compression and Craig noticed that bright

37

red blood began oozing up the tube with each compression until it started dripping from a valve near the reservoir bag. Tanya swore savagely.

"Stop for a second there," said Tanya.

Craig sat back on his haunches, allowing Tanya to check for a carotid pulse. She cursed again, before zipping her med pack up and pulling it onto her back. "It's over, Craig," she said, "he's dead. He has some kind of significant internal trauma, possibly tracheal shear, as a result of the crash."

Nodding, Craig placed a finger over the man's half-open, dry eye and dragged it shut. When he pulled his hand away, the eye slowly re-opened, the dilated pupil seeming to stare at Craig.

Standing and clasping the man's harness, he dragged the body away from the chopper, towards his injured comrade, still hunkered down behind the tree nearby. The American was standing on the upper side of the Apache, two incendiary grenades in his hands. Dropping one onto each instrument panel, he jumped down from the helicopter, pulled a third incendiary grenade from his webbing and threw it up onto the engine block, before retreating towards Craig. The grenades hissed and spat into life, their dull glow eventually brightening to the point of giving a welding arc a run for its money. Looking into the depths of an activated thermite grenade was not advisable.

"Only had three on me," said the American, brushing past Craig and taking up a firing position behind a tree nearby.

"I got one on me," said Craig.

The American held up a hand. "No problem, guy, three should do it."

"Name's Craig," he said, grunting as he dragged the dead weight of the corpse behind him. Momentum was the key. Pulling the pilot's body at a slow trot meant less exertion.

"Spook," replied the SEAL, over his shoulder.

With a few quiet words, Tanya managed to coax the injured pilot from behind the tree. She held her rifle to her shoulder as she moved ahead of the group, disappearing into the forest beyond, in search of a potential landing zone for the chopper, which was still faintly audible in the near distance.

Shots erupted behind them, and turning mid-stride, Craig brought his weapon to bear one handed as he continued dragging the body towards the tree line.

"Get your ass movin', Craig!" Spook shouted, "they're on us!"

Spook's silenced weapon sounded like a cap gun compared to the fire coming downrange. Only two rounds snapped close to Craig, the remainder intended for Spook.

"Keep goin' mate!" panted Craig, watching the injured pilot in front of him slowing down, blood beginning to soak through the uniform covering his right arm. The man shook his head and was about to reply, but Craig beat him to the mark.

"Get your arse in gear, mate!"

An explosion thundered nearby, almost throwing Craig to the ground. The incendiary grenades had reached the fuel tank of the chopper. The explosion had started several grass fires and one serious fire, which had streaked its way into the canopy of a eucalyptus ten metres above the ground, making for all the hallmarks of a bushfire. The thickening smoke and worsening visibility allowed Spook to break contact. Within minutes he had re-joined the group. Taking hold of the pilot's webbing, he pushed Craig aside.

"I got him Craig, you have a rest."

Craig ran back, taking cover behind a tree, ready to give covering fire for the retreating group.

"Over here!" he heard Tanya call in the distance.

"You heard her!" growled Spook, "get moving," probably to the injured pilot.

As Craig was about to chance a glance over his shoulder, he watched a large group of Indonesian soldiers advancing through the smoke at a run. Two were coughing, one badly, to the point he dropped to the ground. Allowing his sights to glide over the pair, Craig allowed his weapon's target reticule to rest upon the front most enemy. One silenced shot dropped the man's lifeless corpse to the ground. Watching their reaction carefully, Craig saw with dismay that their contact drill was smooth, well-rehearsed and professional. Although they did not know from where the shot came, they advanced in good order, using cover and concealment to their advantage.

Pulling a smoke grenade from a pouch, Craig pulled the pin, threw it as far as possible and waited. When the orange smoke began puffing across the enemy's axis of advance, he opened fire with lethal efficiency upon those who were still visible. Firing blindly into the forest before them, the Indonesians began to panic. Some of them retreated away from the smoke to wait for it to clear. Others pushed on and were systematically shot.

With adrenaline and fear pumping through him, Craig took the opportunity to sprint back towards his group, taking cover behind another tree. Still the orange smoke was spewing its blanketing cover. At the far right flank, one enemy soldier sprinted clear of the smoke, making for the cover of a fallen tree nearby. Craig brought his weapon to bear, aimed and released a shot in less than a second. The bullet hammered through the centre of the man's chest. The soldier dropped to the ground, lying still and lifeless.

Calculating his magazine as three quarters empty, he ripped it clear and slammed a fresh one home. The smoke grenade spluttered, spat back into life for a few seconds and then died, the smoke quickly dispersing. As the fading cloud drifted up into the tree tops, a large group of Indonesians came into view, walking in an extended line towards him.

Five died in quick succession, before effective enemy fire began hissing and whizzing near Craig's position. Several rounds thudded into the tree trunk, forcing him to cease fire and seek complete cover behind the tree. *Fuck me, this might be it,* Craig thought as a bullet ricochet off the ground beside him with a loud whine.

Pulling his last smoke grenade from a pouch, Craig dragged the pin clear and dropped the grenade nearby. Within seconds it was hissing noisily, releasing a thick, choking, bright green fog which drifted across Craig's position. Reaching into another pouch, Craig pulled clear a high explosive grenade, disengaged the pin and threw the bomb with a grunt, before springing to his feet and sprinting back, away from the fight.

Exploding with a dull thump, the grenade indicated its effectiveness as incoming fire dwindled and screams rent the air. Craig took cover behind a large fallen tree. Making sure no enemy had appeared through the blanket of coloured smoke, Craig leapt back to his feet and sprinted across a patch of open ground towards Tanya, in the near distance. She was knelt behind a tree, her assault rifle pulled into her shoulder as she provided cover for Craig.

She motioned for him to move quicker. Craig sprinted as fast as his legs would allow, watching as Tanya's head dropped so she was able to stare down the scope of the rifle. He did not need to look behind him to know enemy were advancing, or the smoke grenade had given up the ghost, or both. It seemed to happen all at once. Enemy bullets cracked and whizzed past his head as Tanya opened fire, sending bullets in the opposite direction, but just as close to Craig's face.

As he closed on the friendly position, relief washed over him as the noise of the helicopter slowly increased with each step. Spook came sprinting over a rise in the ground and dived into cover behind a massive pine where he opened fire. Tanya threw a smoke grenade and as the thick blanket of orange wafted across their position, hiding them from the Indonesian advance, the trio retreated in good order towards the waiting chopper.

Craig climbed on board, pulled the headset down over his ears and as he was buckling himself in, the chopper was ascending, turning and accelerating, throwing dirt, rocks, twigs and leaves in a storm behind them.

"That was close," said Craig, grinning.

"It aint over yet," one of the aircrew muttered.

As the chopper accelerated out of the brownout towards home, Craig noticed a dark, distant blob quickly gaining on them from behind. Within minutes the blob had taken definition. It was an enemy gunship.

Chapter 4

"Indonesian President Joko Wahid assassinated in his home yesterday. Indonesian Secret Police suspect British SAS." – *The Scotsman (UK)*

The muster progressed painfully slow, with cattle breaking clear and sprinting for freedom once or twice every half hour. Mick had explained how unusual that was. Normally the herd would walk calmly for kilometres before any of them broke clear in frustration. Being a grazing animal, cows were prone to eat grass, rest and move along a bit before doing more of the same. Especially farming cattle. Walking endlessly was foreign to the animals. So normally several would break clear every few hours, but never as often as they currently were. They seemed frightened.

For good reason, too, thought Ben. Over the last five months, the only people they saw had been trying to shoot them. So it was that as the sun began sinking towards the western horizon, a small group of cattle ran for a small area of bushland nearby.

"Go, son!" Mick roared with a grin as Ben chased them.

Ben had become accustomed to the motorbike now and felt more confident as he accelerated after the fast-moving animals. Three times he attempted to cut off and turn them, but failed on each occasion. They were utterly determined to reach the safety of the small area of bush, which was fast approaching. If he was to succeed, he needed to turn them within the next few minutes.

"Come on ya stupid bastards!" shouted Ben, steering the four-wheeler closer to the cow leading the charge. He could hear her short, sharp exhalations over the noise of the engine. She was tired, almost winded, but keeping up the pace, and it was in that moment it dawned on Ben he'd likely never turn them.

"Shit!" Ben yelled, as he turned his attention from the cow running beside him to the thick eucalyptus directly in front of him. Turning away hard and feeling the rear end beginning to slide around, he managed to just miss the tree, but plunged into the thick, native shrub beside it. The branches and leaves whipped across the skin of his hands and arms, and a thicker branch snapped against the pressure of the handle bars. As the bike pushed past, part of the branch somehow managed to break and wedge itself against the handlebars and the throttle.

The engine screamed in response, the front wheels leaving the ground and, once again, Ben was left hanging on for dear life. He took his thumb off the throttle, but the bike continued to accelerate at full throttle. Ben yelled, adrenaline fuelling his body as he weaved through the forest, trying desperately to avoid colliding with trees or fallen logs. The cattle were long forgotten as trees, shrubs and tall grass whipped by either side. He rode through a spider's web, which stuck to his face, the large Golden Orb spider clamping desperately to his nose. Going almost cross-eyed as he tried to focus on the spider, Ben's high-pitched scream sounded almost inhuman.

*****

"My God that boy can ride," muttered Mick, leaning forward in the saddle to stretch his back. With several degenerated discs in his spine, it only took a few hours of mustering before the pain began. A day in the saddle usually put him in bed recovering for most of the next day. Nurofen and Paracetamol were his best friends on those particular days. So as Mick watched Ben's progress as the young man steered the four-wheeler at high speed, masterfully through the bushland, he willed for the chase to soon be over. The faster they drove the cattle home, the less likely he was of being bedridden.

Mick had been riding motorbikes most of his life, and there was no chance he could negotiate through the scrub with the skill and pure speed Ben seemed to be doing. The young man was riding the four-wheeler to the vehicle's absolute limit.

"He's having a bloody ball!" said Mick quietly, patting the mare's neck, his eyes fixed on Ben as he fish tailed between trees, or slid sideways around large shrubs. Ben was yelling and yahooing, but Mick could not quite make out the words.

*****

"I'm gonna die!" screamed Ben, eyes wide as dinner plates as he narrowly missed the trunk of an Iron Bark.

The spider had climbed up onto his head to gain a better purchase. Twice Ben attempted to brush the spider away, but when his hand left the handle bars, a tree, shrub or fallen log seemed destined to be his final resting place. So he ignored the spider for now, although he could still feel it crawling over his head.

"Stupid bloody thing!" he yelled, trying to dislodge the branch which had wedged the throttle fully open.

His last hope of survival was to ride back to Mick, who might at least be able to help him during what could be his last minutes on earth. Bringing the motorbike around, trying desperately to remain in control as the rear end began sliding out, Ben narrowly missed a Paperbark. Careening between a fallen tree and an Iron Bark, the trunk of which was as wide as a family car was long; Ben's heart was in his throat.

He realised too late a steep cliff was right in front of him. Trying to steer the four-wheeler away from the sheer drop, he failed, and the ground disappeared beneath him. Ben shrieked with terror.

* * * * *

"Crazy bastard!" Mick snarled, watching Ben shriek with joy as the four-wheeler went airborne, disappeared from view and then reappeared in a cloud of dust as the motorbike launched up the opposite side of the creek bed. Ben was standing up off the seat as the four-wheeler slammed back onto terra firma and almost skidded out of control.

"Righto, that's enough now, Ben!" Mick yelled. The mare shied slightly at Mick's voice, but relaxed as he stroked her neck. He realised the young man was heading towards him like a bull out a gate, dust trail following.

"Slow down, ya galah, you'll spook the cattle!" Mick yelled.

But Ben kept coming, ignoring him. Cursing under his breath, he watched the young man cut a large circle around the herd, the four-wheeler only just managing to maintain traction on the loose, bone-dry soil. The second time around Ben steered it much more tightly around the herd, the motorbike only passing within metres of the beasts on the outer edge. He was yelling and waving his arms shouting something, but Mick was too busy trying to control the mare to take notice.

"You bloody idiot!" roared Mick, struggling to maintain control of the horse as she skittered away from the motorbike, throwing her head, her ears flat back against her skull in fear.

"What the frigg'n hell are you trying to prove? You're gonna get me killed!"

* * * * *

Mick was shouting instructions, but Ben could not make out the words.

"What'd ya say?" yelled Ben, knuckles white as he struggled to control the four-wheeler.

"I bloody said—" but the rest was lost as Ben skidded around the far side of the herd, the engine continuing to red line. The cattle were growing restless, more skittish animals pushing their way into the centre of the herd, away from the noise of the fast moving motorbike as it continued to cut tight circles around them.

The rear end almost skidded out, but Ben managed to steer out of the slide, using his body weight to help keep control. The older man appeared again, still trying to calm the horse, which was growing more and more restless with each circle Ben travelled. Would this be his last time around before he crashed and died?

"Say it again?" Ben shouted, holding a hand up to his ear, fear now encompassing every fibre of his being.

Mick punched the air above his head, but the signal meant nothing to Ben.

* * * * *

"Say it again!" Ben seemed to be taunting Mick, screaming past on the motorbike, bringing his hand up to his ear. Was he grinning?

"You bloody little smart arse!" shrieked Mick holding his fist up before Ben disappeared behind the cattle.

* * * * *

Trying once again to pluck the branch stuck in the throttle lever, Ben almost lost control. Terrified of rolling, he ignored the branch for now, clamping down on the handle bars like a vice and wrestling to keep the machine from sliding out beneath him. As Mick appeared once more, an idea came to him. Steering the four-wheeler directly at Mick, who was continuing to shout commands at him, punching the air, or raking an index finger across his throat. He knew that hand signal! Mick wanted him to kill the engine!

"I don't know how to turn it off!" he yelled, rapidly closing the distance. "Hang on, I've got an idea!"

He needed to get close to Mick so that the older man could hear him. As it was, neither of them could hear one another.

* * * * *

"You mad bugger! What the bloody hell are you doing?" Mick kicked the mare, allowing her to gallop clear of the closing threat.

* * * * *

"Oh shit!" Ben muttered to himself. Then he realised Mick's plan. And it was brilliant!

"You bloody legend, Mick!" Ben shouted, giving chase to the mare who was galloping away, carrying the older man clear. Mick throwing glances over his shoulder every few seconds.

With the mare at full gallop, Ben would be able to come alongside and they would be able to discuss an action plan. Perhaps today was not the day he died.

"Thank God!" he said.

* * * * *

"Mad little prick," Mick muttered, as he pushed the mare harder in an attempt to outrun the motorbike.

Casting a glance over his shoulder, he saw that Ben had closed the distance. With all thought of mustering long gone, Mick was now completely concentrating on outrunning the young daredevil.

"Get outta 'ere!" Mick roared over his shoulder, waving his arm.

* * * * *

"Get up 'ere!" Ben heard Mick yell, almost inaudible over the screaming engine.

"Yeah, keep your knickers on!" shouted Ben. "Don't slow down, will ya!" he roared in sarcasm.

Mick always had to be awkward. If he at least slowed a little, Ben could come alongside much easier.

* * * * *

"Don't slow down, will ya?" warned Ben. Mick looked back to see Ben grinning.

"Bloody galah!" yelled Mick. He knew this must have been some kind of payback for the way he had treated the younger man when they first met.

"You're gonna get me killed!"

The mare was blowing hard; she was losing speed as she tired.

* * * * *

Finally, Ben saw Mick was slowing down. He came alongside, and with the engine still redlining, passed the horse and rider.

"The throttle's stuck!" Ben yelled as he flew passed.

* * * * *

"Oh shit," said Mick, realisation dawning on him, a sickening feeling taking a tight grip. "Hang on son!" he yelled, kicking the mare back into a gallop. "Come on girl, one last time," he urged the horse.

Several years ago, Pete, a cattle farmer on a nearby farm, had been killed whilst riding a four wheeler. Pete had been checking fence lines when for some unknown reason the throttle had become stuck fully open. The four-wheeler, a cheap Chinese contraption, had eventually skidded out of control and rolled, sending Pete cartwheeling at high speed across the ground.

Sally, Pete's wife, had called Mick that evening asking to help search for her husband, after he'd failed to return home. It had taken Mick almost twenty four hours to find his friend. Exhausted, hungry and thirsty, he eventually came upon Pete's final resting place. The motorbike was upside down lying on a patch of oil and petrol-stained ground. With handle bars twisted at impossible angles, the seat lay nearby, and fifty metres further, partially hidden amongst a stand of Billy Goat Weed, was one of the wheels.

Mick found his mate's bloated body lying supine, dry eyes staring at the sky, his right leg twisted at an unnatural angle, dried blood caking his mouth, nostrils and ears. He would have died instantly, Mick knew.

The memories flooded his mind as he gave chase, ever so slowly gaining ground on Ben, who was shouting something back at him.

"Hang in there, son!" Mick yelled back. "Hang in there, for Christ sake," he muttered to himself, pushing the horse on. "Come on girl," he urged the mare on, leaning forward in the saddle.

With great effort, the horse managed to slowly close the gap, metre by metre. At the same time, Mick noticed Ben was heading for a thick stand of trees. There was no way he would be able to reach the boy in time.

"Hit the brakes, Ben!"

* * * * *

Ben slammed his foot onto the rear brake as hard as he could. The four-wheeler slowed substantially as the smell of burning brakes filled the air. The engine screamed in defiance, and with a small thud, the rear brakes failed as the pads were ripped clear of their mounts. Once again the motorbike began accelerating, and as the trees closed upon him, he noticed Mick was now beside him.

"It's alright, son," shouted Mick.

Ben did not feel like it was alright. In ten seconds he would either be embedded within the trunk of a eucalypt, or spattered across the forest canopy.

* * * * *

Even though he was panicked, Mick made himself sound calm as the forest grew closer. Ben was travelling too fast to turn now. Any sudden deviation in direction would cause the bike to roll, spilling him across the ground at high speed. Shaking the memories of Pete's bloated corpse clear, Mick concentrated on the task at hand.

"Hold her steady, Ben!" he yelled, leaning across in an attempt to pluck the offending branch clear of the accelerator.

Ben glanced across and the bike swerved slightly as he lost concentration. "What?" the younger man shouted back.

Having almost fallen out of the saddle, Mick clenched his jaw, righted his balance and tried again. "Hold her fuck'n steady I said!" he roared.

Less than fifty metres of open ground now remained between them and the unforgiving forest.

After all we've bloody been through, thought Mick, *I'll be buggered if I'll let it end like this!*

Clenching his thighs tight around the girth of the mare, he leaned as far across as he dared, grasped a tight hold of the offending branch and pulled. It remained wedged in place.

"We're gonna die!" yelled Ben.

"We aint gonna die!" replied Mick, snarling as he tightened his grip on the branch, twisted it until it snapped, and then dragged it clear. Immediately the bike began to slow, the engine finally beginning to idle.

"Now, slowly pull on your front brakes!"

* * * * *

Ben obeyed, his left hand gently squeezing the lever which controlled the brakes attached to the front wheels. Too hard would mean a nosedive over the handle bars. Too soft and Ben would make a close acquaintance with a tree trunk at moderate speed. The best he could expect were broken bones.

Pulling harder on the brake lever, Ben almost left the seat, but the bike slowed to a manageable speed. He turned the four-wheeler, but it came to a sudden halt as one of the front wheels struck the trunk of a Blood Wood. Sitting back on the seat and breathing a sigh of relief, Ben switched the engine off.

"Good girl," said Mick softly, dismounting the horse, patting her neck. "Good girl." The animal was still gaining her breath, her flanks glistening with sweat.

"Alright mate, off you get," said the older man.

Ben tentatively swung his leg over the seat and stepped off the bike, his legs weak, his fear still strong.

"Thanks Mick," he muttered, holding out a shaking hand.

"You're right son, no worries," he said, taking the younger man's clammy, trembling hand.

Surveying the massive paddock, hands on hips, Mick watched the cattle in the distance, grazing quietly. The animals had scattered in all directions. It would take the best part of an hour to herd them back together to continue the muster. With the sun sinking and light fading, it might be possible to reach the homestead by nightfall. Mick glanced around at the mare, and although her breathing had slowed, the slick sheen of sweat still soaked her coat. She held her head low to the ground, trying to gather strength. That in itself was enough to sway his decision.

"We'll sleep here tonight," Mick said, beginning to unstrap the saddle.

Ben simply nodded. "Yeah, okay."

Ever since the invasion, Ben's resolve had strengthened. What had once seemed too difficult or dangerous, causing abject fear, hesitation, or outright refusal had now become second nature.

"Good lad," Mick said, slapping the young man on the back.

Turning to the mare, Mick lifted the saddle clear and placed it on the quad bike. Rubbing her back, he felt the heat emanating from her coat.

"She needs water. You stay here if you want Ben, I'm taking Daisy for a drink. There's a dam about a kilometre away."

Ben looked incredulous. "Daisy?"

Mick looked affronted. "Yeah?"

"You named your horse Daisy?"

"So what?"

"Oh, nothing Mick, nothing," Ben smirked. "I just expected the horse to be called something a little bit more…well different."

"You thought wrong, son, now you comin' or not?"

"Yeah, I'll come for a walk," replied Ben. "Christ knows I need it," he added, throwing a glance back at the four-wheeler.

It took almost twenty minutes to cover the distance, Mick unwilling to press Daisy too hard, as she was already exhausted and overheated. The dam was half an acre in size and, Mick claimed, twenty feet deep in the centre. Daisy immediately drank her fill, stood quietly for five minutes and then drank deeply once more.

"You ever think Australia will be the same after all this?" asked Ben.

"Course it will!"

"You seem pretty sure about that, old man."

"In fact, there's a chance Australia will be better than it's ever been."

"How's that?" Ben asked, watching Daisy wade into the water. She rolled, soaking her body in the cool water.

"This is gunna sound harsh," explained Mick, crossing his arms, watching Daisy enjoy herself. "The weakest amongst us, those unwilling to defend what they love, are gone, either killed outright, or dying later at the hands of Indo soldiers. The only Australians who will come out of this are those with the gumption to stand up and fight outright, or resist in some way.

"Only the strong have survived, and only the tough will continue to survive. Australia's never been invaded before. Well…" Mick said as he pulled a length of grass free and chewed the end, "Jimmy would probably disagree with me there," he shrugged.

"Probably," chuckled Ben.

"Alright, for Jimmy's sake, wherever he may be… still kicking about I hope… this is the second time Australia's been invaded. So in many ways, it's a good thing. Those lazy, useless bastards taking every bit of money offered by the government and giving nothing back will have scampered when the invasion happened. They'd have probably survived a week," Mick bit the end of the grass and chewed. "Actually, no. I'll give 'em the benefit of the doubt." He grinned, watching Daisy taking a deep, refreshing drink. "I'll give 'em two weeks. Two weeks post invasion and most of 'em would have been killed."

"Pretty harsh outlook," observed Ben.

Mick shrugged again. "Tell me which part of the invasion wasn't harsh?"

"True."

"So when this is all over, and don't mistake me, Ben…" Mick flicked the piece of grass away. "… this invasion is far from over, but when it's all over, Australia will be better for it. We've got a lot of re-building to do. Our debt will be extortionate. Probably like nothing we've had in the past. But at least the people doing the rebuilding will be robust, driven and focused. The dead wood will be long buried."

"Along with some of the robust, driven and focused ones too," Ben added softly.

Mick nodded, instantly regretting the last statement, thinking of Kane and all the other men and women who had died defending their country thus far. "Very true, young fella," Mick said quietly. Then, unbidden, the face of Jonny Hargraves arrived in his mind's eye. He attempted to fend off the flashback, but failed.

"We're gett'n bogged down!" shouted Jonny, his voice only just audible over the fire fight. "Guns go!"

With bullets cracking close overhead, Mick hefted the Mag-58 heavy machine gun, climbed to his feet and sprinted forward a few paces before throwing himself to the ground. Pulling the gun's butt into his shoulder, he put down a withering amount of fire on the enemy, visible only by their muzzle flashes amongst the jungle's foliage. The two other men of his group were also taking well-aimed shots with their SLRs. Then, before he knew it, the scout group were on their guts beside them, adding support for the rifle group who were sprinting forward to join them.

Then the advance halted completely. Snapping his head around, Mick searched for Jonny. Glancing over his shoulder, Mick saw his mate lying supine. Gibbo the signaller knelt over him with a combat dressing in his hand, trying to stem the bleeding.

If they didn't keep the momentum up, they'd all die, Mick knew.

"Scouts go!" he roared, taking over command.

It took half an hour to push through the enemy position, killing those who remained to fight. Once they had re-organised themselves, the section, under Mick's command, covertly made their way back to their wounded section commander. Jonny was in a bad way. He was ghost white, the jungle around him stained in places with the ochre of dried blood, and bright red in others where fresh blood was still oozing from the terrible wound in Jonny's abdomen.

"Mick, you hear what I said?" Ben asked, but it was obvious the older man was in another place, his vacant eyes staring at the horizon.

"Mick!" Ben tapped his shoulder and Mick pulled away violently, his eyes wide, chest rising and falling rapidly. For one split second it seemed Mick was about to attack him.

"Jesus mate, you alright?" Ben asked, taking a step back.

"Yeah, son, yeah," replied Mick, seeming to snap out of it. Running a hand over his face, he shook his head, took a deep breath and let it out quickly. "Yeah I'm fine," he muttered.

Ben thought better than to ask more of the incident. Katie had spoken often about her father's flashbacks to the Vietnam War. She heard him moaning, talking, shouting or screaming in his sleep. He never spoke to her about what had happened that affected him in such a way. She never asked, either, but it was obvious, even now, the memories were as fresh as a daisy.

"Come on, mate, let's get crackin'," Mick said, slapping Ben on the back.

Mick led Daisy out of the dam, the horse now looking much more content. Her breathing had settled; cool water now glistened along her flanks where, more recently, rivulets of sweat had trickled. It was a beautiful, clear, calm day, thought Ben as he looked up, watching a flock of finches scud past disappearing into the treetops seconds later.

However, twelve kilometres above them, the soft, almost inaudible sound of fast-moving fighter jets ripped across the sky.

Chapter 5

"Indonesia signs peace treaty; withdraws from Australian soil. Victory at long last! " – *The Irish Times (UK)*

Craig blocked out the aircrew's chatter, their voices quickly becoming background noise as he focused on the inbound enemy gunship. The Blackhawk pilot was better than good, throwing the utility helicopter around like a fighter jet, following the contours of the earth, dodging between mountains, into valleys, down into dry creek beds, flying so low that they were below the forest canopy either side of them. Yet, the enemy pilot was just as determined, and almost as skilled. The distance narrowed.

The injured Apache pilot looked pale, his face lined with both pain and exhaustion. One hand clamped a pad over his right arm to help stem the bleeding. It was the best Tanya could do given their situation. In order to clean and dress the wound properly, she would need to unstrap from her seat to gain better access. The way the helicopter was being thrown around, that was simply not possible.

A flickering light beneath the chasing gunship indicated the main gun was now in range. Tracer rounds streaked passed the Blackhawk. No bullets struck, but they were close enough to cause concern. A second storm of metal raced past them, this time closer. With seat belts tightening across his chest and stomach, Craig clenched his teeth as the Blackhawk peeled hard to the left, descending dangerously close to the forest. Treetops raced by in a green blur only metres beneath them. One wrong judgement by the pilot and it was all over. Craig hated being out of control. A steep right turn brought them less than one metre from the surface of a long river. Stretching in his seat, he could just make out the enemy gunship, desperately giving chase, however, unless Craig was mistaken, they had pulled away a little.

Spook was glaring at the gunship in the distance behind them. His face was impassive, but more than likely, he was equally frustrated at the situation, especially being unable to do anything to help affect their escape.

Stomach descending to his boots, Craig whipped his head around to watch through the front windscreen as the Blackhawk rose sharply out of the river system that was quickly coming to an end. Another hard turn to the left and a farmstead zipped by at close range. Craig thought the house looked familiar, but it was consumed by the forest before he could focus.

Movement inside the cabin caught his attention and he realised Tanya was out of her seat. She was knelt down in front of the now unconscious Apache pilot.

"Tanya, strap yourself in!" said Craig through the headset, but she either could not hear him or was ignoring him. Her communications lead was unplugged, he realised. Cursing, he tried to gain her attention but failed. She was completely focused upon what she was doing. Tightly bandaging the unconscious man's arm, she ensured the bleeding would be greatly reduced, if not ceased completely. Within thirty seconds she'd placed a cannula in the man's arm. Within one minute fluids were up and running.

Quickly, she sat herself back down and strapped herself in, just in time. The Blackhawk once again dived towards earth, pulling out almost at ground level. Craig glimpsed their pursuer open up with its main weapon. The enemy helicopter was close enough that he could hear the dull clicks of the thirty-millimetre chain gun over the whine of the Blackhawk's engine. Another gut-wrenching turn and the gunship disappeared from view. Rising violently over a small knoll, pushing the chopper to its limit, the Blackhawk pilot was determined. It was at that moment Craig knew they would make it to safety. He caught Tanya's eye and smiled reassuringly. She smiled tightly, but the glint of fear swam in her eyes.

Five deafening thuds sounded in rapid succession, followed immediately by a high-pitched screeching sound. The Blackhawk suddenly lost all power, feeling slow and sluggish. Instinctively, Craig knew they had been hit. He could feel them falling. The screeching sounded almost like a dying animal. But Craig knew it was the Blackhawk making the bloodcurdling sound.

"Brace! Brace! Brace!" the voice shouted into Craig's headset.

He was numb; not with fear, but disbelief. So sure was he they would make it to safety. Now with thick, black smoke spewing from the chopper's engines, the aircraft began spinning on its horizontal axis. They seemed to spin slowly at first, but gained momentum as they plunged towards the forest below.

He remembered hearing a mayday spat out like a machine gun prior to impact, calling for any close air support. Then they hit the ground. Hard.

* * * * *

"Good shot," Cutter stated calmly as they accelerated rapidly away from USS *Ronald Reagan*. "Engines normal, systems good."

Jess was bone weary, having flown missions day and night on a rotating roster for weeks on end. But the catapult always seemed to wake her up. If caffeine could be injected directly into a vein, than the thrill of being launched into the air off the end of a super carrier was twice as potent.

Indonesia's main force had retreated inside the first week. With tough international trade sanctions in place, Indonesia was having a tough time of it. There was certainly no scope for them to repair what had survived of their defence force, let alone rebuild a new one. But it was the stoic, fanatical Indonesian soldiers, more than twenty thousand of them, who had remained on Australian soil, melting into the forests, disappearing into already-occupied towns and cities, who were causing the most problem. They were well equipped, resourceful and determined to win. Even as quarter of the western world waded in to assist Australia, the thought of defeat had not crossed their minds.

Today, they were flying alone in support of a US Blackhawk that had come under enemy fire. Scant incoming intel reports suggested the Blackhawk had been hit by ground fire, but was still airworthy and limping away to a safer area. It was a simple support mission. Far removed from the initial missions she had flown off the coast of Australia against enemy shipping lines, surface-to-air missile sites, anti-aircraft gun emplacements and ground vehicles. Today would be a walk in the park. She smiled.

They flew at close to forty thousand feet in altitude. Although oxygen masks were a requirement, the vast distance between themselves and the ground would allow precious seconds to evade should a surface-to-air rocket be fired.

"Five minutes," Cutter said calmly, indicating how far they were to their mission.

"Roger," Jess replied, keeping a constant eye on the radar, weapon systems, and the distant ground below.

Although cloud cover was scarce, occasionally her view of the ground was blocked as the aircraft scudded above a bank of light cloud. Australia was a beautiful country. When the war was over, and the task of rebuilding complete, she intended to return as a tourist. The forest-covered mountain ranges were spectacular, the occasional clear, blue stream cutting its way through the land to marry up with large rivers, meandering into the horizon, towards the now-invisible ocean beyond.

They were so far inland that one could be forgiven for forgetting the year. The distant ground beneath her seemed like some forgotten wilderness; making her think of how the United States might have looked before white man arrived.

At altitude, Australia's countryside looked like a mash of varying shades of green, brown and grey, as rocky knolls gave way to fertile valleys and massive green, pelted mountains. It was a country of diversity, rapidly changing landscapes, and opposing weather patterns from one end of the land to the other. As a result, Australia bred tough people. Although the initial Indonesian invasion had taken Australia by surprise, her people had resisted with resilience, never giving up, constantly taking the fight to the occupiers. Some resistance groups fought without leadership, and although they were motivated, were beaten down with savage atrocity. Others were lucky enough to be mentored by scattered remnants of the Australian Defence Force. These guerrilla groups had the most success. They were not only motivated, but well-trained and well-led, slowing the Indonesian advance.

Jess remembered sitting glued to the television each evening, listening to the reports coming in from Australia. Some of them completely fabricated, others sent from satellite phones from foreign correspondents on the ground. One in particular, which would forever remain burned into Jess' memory, was a British reporter stuck somewhere in the centre of Sydney during the initial invasion. The reporter's voice wavered with fear, but she remained focused on her story, whilst in the background was the distant, yet constant chatter of automatic gunfire.

She had remained disgusted at the inaction of President Baker as he reneged on the ANZUS Treaty, refusing to mobilise US troops to support Australia in her hour of need. Jess remembered the day President Baker had been impeached; she had been at work. The entire crew room had erupted at the news, one pilot almost choking on a sandwich as he roared his approval. Then, less than ten days later, the United States had mobilised in support of Australia. Finally, after hundreds of flight hours, and thousands of training hours, Jess had been on her way to war.

"Two minutes," Cutter spoke quietly.

* * * * *

Unbuckling his belt, Craig rapidly checked himself for injury. Adrenalin had a powerful way of supressing injury, so he made sure to check both arms and legs. When he found both to be intact and uninjured, he pushed himself off the seat, grabbed his weapon and looked for Tanya. She was unconscious. He checked she was alive before unbuckling her belt. Dragging her out of the wreck, he pulled her limp body behind him then trotted away from the devastated Black Hawk. Fifty metres later, he set her down behind the thick trunk of an Iron Bark and rolled her onto her side, so she wouldn't choke on her own vomit in she threw up.

Sprinting back to the crash site, he checked out the wrecked aircraft. It was far worse than he'd expected. Although the chopper had crashed upright, the heavy transmission box, sitting above the passenger cabin and directly below the rotor shaft, had swung down upon impact, crushing one soldier against the rear wall.

"Fuck'n hell," he muttered.

The farthest side of the chopper had impacted a large tree trunk, snapping off the rotor blades and crushing the door gunner. Checking the cockpit, he saw one of the enemy rounds had struck the co-pilot, leaving a hole in his chest wider than a man's fist. As for the Blackhawk pilot, he seemed to carry no external injury, but a brief assessment left Craig in no doubt he was dead. Adjusting the pilot's head back in case he began breathing by himself, Craig moved on. If the guy wasn't breathing yet, it was more productive to check for others who may be more salvageable.

Ducking back into the wreck, Craig squatted and looked around, ignoring the acrid smell of leaking oil, fuel and blood. Even Spook had been killed. The top half of his skull was crushed by part of the drive shaft, which had driven into the cabin upon impact. The Apache pilot remained unconscious, yet alive. Unbuckling him and gently dragging him clear, Craig set him down close by Tanya, rolling him onto his uninjured side. Ensuring what little remained in the fluid bag was running into the unconscious pilot's vein, Craig placed the bag on a low hanging tree branch before returning to the crash site.

Retrieving as many weapons as possible, Craig carried them back to Tanya. she was still out, but was breathing and had a pulse. Same with the Apache pilot. Returning to the doomed chopper, and with great effort, he managed to drag each person away. Only one remained irretrievable, his body crushed by the transmission. Laying the bodies side by side, Craig marked the location on his GPS. He had no tools, much less the time to bury them.

Not being a religious man, Craig stood over the corpses and said nothing; instead, he looked at each man and sent a silent thought to their family, wherever they were in the world. Given the current conflict, it would be weeks, maybe even months, before their bodies were returned home.

As he turned away from the bodies, he heard the enemy chopper approaching from the east. He assumed the enemy helicopter had long since departed the area, in search of other targets, but obviously not. Sprinting for cover, he slid onto his stomach behind a fallen tree, hoping Tanya and the Apache pilot were hidden from view.

The chopper hovered over the crash site for almost thirty seconds, throwing the sparse forest canopy into a blitz; half-dead leaves sent streaking towards the ground in a hail. Losing interest, the chopper slowly accelerated away, its noise gradually fading into silence.

* * * * *

"Radar contact two o'clock low, no friend-or-foe ID," Cutter spoke quickly.

"Roger," acknowledged Jess, double-checking the weapon systems were armed and online.

Pushing the jet faster, they made a low altitude, high-speed pass across the bow of the aircraft and identified it as an enemy chopper.

Trace rounds flickered in the near distance as the helicopter opened fire. Jess saw the rounds in her peripheral vision, but her concentration was total as she selected a rocket on the port wing, before enabling the targeting system, all of which took less than a second. Cutter threw the Super Hornet into a break turn to the left, vapour trails streaking from the wing tips.

Engaging the airbrake, the fighter-bomber turned hard, descended and violently decelerated. Microseconds later, the enemy helicopter was locked onto, the missile had been launched and Cutter was ascending and accelerating on full afterburner.

"Missile gone," said Jess calmly, tracking the progress of the warhead over her right shoulder as the Super Hornet rapidly departed the area. Dropping a string of flares and commencing a break turn of its own in a desperate attempt to evade the incoming missile, the enemy chopper failed. Jess watched the distant fireball fall from the sky like a lead balloon, crashing into the sparse foliage beneath.

* * * * *

Craig ignored the nearby explosion, but managed to glimpse the Super Hornet streak overhead as it ascended at what looked to be a forty-five degree angle, the red orbs of the afterburners visible, powerful engines rumbling as the aircraft departed the area.

Tanya groaned and Craig knelt beside her, ignoring the almost invisible dot high above them that had once been an F-18 Super Hornet. In less than thirty seconds, the deep, powerful rumble of its engines had faded to silence.

"Can you hear me?" Craig asked, shaking her shoulder.

She groaned again, but said nothing. Her eyes fluttered open for a second, before closing again.

He shook her shoulder, harder this time. Her eyelids parted and she looked at him, her bleary eyes gaining focus. Freezing, realisation took control of her face and she rolled away from him, unsteadily rising onto one knee. Clamping a hand to her weapon nearby, she pulled it to her, her master hand naturally curling around the pistol grip. Moving to the Apache pilot, she checked him, motioning Craig to silence as he began to speak.

"Did anyone else survive?" she asked, turning to him.

"No," he answered with a slight shrug. There was no point sugar coating it. No point trying to break the news gently.

She stared at him for a long time, her mouth slightly open, a look on her face half way between doubt and sorrow.

"No one else survived?" her voice a whisper.

"I'm sorry Tanya," Craig replied.

He felt for her in that moment. As a member of combat rescue, it was her duty to preserve life, and he knew that in her mind, she had been unconscious and useless while others were busy dying.

"There's nothing you could have done, mate," he said softly.

She shook her head, clenched her jaw and sat beside the unconscious Apache pilot. She ripped her helmet clear and threw it away contemptuously.

"I could have at least tried," she said.

Turning her attention to the Apache pilot, she checked the bandage on his arm, ensuring no blood had leaked through. The bandage remained stark white, suggesting the bleeding had been arrested, which was at least something. The fluid bag was now empty. Disconnecting the tube from the cannula she had placed in his arm, she pushed it into an empty pouch. Opening another pouch on her chest webbing, she pulled clear a blood pressure cuff. Taking the blood pressure, she nodded, satisfied.

"He's stable at least," she said quietly.

Craig nodded and moved away. Slinging his weapon, he searched the vegetation, eventually finding two sturdy branches. Returning to the deceased, he dismantled straps from personal webbing and retrieved aircraft strops. Keeping the branches shoulder width apart, he created a makeshift stretcher. It would be more to drag behind him than carry like a traditional litter. There were only two of them remaining able-bodied, and with the requirement for outward protection, one of them would need to be patrolling forward, weapon ready.

Lifting the unconscious pilot onto the make-shift stretcher, Craig used another length of webbing to pass across his chest and under his arms, binding him to the stretcher, so that he would not slide off.

"What's that smell?" whispered Tanya.

Craig's first thought was the chopper and dead bodies in the near distance. But a moment later, he smelt it too. Looking up through the canopy of sparse scrub, he saw the thick black smoke and heard the faint crackle of powerful fire as it began spreading through the trees towards them. The downed enemy chopper must have started the fire.

"Time to leave," said Tanya.

"Yup," Craig agreed. "One sec." He ran to the Black Hawk, delved into a pouch and pulled clear two incendiary grenades, dropping one in the cockpit, and the other onto the main radio. The grenades did not explode, rather they sputtered at an incredible heat, melting everything before them, including steel. Casting one last glance at the bodies neatly laid out one beside the other, he departed.

Slinging his weapon and grabbing a branch in each hand, he lifted the stretcher behind him, so that the unconscious pilot's head was close to the small of Craig's back, and his feet were close to the ground. Such technology had worked for the Native Americans for tens of thousands of years. There was no reason it should not work now.

"Let's go," he said, stepping off at a rapid pace. The crackling flames sounded nearer, acrid smoke beginning to settle upon them. If the fire spread, it had the potential, given the dry conditions, to envelope the entire area in a firestorm, which was an environment that created its own wind, driving itself forward in a fury of destruction. Although the sparse vegetation and lack of natural wind reduced the chance of such an event occurring.

Tanya nodded, and pushed well forward of Craig, leading the way as she watched for enemy. Although they did not have an exact plan on where they were heading, their first task was to move clear of the developing bushfire behind them.

It was difficult to evade a full-blown bushfire, but moving downhill was a start, as fire ripped uphill at incredible speeds. Tanya seemed to know this, picking her way downhill wherever she could, even if it was only a slight downward angle in the ground. Heading downhill was also following the path of least resistance, the catchcry of water. If the fire did build into an inferno, a deep spring of water may be their saviour; that was if not all oxygen was sucked out of the air around them.

Clenching his teeth, Craig pulled the unconscious man behind him at a rapid pace. Glancing over his shoulder, he saw although the distant fire was spreading, it had certainly not reached the irrevocable heights of a firestorm. Sweat beaded his forehead, slid down his cheeks in rivulets, or dripped from his chin. Tanya moved through the undergrowth towards him. She moved quietly, but with confidence. Signalling for Craig to stop, she knelt by the unconscious Apache pilot, checked his pulse, counted his respirations and checked blood pressure. Making sure the straps were still holding him on the stretcher, she seemed satisfied, moving past Craig with a smile and a wink.

Tanya was back, he decided, watching her walk into the distance, drawn to the seductive sway of her hips. He stood watching her until she disappeared behind a clump of tall grass, before remembering he should be following her. Dragging the unconscious man, he shuffled forward at a sedate trot, faster than a rapid walk and slower than a run. He found the pace, combined with the forward momentum, combined with the slight downward lay of the land, easy to maintain.

The loud crump of an explosion echoed across the landscape and Craig knew the fire had found the fuel tank of the enemy chopper. Glancing over his shoulder, the fire itself was no longer visible, but the thick, black plume of smoke was massive, much larger than it had been. Craig felt the shockwave pass through him as another explosion rocked the bushland.

"Fuck'n hell," he muttered, continuing to trot, keeping Tanya's distant figure visible.

The fire must have found the decimated corpse of the Black Hawk, meaning it had not only spread, but was picking up pace. Glancing back, Craig was shocked to see the smoke now blotted out half the horizon. He pushed on harder, moving into a run, his legs burning, lungs straining. His foot struck a hidden rock and he almost tripped, but righted himself at the last second. With a soft curse continued on, sweat pouring down his face and soaking his uniform.

"That fire's comin'," said Tanya, jogging towards him. She quickly checked the unconscious man, ensuring he was still alive and then squeezed Craig's arm. "You want a break?"

"No," Craig said, nodding back the way Tanya had come, "you get going. Find some water or something, we don't have much time."

Tanya nodded and jogged away, Craig following at a rapid pace. He could hear the flames. So powerful was the fire, that individual crackles were no longer audible. The sound had built into a fierce roar. Slowing his pace, he watched a small mob of kangaroos bound between him and Tanya, oblivious to his presence, simply concentrating on one task; outrunning the fire.

Snapping a look over his shoulder, Craig could see flames high up in the treetops behind him, the fire not only sliding across the ground, but also jumping through the canopy above, assaulting the dry Australian bush from two fronts. Smoke had descended upon their position, assaulting Craig's nostrils, burning his eyes, causing him to squint in order to keep Tanya in view. With a snarl, he pushed harder, increasing his pace, almost losing his footing for a second time.

"Down this way!" he heard Tanya's voice, although by now, he had lost sight of her. The roar of the flames almost drowned out her voice. He could feel the heat behind him, growing more intense by the minute.

"Craig, down this way!" she shouted again.

It was then, as he pushed through a dilapidated shrub, he caught sight of her. She was below him, standing chest deep in a body of water. But to get there, he would have to negotiate a steep slope. The rapid advance of the fire would not allow him the time to carefully pick his way down.

"Hold on, mate," he muttered to the unconscious Apache pilot behind him.

Taking a step forward, he slid down the steep slope on his arse, holding the makeshift stretcher behind him, struggling to keep it from flipping. He hit the water hard, and a second later, Tanya was beside him, taking control of the unconscious man's head, ensuring it did not disappear below the surface.

"Best I could do," said Tanya.

"I guess it'll do," he grinned, ducking his head under, enjoying the cool water against his face. The spring was five feet deep at its centre, Craig approximated. It was oval, about fifty metres long and twenty metres wide.

He went to help Tanya hold the makeshift stretcher, ensuring the unconscious man remained above the surface. She checked his pulse, listened to his breathing, and seemed satisfied. Although the bandage around his arm was wet, it remained white, no blood leaking through.

The heat was intense, fire enclosing the body of water from one end to the other, flames licking the edges, or roaring through the canopy, skipping from one tree to another with fearsome speed. A tree, trunk as thick as a small car, black, smoking and defeated, came crashing down, slamming into the water five metres from them. Neither of them knew if they'd survive.

Instead, they remained silent… and watched the world burn.

Chapter 6

"**Munduberra:** Hundreds of Australian civilians slaughtered as they return to their homes! We can report US Marines, who arrived at the horrific scene later in the day, became embroiled in a nineteen-hour long gunfight with Indonesian soldiers. The war it seems is not over." – *L'Indépendant (translated by ADÉLAÏDE TILDE) (France)*

Distant shouting tore Finn awake. He had fallen asleep on the leeward side of a dry creek bed, beneath what remained of the root system of a monstrous tree. The soil that once anchored the giant into the earth having long been eroded in some flood. It was still pitch dark, the half-moon partially visible through the tree's canopy.

Following his escape from the Indonesians, Finn had enjoyed almost twenty minutes freedom of movement before the shouting had started, indicating they'd found the soldier Finn killed. With no idea of their tracking skill or capability, he'd been progressing with caution, covering his tracks where possible. Finally, exhaustion had engulfed him.

The shouting, much closer, had ripped him from the soft grips of slumber. Their tracking was better than he thought.

"This is a cluster fuck," he whispered.

Finn pushed himself out of the protection of the tree's root system. Standing, the Royal Marine Commando crossed the dry creek bed in several strides and climbed up the opposite bank. He held his weapon close, safety catch off, index finger resting lightly upon the trigger. He felt alone.

Switch's easy laugh, Mike always farting and blaming some unseen frog, Orms' practical jokes that made everyone laugh, Sacker always a serious bootneck. He did not joke much, but he was thoroughly professional. *All dead*, thought Finn. *All fucking dead*. The Indonesian shouts were closer. They were gaining ground. Although they had night vision, Finn was struggling to understand how they were tracking him, until the intermittent bark of a dog, almost inaudible amongst the shouted foreign language, explained everything.

He pushed on faster, weaving through trees and avoiding shrubs in order to reduce sound. Occasionally, he lost his footing on protruding rocks and roots. Once, he slammed his shin into a fallen tree trunk, causing him to hiss under his breath as he clambered over the log. It was then he heard the noise. Stopping, Finn allowed his ears to take command, and he heard the sound that may just save him. Running water.

Ignoring the shouts behind him, Finn changed direction, pushed through a spider's web, wiped the spider from his neck and hopped over another long-fallen tree. Within minutes, he stumbled knee deep into the creek, feet slipping on the rocky floor. Making his way downstream, he ignored the cold water as it soaked through his uniform and assaulted his skin. Better to be cold than captured. Better to be uncomfortable than tortured or dead.

He continued to stride downstream, water soaking through his supposedly waterproof boots, wetting socks and feet beneath. But it was a small price to pay in order to throw off the dog's trail. At least he hoped it would throw off the canine. For the first few minutes, the enemy voices sounded louder again, probably within two hundred yards. But ten minutes later, his legs numb with cold, feet feeling like blocks of ice, the enemy departed into the distance, their voices eventually fading to silence. Rather than allow the dog to regain a trail, Finn clenched his teeth to stop them from chattering and continued downstream.

Eyes gritty with fatigue, body resisting the ever-increasing strength of exhaustion, he slowly plodded on through the creek. Parts of the creek bed were slime-covered pebbles and rocks, forcing him to concentrate in an effort to avoid slipping over. Other areas were covered in thick, soft, sticky mud, which clung to his boots, weighing down his feet and ensuring he progressed at no more than a snail's pace.

Occasionally he felt fish, startled by his presence, brush against his pants as they rushed away. At least he thought they were fish. Stopping in a waist deep part of the creek, Finn rested his forearms on a large, half-rotten log. Years, maybe even decades before, it must have been a vibrant tree, but now all that remained was the trunk, as thick as a man's leg.

Resting on his feet, Finn felt sleep approaching, like some silent assassin. Closing his eyes, he began to sway, legs losing their will to hold him upright as sleep worked its soft, silent magic. Suddenly, the surrounding forest exploded with deafening gunshots, and before he knew it, Finn was reliving the firefight. He watched Mike shot through the leg. Moments later another round slammed into his chest. With a jerk, Finn came to, eyes flicking wide open, adrenalin pumping through his body defeating slumber. He felt something cold slide over the skin of his arms and he looked down. In the dim light thrown by the half-moon, he watched a snake, oblivious to his presence, slither across his arms, down the log and disappear into the water, swimming away behind him.

Finn rubbed his eyes, Mike's corpse still at the back of his mind. The position in which his mate died, forever etched into the banks of his memory. Forehead resting on the leaf litter, left arm splayed out beside him, right hand clasping his rifle.

"Mike!" Finn had shouted at the deceased man no more than ten yards from him. "Mike!"

Finn shook his head and became aware of the creek around him, the vivid memories rapidly retreating to silence. He shivered as he felt the ice-cold water.

Get a grip, you twat! He slapped the palm of his hand against his forehead. *Get a fucking grip!*

Brushing past the log, he continued and almost collapsed, realising he could no longer feel his legs. He needed to find shelter and dry off. Groggily, he checked his watch. 04:17 hrs. Dawn was not far away.

Stumbling up the creek bank, Finn felt clumsy, his waterlogged boots, like heavy cumbersome bricks, causing him to trip on every stick, rock or exposed tree root. Combined with exhaustion, he was brought to his knees, but within seconds, silently pushed himself back to his feet, refusing to be beaten.

The smell of a decomposing body filled the air. Eventually, he came across a dead kangaroo. The animal was partially decomposed, half the rib cage exposed, the other half hidden behind a thin layer of putrid skin.

"Fuck'n goppin'," he coughed, a look of disgust on his face. But as foul as the smell might be, Finn knew it would be a good place to settle down and hide.

Searching around the area, he found a thin pine had snapped at the base and fallen to the ground. Finn sat down against what was left of the upright trunk, careful not to snap the few brittle tendrils still attaching the trunk from the main tree lying almost at ninety degrees. Sliding forward on his arse, he was forced into a sitting position, and before long onto his back as he negotiated his way amongst the upper branches of the fallen pine lying on the forest floor. Snapping a few branches to make way, he pushed his way into the thickest foliage, although he was careful to lay them back in place behind him once he had passed through.

Finally, he lay still amongst the thickest part of the fallen pine. Needles brushed his face, soft wind teased the branches and the stink of dead kangaroo filled his nostrils. Although the cold still assaulted his body, being out of the water and in some kind of rudimentary shelter seemed to help. He could feel his uniform slowly drying, and clasping his arms across his chest held in some heat. Moving his right leg slightly, he was comforted by the cold metal of his rifle lying on the ground beside him. Although his stomach growled, Finn ignored the feeling. Warmth took priority. Realistically, he could go without food for another three weeks, and without water for up to one week without exertion. Although that would be difficult. In fact, it would be almost impossible.

As his eyelids grew heavy, Finn attempted to remain awake, forcing his eyes open and remaining alert for nearby sounds which might indicate the presence of enemy. It worked for a time; a short time, before sleep crept over him.

Mike, forehead resting on the leaf litter, lay with his left arm splayed out beside him, right hand clasping his rifle.

"Mike, wake up," whispered Finn, gently shaking the man's shoulder.

No response.

"Mike, you twat! Wake up, time to go," he spoke louder this time, punching him.

"Oi, mucker! We're moving!" Finn insisted. But his friend remained silent and still.

Then Mike moved. He looked slowly across at Finn, great globules of coagulated blood dripping from his mouth, lips peeled back in a snarl to reveal red teeth. His dead, dry, sightless eyes staring over Finn's shoulder.

"Let me rest in peace," he hissed slowly, before resting his head back onto the leaf litter, a trickle of blood oozing from the corner of his mouth.

Finn flinched and his eyes snapped open, sleep rapidly departing, heart thundering in his ears. Darkness enveloped him and he looked up at the partially obscured night sky above. The gentle wind continued to caress the fallen pine under which he lay.

Trying to relax, he listened to the sounds of the night for what seemed an age, before his eyes began fluttering as sleep reached for him. This time he slept dreamlessly, blissfully unaware of a fox scavenging amongst what was left of the rotting kangaroo carcass nearby. Clueless to the owl as it swooped down, pouncing upon a rat within metres of his boots. Usually Finn was a light sleeper, alert to the smallest noise. But exhaustion had enveloped him.

* * * * *

In the distance, there were faint shouts followed by the long staccato of two dogs barking. The shouting grew louder as the search party slowly wended through the sparse scrub towards Finn's position.

Occasionally, the dogs began barking again as they regained a strong scent trail, before concentration reigned supreme and they resorted to a slow trot, noses centimetres from the creek bank. Finn, snoring softly, had no idea that the dogs would lose his trail for almost two hours, forcing the soldiers to lead the animals back to the last known trail. Three times they were forced to repeat the procedure. He would never know that the Indonesians, tired, hungry and thirsty, had almost abandoned the search. Almost. Sitting against a monstrous Ghost Gum, they muttered amongst themselves as the dogs lay panting nearby. An argument broke out, and finally, the search recommenced, one soldier rising with a shake of his head and a curse, kicking a broken branch across the ground.

Then, as the sun gave forewarning of its coming in the eastern sky, forcing stars to silently retreat, the dogs crossed the creek and regained their strongest trail yet. Their barks sounded more like howls, forcing the Indonesians into a run just to keep pace with the canines. They shouted in an effort to recall or slow the animals, but without avail. They were on the trail, the soldiers knew it, and they unslung weapons, flicking safety catches off.

* * * * *

Finn snorted, snapping his eyes open, his heart thundering. Sitting up, he lifted his rifle, flicked off the safety catch and listened intently. The eastern sky showed gunmetal grey, silhouetting a few clouds, that would, within half an hour, be thrown into hues of pink and purple as the sun rose. With images of Mike fading in his mind, Finn pushed himself clear of the pine, weapon in hand, and stood up. Taking in a deep breath of fresh air, he let it out slowly and felt his heart beat begin to slow. The adrenalin helped warm his body against the cold air assaulting his damp clothing.

Shivering, he knelt, still acutely aware that something was amiss. Without even being aware, Finn's index finger had gently dropped onto the trigger applying ever so slight pressure. Dawn's gentle silence was shattered as barking echoed across the scrub. The dogs were close. With no time to evade and lacking the speed to outrun a canine, Finn knew the game was up.

"What a cluster fuck!" he snarled, pushing himself to his feet and sprinting towards the kangaroo carcass.

Diving onto the stinking remains, he rolled amongst the putrid mess, smearing maggot-ridden flesh over his clothes and holding vomit at bay. Pulling the rib cage in front of him, Finn lay prone amongst the deceased kangaroo, the muzzle of his weapon protruding between the ribs. The barking was louder, and he could now hear the animals sprinting across the leaf litter towards him. They were breathing hard, but enthusiastic.

Breathing through his mouth so as not to smell the putrid stink of the corpse into which he so recently immersed himself, Finn lay still and silent. He glimpsed the first dog burst through nearby shrubs, closely followed by the second. They were at full sprint, tongues lolling from their mouths, their breath coming in rhythmic pants. He lost sight of them as they sprinted behind him, but he could hear them slow and begin trotting through the leaf litter. He knew they had located his immediate scent, however he hoped the decomposing kangaroo helped to throw the trail off, or at least confuse the canines.

Closing his eyes and clenching his jaw, Finn felt a wet nose sniffing the stinking intestine lying across his right ear. The dogs might not realise he was lying amongst what remained of the kangaroo, but the Indonesian soldiers would be able to see his legs protruding from the corpse. Capture or death would follow with minutes. At some point, he needed to make a break, and he knew it. For the time being, however, he remained silent, listening to the dogs circle the corpse, panting softly. They knew their quarry was close, but the putrid corpse was throwing them.

The only part of Finn's body now moving was his eyes, as he scanned the scrub in front of him, trying to ignore the canines padding around him close by. Clumsy footfalls issued through the dry leaf litter towards him, branches snapping, voices calling, or cursing, Finn could not tell which. The Indonesian soldiers were the next to appear on the scene. The first blundered over a large, fallen log, whilst the second brushed quietly past a grass tree, his eyes alert,. The second to appear seemed to be the leader. Finn ever so slowly bringing his weapon to bear so the target reticule rested over the enemy's chest.

He waited until the last soldier appeared; winded, hands resting on knees, sweat dripping from his face. Finn smirked as he watched the grossly unfit soldier. Train hard, fight easy was a method of thinking lost on the third enemy soldier. Finn returned his attention to the second soldier, the leader. He was staring hard at the dead kangaroo. Realisation dawned on him, mouth opening to shout an order, and weapon beginning to rise. Finn shot him in the chest three times in quick succession. The Indonesian crumpled to the ground. Finn swung his aim to the second soldier and shot him, too. As he went to drop the third, he felt a powerful jaw close upon his right boot. Rolling onto his back, he kicked the dog in the head with his left foot. With a yelp, it released its grip. Rolling back into the prone position, Finn's peripheral vision picked up the second dog charging in towards him. But ignore it he must. The third and final enemy soldier, who had now shouldered his weapon, was the most dangerous. Rounds cracked over Finn's head and stitched the ground beside him. Ignoring them, he fired twice. The first bullet snapped passed the enemy soldier's head, but the second ripped through his throat in a bloody swathe.

Pushing himself into a kneeling himself, he was about to stand before the second dog him in the side, slamming him to the ground. Keeping a firm grip on his weapon, Finn felt burning pain as the animal's powerful jaws latched on. Feeling the second dog reclaim his boot, he knew he stood the possibility of being torn apart. Ignoring the pain, Finn knew he needed to stand up. If one or both dogs latched onto his throat, it was over.

Forcing himself to kneel, he tried to elbow the closest dog away but failed. Kicking the second dog away, he was able to stand. Losing its grip on his arm, the first animal fell back too. Without losing a moment, Finn swivelled around and slammed the butt of his rifle into the canine's head. It flopped to the ground unconscious. With pain racking his arm, and discomfort assaulting his foot, he turned on the remaining dog.

"Come on then Fido, let's have ya!" he snarled, although he refrained from shooting. He hated killing animals. Finn would rather cut a man's throat than shoot a dog.

Circling him, the canine was alert, although unsure, its eyes continuously glancing at its downed comrade. Finn slowly began backing away from the area. He was tempted to search the enemy dead for ammunition, food, water and additional weapons, but he had enough provisions on him to last another few days at least. Departing the area and putting distance between himself and the altercation would be in his best interests.

* * * * *

Ben's eyes snapped open and he took in a sharp breath. Heart thundering, he blinked, wiped sleep from his eyes and sat up in bed. Katie slept beside him, breathing quietly, the warmth of her body pressed against him. Moving slowly so as not to wake her, he padded to the bedroom window and opened it fully, looking out at the distant forest. Ben was sure he heard a series of gunshots. Passing a hand over his face, he supposed it may have been part of a dream.

He stood for several minutes, listening and watching, although the homestead remained awash with nothing but bird calls as they greeted the morning. Hearing Katie roll over he glanced back at her, but she remained asleep. He watched her. She was a beautiful woman. He had no idea what she saw in him. The bedroom door exploded open and Mick walked in, ripping Ben from his thoughts.

"You can't just walk in here, old man!" hissed Ben.

"My house aint it?" Mick asked, grinning. "You hear those gunshots as well?"

Ben's heart began thundering again as he realised it had been no dream. "Yeah," he said.

"Get your rifle," said Mick, "get your boots, and —"

"Yeah, yeah," said Ben stifling a yawn, "I know Mick, right behind ya mate."

"By the way," said Mick turning in the doorway. "Nice undies, Ben, do they make them for men?"

Ben smirked, gave the older man the finger and closed the door in his face.

"Fuck'n smart arse," he chuckled quietly as he dressed, shaking his head. His boots were out on the veranda; Katie would not allow either man to wear them inside.

He slipped out the room and closed the door silently behind him, leaving Katie sleeping peacefully. Mick was already waiting for him outside. Ben sat on a chair and pulled on his boots, accepting the familiar rifle the older man pushed towards him. His hands caressed the weapon with familiarity, the cold, wooden butt stock and faint scent of gun oil bringing some semblance of order to the world. He felt naked without it.

"We'll go quiet, I'd like—"

"Oh, I thought we'd start singing the national anthem," interposed Ben, a serious look on his face. "Yeah, I thought we'd go running in there shouting and laughing? Did you plan different?"

Mick grinned and shook his head. "You're a little prick," he chuckled. "Yes, as a matter of fuck'n fact, I did plan different!"

The younger man chuckled and slapped Mick on the back.

"You know the drill," said Mick.

"Yeah, mate," replied Ben quietly. "I know the drill. By the way, you taken your medication this morning?"

"No, that can wait 'til—"

"No it can't, Mick," said Ben. "Katie'll crucify you if she found out, you know that! Go take your medication mate, I'll wait here."

Mick hesitated for a moment and looked ready to argue.

"Go!" said Ben.

Nodding, the older man wordlessly disappeared inside.

With heart trouble and blood pressure problems, it was imperative Mick take his medications. Mick probably only had enough medication for one more month, at the outside. If the national situation didn't resolve sometime soon, he'd be quite sick in a short space of time.

Sitting on a nearby chair, Ben looked out at the forest and remembered Mat and Craig. Both were incredibly skilled soldiers. So many times one or the other, or both, had pulled him out of dire situations. Usually with a quiet word, pat on the shoulder, wink, or after having killed half an enemy platoon, lectured on where he went wrong.

The invasion of Australia had been an incredibly terrible event, killing hundreds of thousands, displacing millions, and affecting the entire population. Before the Indonesians made landfall, Ben had been an information technology consultant. A bad day for him consisted of a late coffee, or a particularly stressful conversation with a client who should have packed their computer into the closest box and returned it to sender. Some people just should not own computers, or technology of any sort. At least, that had been Ben's assumption prior to the invasion.

However, his idea of a stressful day had been forever changed following the invasion. A late coffee would mean nothing, and a telephone conversation with some witless clown who was having trouble understanding what a keyboard was would make for endless entertainment rather than creating an early receding hairline.

Everything was relative. A person, who had not experienced true hardship, owned a limited capacity for intestinal fortitude when the proverbial hit the fan. The invasion had tried, tested and broken many Australians used to living a comfortable lifestyle. When a truly terrible day started with a flat tyre on the way to work, individuals found themselves in a crisis when, after the Indonesian arrival, they were wondering from where their next meal was coming, or if they were going to survive the night. Many floundered under the new pressure, but some accepted the new lifestyle and worked through it as best as possible.

It was those individuals, with the gumption to climb back onto their feet and brush themselves off, who not only became resistance fighters, but they would be the ones to rebuild Australia when it was all over. The thoughts churned through Ben's mind as he stared off into the forest, vaguely aware of Mick's soft footfalls inside as he moved to the medicine cabinet in the kitchen.

"You right, mate?" Mick asked quietly as he closed the front door behind him.

"Yeah, let's go."

The pair moved off quietly into the forest towards where the distant gunshots had first been heard. Ben was mindful of spacing, keeping at least ten metres between himself and Mick, who was leading the way. He made sure he was not only behind but also slightly to one side of the older man. A lesson learned from Craig, who often took the time to explain tactics and why certain patrol formations were better than others given weather or terrain. Walking diagonally behind Mick ensured that if they were ambushed from either front or rear, either man could go to ground and offer immediate supressing fire for the other without fear of accidentally shooting the other.

Had Ben been following directly behind the older man, were they to come under ambush from the front, he would run to one side and drop to return fire. Diagonal spacing offered expanded, yet safe, fields of fire for smaller patrols.

Micked stopped and went to one knee. Ben followed suit, dropping onto one knee amongst the leaf litter of the forest. He brought the rifle into his shoulder and stared out over the sights. With a soft whistle, Mick gained the young man's attention and signalled to move forward. Brushing passed a long dead eucalypt sapling, he saw the small mob of kangaroos grazing in the near distance, their movement amongst the forest likely the reason Mick stopped.

As they neared, the animals pushed themselves up on their legs and stood tall, watching the pair with alert eyes. As they neared, the kangaroos departed in rapid bounds. The men crouched once more, allowing the mob to leave the area. When he thought they were once more alone, Mick stood, withholding a grunt, and signalled Ben forward.

They progressed through the scrub slowly, picking their way carefully through the underbrush to eliminate as much noise as possible. A flock of Kookaburras, oblivious to the men's presence, began laughing nearby, marking their territory. Smaller birds twittered and called as they flew overhead in small groups, or sat high up in trees looking down upon the pair. The world was waking up. Ben lost his footing on the edge of a rabbit hole and fell to the ground with a grunt, landing face first in a clump of grass.

Mick stopped and turned slowly. He shook his head, his face somewhere halfway between smirk and frown.

"Get up," the older man mouthed.

"Get fucked," the younger man mouthed back, pushing himself back onto his feet quietly.

Mick looked at him sternly, as if daring Ben to repeat himself.

"What?" the younger man mimed, a look of innocence crossing his face.

Mick shook his head and turned away, continuing slowly. Ben followed, almost losing his footing on the same rabbit hole, before trotting forward a couple of steps and continuing on his way.

Hearing the commotion, the older man turned around again, but Ben made sure he was paying particular attention somewhere else.

The pair made good progress for almost twenty minutes before nearby gunfire brought them to a halt. They waded through the hip length grass at a half crouch, eyes alert, safety catches off and index fingers gently resting on triggers.

A loud crash issued from the bush directly to their front and Mick went down on one knee, signalling for Ben to do the same. Fast footfalls crunched through the leaf litter towards them at a pace suggesting the individual was progressing at a fast run.

Ben moved up beside Mick and brought his weapon to bear.

A gentle hand on his shoulder and a reassuring nod from Mick suggested he relax. Itchy trigger fingers did not win battles, they started them. The man ploughed into view as he sprinted between the trunks of two trees. He stopped, breathless and looked behind him, as if expecting a follow up. One of the sleeves of his camouflaged uniform was ripped, the skin beneath stained dark red, blood dripping from his fingertips.

Mick stood, weapon pulled into his shoulder. "Halt!" he challenged.

The intruder stiffened, slowly looking around towards the new threat.

Ben also stood, staring down the sight of his weapon at the soldier.

Slinging his weapon, the soldier held his hands up, a look of relief crossing his face.

"Thank Christ," he said in a thick British accent.

Mick and Ben looked at one another.

"Advance slowly," advised Mick. "Nothing stupid, you know the drill."

"My name's Finn," offered the newcomer as he slowly walked towards them.

Mick introduced himself and Ben.

"Stop there," said Mick. "Turn around, keep your hands visible."

Finn obeyed, knowing well that these men, after months of siege, would probably think nothing of killing him and leaving him to rot amongst the forest. Better to simply do what they wanted. Given the situation, he would rather be captured by Australian civilians, than Indonesian soldiers.

"You British Army?" asked Mick.

"Royal Marines," Finn answered, trying not to sound affronted.

"Righto, relax," offered Mick, after stripping Finn of his rifle and searching him for any other weapons.

"Welcome to Australia," Mick offered. "How have you enjoyed your stay so far?"

Chapter 7

"Queensland remains the last great battlefield for Indonesian resistance. The government of Indonesia denies all responsibility for their soldiers (thought to number in their thousands) who remain on Australian soil." – *The Times (UK)*

The charred bodies, which had since been placed in body bags, were carried gently from the Blackhawk under the watchful eye of Craig.

Hours after the fire had swept through, three Blackhawk helicopters, escorted by an Apache gunship had swept the area, finally spotting Tanya and Craig in the dam. They landed nearby and loaded them aboard, securing the still unconscious Apache pilot to the deck, where Tanya maintained a vigilant watch over him.

"Good work on bringing the pilot back, mate," Craig heard a voice behind him, followed by a slap on the back. He turned to see Colonel Mal Tabb, the Australian Medical Officer in charge of the tiny Air Transportable Hospital (ATH) situated upon the Redcliffe showgrounds near Brisbane. Colonel Tabb was a man of average height, dark eyes filled with humour and brown hair streaked with grey. He was the man responsible for running the ATH, and he ran it with a fierce efficiency. The operation at the Redcliffe showgrounds ran like clockwork, and even now, as Craig stood talking to the Colonel, the Apache pilot, who remained nameless, was being operated on inside the hospital.

The ATH took up almost the entire show grounds. Initially the hospital had been airdropped in sections. Once pieced together, it was inflated and within four hours was capable of providing care for basic complaints. More severe ailments could be addressed within twenty-four hours, and complex surgical procedures would be underway within forty-eight hours. Almost two hundred ATHs were scattered around Australia's coast.

The ATH held twenty-eight beds, an operating theatre and an intensive care unit. It was air-conditioned to maintain a constant temperature and the operating theatre was maintained in a negative pressure environment.

Redcliffe, being on the coast, made it easy for medical supplies to be flown in from USS George Washington steaming off the coast of Queensland.

"Yeah, pity about the others," replied Craig, trying to sound less downhearted than he actually felt.

"Not your fault, mate," said Mal. "For the love of fuck, you got shot out of the sky, it's lucky any of you pricks survived!"

"True," replied Craig.

"Sir, phone call, they want to speak to you," said a private running towards them, a satellite phone in his hand.

"For fuck sake," said Mal, taking the phone from the private and glaring until the young soldier turned and trotted away.

The colonel held the handset to his ear. "Yup," he said, then paused for a second. "This *is* Colonel Tabb you idiot!" Mal said matter-of-factly.

Craig grinned as he stared out to sea, where USS George Washington was just visible upon the horizon. He liked the way Colonel Tabb didn't tip toe across eggshells, he was matter of fact. It was probably why the ATH ran so well.

"I—" Mal shoved a hand in his pocket, anger glinting in his eyes.

"Well if you let me—"

"You can—"

"I see, well the problem—"

Craig was struggling to remain from bursting out laughing as he watched the one-way conversation Mal was having with whoever was on the other end of the phone. Colonel Tabb caught Craig's eye and shook his head, silently mouthing, "Fuck me".

"I thought that—"

There was an extended silence as Mal impatiently listened before he exploded.

"Listen you cock wielding fuck-weasel, no, no, I'm done listening you fuckin' turbomong. I've had it up to here with your shit bag antics. Up to here! You hear me? I wanted that order put in for those supplies at zero seven hundred this morning, and here we are, four, no—" Mal checked his watch, "five hours later, and it still hasn't been submitted!"

There was silence again as Mal listened.

"*You're* offended? Are you fucking serious? Well you may as well amend the order form and add on a box of tissues!" He hung up and dropped the satellite phone into a pocket. Letting out a harsh sigh, he shook his head and chuckled. "Un-fuck'n'-believable."

"Trouble in paradise?" asked Craig.

"Nah, not really," grinned Mal. "I wish they had a bloody private in charge of the orders though, not another colonel. That fuck knuckle is hard pressed to wipe his arse after having a shit, let alone order life-saving gear we desperately need for the hospital. If we had a private in charge, the order form would have been submitted at zero six hundred this morning. Ah well, can't complain too much; the thunder fuck is submitting it as we speak."

Craig noticed Colonel Tabb loved to offend people in the most colourful ways, all the while that humorous glint never left his eyes.

Mal pulled a small square of bubble wrap from his pocket and began popping the bubbles, one by one. He sighed when he had finished and pushed the spent piece of bubble wrap back into his pocket.

Craig looked at him, eyebrows raised in question.

Mal smiled and shrugged. "It's my thing, mate. It's what I do."

"Think of it like a stress ball," said Tanya sitting down beside him and sighing, shoulders slumped, eyes glazed.

"You look exhausted," said Craig.

"Thanks," she chuckled. "I feel it."

He watched her as she stared out to sea, silently watched a flock of gulls wheeling and diving towards the ocean's surface, where small fish were boiling the surface. Hugging her knees to her chest, she slowly lowered her head, tears sliding down her cheeks. Her shoulders shuddered, but she maintained her silence.

When he touched her back, she inhaled a shuddering breath.

"Sorry," she said quietly, voice thick with emotion.

"No need to apologise," said Craig, stroking her back. "We've been through a lot; it's bound to catch up some time."

"It's just... I could have... Oh, I don't know..." She shook her head, her voice trailing to silence. Sniffing, she wiped tears from her cheeks.

"You could have what?" Asked Craig. But before she could respond, Craig continued. "Could you have stopped the chopper from being shot down?"

"No."

"No, of course not. Could you have saved the lives of any of the soldiers who were killed on impact?"

"Probably not."

"No, no way in hell. Is any of what happened your fault?"

She looked over at him, red-rimmed eyes glistening with tears, cheeks wet. "I don't think so," she replied.

"No it's not, I know that for a fact," he said. "You need to know that too," Craig said turning and grasping her shoulders. "You did everything humanly possible. None of what happened is your fault, you didn't influence any of the events and you certainly couldn't have changed them once everything went to piss. You are not to blame." He squeezed her shoulders. "Understand? You are not to blame."

She nodded and managed a weak smile.

"Oi, you pair of shit lips, when you've finished canoodling," said Mal, approaching the couple, grinning. He gestured at the ATH in the near distance. "Just got a phone call from the head surgeon. The Apache pilot's out of surgery. He's in a stable condition and expected to survive. He needed four units of blood, though. The surgeon had his ring gear hanging out it sounds, but the boy's gonna pull through. Wouldn't have made it if it wasn't for you," said Mal, looking at Tanya purposefully. He stopped short of saying any more, but his eyes seemed to say chin up, dust yourself off and back on your feet. We still need you.

"Good work," smiled Craig. "You saved a life today."

"Thanks," said Tanya. She leaned forward and kissed him on the cheek. "I mean that. Thanks."

"Christ on a popsicle, you two are making me blush. I'm outta here!" said Mal throwing his arms up in the air, although no one could miss the grin on his face as he turned away.

*****

Four hours later, Craig and Tanya found themselves on-board another helicopter amongst a small group of US Marines heading back out into the Australian scrub where another TIC was taking place. Two friendlies were reported wounded, one possibly dead. They flew low, trees dangerously close to the underside of the aircraft whipping past in blurs of green and brown.

It became obvious as they touched down that the firefight was over, the Indonesian force overrun. Most lay dead, the bodies organised into neat rows where they were checked for intelligence, such as notepads, marked maps, radios, digital cameras or phones. A quick exchange between the small Marine force aboard the chopper and the Marine in command of the men on the ground ensued while Tanya worked on the wounded men. One had suffered a bullet wound to the shoulder, the other a fractured leg, as a result of accidentally finding a wombat burrow with his foot as he sprinted towards cover. The third had passed away because of blood loss. He had been struck by a large bullet in the abdomen, which Tanya guessed had dissected his descending aorta. At least the death would have been fast.

Craig helped where possible, and within ten short minutes both Marines were stable, pain relief working its magic as one dozed and the other, his leg splinted, stared silently up at the roof of the helicopter, hands clasped together and resting on his chest. Over the noise of the engine and rotor blades, neither Craig nor Tanya could hear what the Marines were discussing. After a chuckle and a few slaps on the back, the Marine commander turned away to re-join his men nearby, while the small group climbed back on board the chopper. Moments later, they were airborne again, heading for the Supercarrier.

Once the wounded Marines were triaged and allocated beds in the emergency section of the ship, Tanya and Craig headed for the closest crew room for coffee.

"How do you take your coffee?" Tanya asked. "I know, I know, I should know by now!"

"Black with milk," replied Craig.

She nodded. "Black with milk," she repeated, trying to commit it to memory in preparation for the next time it was her turn to make the brews. Then she paused as she realised what Craig had said. Turning back, she looked at him with one eyebrow raised, hands on hips.

He grinned and winked at her.

The coffee was cheap instant and the milk was powdered, but the brew still tasted mighty fine. Tanya leaned back into the soft sofa, closed her eyes and breathed a sigh of relief as she savoured the taste.

"God that's good," she said, closing her eyes and taking another sip.

Craig nodded but remained silent, enjoying the silence, or as silent as was possible considering the powerful hum of the ship's engines many decks beneath them.

"You need to get some sleep," he said, noticing how exhausted she looked.

"I'll sleep when I'm dead," she replied quietly.

He chuckled, watching as her breathing began to deepen. Gently removing the half-finished cup of coffee from her hands before she dropped it, he placed it on a nearby table. Within minutes she was sleeping like a baby, head rested back against the chair.

Craig finished his coffee, placed the cup beside Tanya's and closed his eyes. He too needed sleep and it was wise to get as much as possible whenever the opportunity raised its head.

* * * * *

"Rise and shine you two." The loud voice startled Craig awake. It felt like he'd been asleep for mere minutes, but a quick check of his watch revealed he had been sleeping for nearly four hours. He felt better for it too.

Stifling a yawn, he looked up to see an officer standing over them, hands on hips. The bags under his eyes and creased uniform told he had experienced just as much sleep deprivation as them.

"I'm up," mumbled Tanya, passing a hand over her face. Rubbing her eyes, she yawned and stretched, before slowly standing. "What can we do for you lieutenant?"

"I've been told to bring you both to see the Colonel," the young lieutenant shrugged, "I don't know why, was just asked to find you and bring you. Took me almost an hour!"

"Good," said Craig, standing beside Tanya, "we needed the sleep."

* * * * *

Colonel Broadhurst was a tall, powerful looking man, his sharp blue eyes glinting with experience that spoke of countless deployments to various parts of the world.

"Good morning to you both," he said, closing the door behind the pair as they entered.

Tanya was about to snap of a crisp salute, but the colonel gestured for her not to bother.

"Take a seat."

When they sat, the commander of the Marine detachment aboard USS *Ronald Reagan* stared at them for a long time.

"Time and time again, your names are mentioned," he began. "At the completion of almost every medevac mission, you two are mentioned in some context. Hell, there's an Apache pilot in recovery owes his damn life to you! You've done some great work out there. But it's not over."

Broadhurst spread out a map. Marked on the map were various areas of Australia. Allied aircraft carriers were tagged around various areas of the country's coastline, with lines along the coast showing what ground the allies had made against the Indonesian adversary. For the most part, it was good news. The Indonesians appeared to be in full retreat in most states of Australia. Except in Queensland, Craig noticed as his eyes came to rest upon their area of responsibility.

"We've gained a good foothold in our area, but the Brits, north of us, are having a hell of a time of it. Preliminary intelligence reports suggest the vast majority of Indonesian soldiers are shacked up in the forests of the British area of responsibility."

Craig noticed a large blue circle dubbed 'Churchill' north of their location. That must have been the name of the designation area given to the British forces. In that moment, Craig felt like a mushroom. Kept in the dark and fed bullshit. The map before them showed just how much was going on around the country outside their little bubble.

"They've requested help," continued the colonel, looking up at them. "We're sending eight F-18s to conduct missions from the HMS *Illustrious*, which they've redeployed from the Northern Territory down to Queensland. The Northern Territory is a forgone conclusion by the way." Broadhurst, tapped the map. "The entire state is now Indonesian-free, so to speak. Queensland appears to be their last true stronghold. The tide has turned for us here in southern Queensland, but the Brits are still fighting hard. There're also a few pockets of die-hard Aussie freedom fighters resisting the Indonesians with mixed success."

The colonel waved in a sailor who carried a plate holding three steaming cups of coffee and some cake. "Please, help yourselves," offered the colonel.

"As I was saying, we've sent up some fighter bombers, a large Marine contingent who do have corpsmen amongst them, but they will only operate amongst the Marines themselves. The Brits have asked specifically for independent medics who will operate flexibly amongst UK forces. When I read the request, I immediately thought of you both."

"We're going to need some time to think about this, sir," said Tanya.

As for Craig, the Australian Special Operations Command had been out of touch with both him and Mat for an extended period, so he assumed he was free to operate as needed.

"I'll give you seventy-two hours," replied the colonel

* * * * *

Craig stood by the hospital bed. Still sedated, Mat was breathing quietly. His head had been shaved and a small, clean wound held closed by surgical staples ran along the top of his scalp.

"He's recovering well," spoke the nurse softly with a reassuring smile. She checked the machines, ran a watchful eye over Mat and then left to check her other patients.

Craig nodded, but remained silent, watching his mate, unsure how much truth the nurse spoke. Would he wake up? If he did, would he be brain damaged? Or would his wife be hand feeding him and wiping his arse for him the rest of his life?

"Looks like I'm going away for a bit mate," Craig said to the unconscious soldier. "Tanya and I are heading up north to help the Brits. Back to our old stomping ground. We had a few near misses there I can tell you!" He grinned as the memories came flooding back, some good, others dark, bloody and violent. His thoughts turned to Tanya. He made sure he mentioned her each time he visited Mat. "You'll like Tanya, mate. She's one top chick. Tough as old leather, but hot as hell!"

The nurse came bustling back in, picked up Mat's chart and scribbled some notes, occasionally looking up at the bank of machines humming and beeping beside Mat's bed.

86

"You get better soon mate, I'll check on you when I get back." He patted the soldier's shoulder, nodded at the nurse and departed.

* * * * *

Flying close to the ocean's surface, the view from the Blackhawk was spectacular. In the distance, kilometre upon kilometre of empty beach slid by. Gently clasping his M-4 between his legs, muzzle resting on the floor, Craig allowed his eyes to take in the clear, blue sky. High above them, he caught a brief glimpse of a flock of birds in close formation heading towards land. Nearby were some marines. Tanya sat beside him, dozing, her head rested back, occasionally rolling from side to side as the chopper changed direction or hit pockets of turbulence. She was a beautiful woman, with soft, smooth skin and although she was fit, she still carried a womanly figure. Often he caught himself checking her out if she was walking in front of him. Only once she caught him in the act, but she just smiled and winked.

Movement captured his attention and Craig leaned forward in his seat so he could better focus. The dark blots were flying high and fast, but they were undoubtedly fighter jets. They banked together and changed direction, disappearing over the land within seconds. As Craig drifted away into his thoughts, he noticed a British destroyer in the near distance. The ship was cutting slowly through the ocean, heading north. Moments later, Craig spotted another destroyer, followed by two missile frigates, and a smaller ship he assumed was possibly an anti-submarine ship. The ships formed part of a British carrier strike group, he realised. Feeling the seat belts digging into shoulders, he watched as the sky disappeared to be replaced with ocean as the Blackhawk banked hard. Looking through the front windscreen, he saw they were approaching the HMS *Illustrious*. Reducing speed and descending, it was only a matter of minutes before they were touching down upon the aircraft carrier's deck.

As the Blackhawk's engines shut down, their powerful whine was replaced by an incessant noise. Two Chinooks and an Apache were outbound towards the coast, whilst three RAF F-35B fighter-bombers were patiently waiting for the choppers to depart a safe distance from the ship. Craig climbed out onto the ship's deck and turned to help Tanya, but she ignored him. Jumping clear of the

87

Blackhawk she stood beside him, wisely leaving her hearing protection pushed into her ear cavities.

Flight line ground crew had signalled for the Blackhawk's aircrew and passengers to remain where they stood. A dull, powerful thud reverberated across the aircraft carrier's deck and the first F-35 was catapulted airborne, afterburners glowing red. The remaining two closely followed the first and within moments they were a trio of black dots streaking towards the coastline. With the all clear given, the small group walked swiftly across the deck towards a waiting British officer.

He welcomed them with a smile and nod, although as several helicopters began start up procedures nearby, didn't speak until they were below decks. The group spent nearly an hour and a half in a briefing room being familiarised with the carrier, locations of toilets, meal timings, locations of fire extinguishers, emergency drills, locations of life rafts around the ship, actions on the 'abandon ship' command.

"Never thought that lecture'd bloody end," said Craig later as he sat with Tanya eating a meal in the mess hall.

"Tell me about it, I was crossing my legs towards the end!"

"Food's not bad," said Craig, cutting into a thin slice of steak.

"You mean chow?" asked Tanya, a cheeky gleam in her eye.

"No, he means scran," said a British sailor nearby, grinning.

"For Christ sake, both of you are weird, it's called *food*!" Craig acted outraged, but could not keep a straight face.

With the meal finished, they found their sleeping quarters. Tanya was bunked with several female sailors, whilst Craig found himself in a large room the Navy termed a Troops' Mess. The room could sleep one hundred soldiers, but was about half full right now. The bunks were four beds high, each soldier being allocated about fifty centimetres of space; enough room to roll over. The bed even came decked out with a belt, to stop one from being thrown if rough weather was encountered. Towels and clothes not being worn were pinned into place around a rail with a safety pin larger than a man's hand. If the carrier were to be subject to an enemy strike and begin taking on water, huge pumps would begin evacuating water back out into the ocean. The pumps would malfunction or fail if the drainage pipes were to become blocked with towels and clothes.

Craig climbed into bed and strapped himself in. Closing his eyes, he tried to relax, but sleep wouldn't come. Disconnecting the strap, he immediately felt more comfortable and less restricted. HMS *Illustrious'* mighty engines growled gently, strangely helping him to relax. As sleep began to envelope him, his thoughts, slug-like, turned to Mat once more. Craig knew he would never forgive himself if his comrade did not pull through.

A dull thud reverberated throughout the ship as, high above the Troop's Mess, another F-35 was catapulted outbound.

* * * * *

Sipping coffee, Craig sat in the mess hall, his breakfast in front of him. He had been corrected several times by sailors, who referred to it as a scran hall, but Craig refused to bow to peer-pressure. It also amused him how it seemed to offend the Navy. Tanya still remained absent. Craig knew she would appear before long. He finished his coffee, enjoying the taste.

"Howdy stranger," a familiar voice spoke.

Craig looked up at Tanya, his mouth full of cereal. He grunted, nodded and then gestured at his mouth to indicate he could not speak. She chuckled and moved away to join the line of sailors, soldiers and airmen waiting for their breakfast.

"Give me some more bacon," demanded a corporal.

The cook looked up at the soldier, paused for a moment and then calmly removed the two pieces of bacon from his plate, and gave him a large serving of mushrooms.

"Oi, is that all I'm gettin'?" asked the corporal, incredulous.

"Yup," replied the cook, smiling pleasantly. "Next!" he called.

Tanya supressed a smile, it always paid never to piss off the cooks. Regardless of which force or country they served, military cooks were the same the world over. One could treat them with disdain and disrespect, but only at their peril. Napoleon coined the phrase, 'an army marches on its stomach.' It was as true in the modern day as it was in Bonaparte's time.

Tanya carried the food and a coffee back to Craig's table.

"Morning," he smiled, his breakfast now finished.

"Oh, you can talk now, huh?"

"I could talk before, but I would have been wearing my breakfast down my shirt."

"New fashion?" she asked.

Craig nodded, a thoughtful expression settling upon his face. "Could make a mint."

"We could."

"We?" Craig asked, raising his eyebrows.

"Well, I thought of it," Tanya reminded him.

"Alright, alright." Craig set his hands on the table. "I'll give you five percent of the profits."

Tanya stifled a laugh, smirking she winked at him.

The pair sat for some time, chatting about their lives at home, what life was like in their respective units. More than once, Craig became lost in her eyes as she talked, only snapping out of it when he realised she had actually asked a question.

"Excuse me, sir, ma'am?" A royal marine stood before them.

"Sir?" asked Craig. "Shit, I work for a living, mate, just call me Craig."

The Marine nodded, committing the name to memory. "Lieutenant Colonel Lacey would like to see you both, if of course, you've finished breakfast."

"Yeah mate, we're finished, just give us a tick," said Craig as he carried the serving trays across to the kitchen where personnel were already beginning the tedious process of washing up.

"Do you know what it's about?" Tanya asked.

The man looked troubled. "Yes ma'am, it's pretty bad. But I'll allow the colonel to elaborate."

The pair followed the royal marine, knowing they were likely less than an hour or two away from being deployed out somewhere into the Australian bush or any one of the countless towns and cities within striking distance of the carrier. As enjoyable as breakfast had been, the interruption had been a cold reminder that war still raged around Australia.

Chapter 8

Lieutenant Colonel Lacey was a short man, well-built with sharp, intelligent, blue eyes and quick to smile. Craig immediately liked him. Also present in the cramped office were several Royal Marine Commandos and a handful of heavily bearded, rough-looking men who were more than likely either British Army Special Air Service, or Navy Special Boat Service. Lacey introduced himself and spared no time on small talk before launching straight into their next mission. Attached to the wall of his office was a large map of Queensland, pertinent to their area of operations (AO). On the map, far inland and marked amongst a section of dark green, was a small circle.

"We're unsure whether this is going to be a rescue mission or body recovery, I'm afraid," began Lacey, a feeling of sobriety suddenly settling on the room.

"One of the close combat sections of Forty Royal Marines Commando unit has failed to make radio contact for nearly forty-eight hours now." Lacey's face remained staunch as he turned to the map and gestured towards the small circle amongst the immense patches of green. "This is where we last received radio transmissions from them."

"What was the transmission, sir?" asked one of the bearded men.

"'Contact, wait out'," replied Lacey.

Someone nearby swore softly.

Usually an enemy force would have had to have been intercepted, either intentionally or otherwise, and a firefight ensued for a signaller to call contact, wait out, over the radio net. Following the firefight, a contact report was usually transmitted to headquarters, updating them on numbers of enemy dead, enemy captured, friendly casualties, if any, the state of remaining ammunition, and current grid reference of section's location. A firefight could take place between twenty metres and up to five hundred metres, particularly if a pursued fighting withdrawal was taking place. If the grid reference was not updated frequently, an exfil or resupply mission would fail.

"Nothing else heard?" another asked.

Lacey shrugged and shook his head. "Afraid not," he muttered. "We've had fast air on rotating missions throughout the AO. One of the strike missions kindly made a pass over the section of forest in question on their return to the carrier, but saw nothing noteworthy. We're hoping the section's radio was just inoperable and they were able to break contact before clearing the area."

Craig remained silent, but as he gazed at the small circle on the huge map running the length of Lieutenant Colonel Lacey's wall, he held grim doubts in his mind about the section's welfare. Wisely, he kept the thoughts to himself, although he knew most people in the room more than likely held similar thoughts.

"So, we're organising you lot to go in and have a look." He smiled half-heartedly for the first time since introducing himself to Craig and Tanya. "You Fa2 medics are spread thin,"—Lacey motioned towards one of the Marines—"and there may be quite a few casualties, so we're bringing along Tanya, a US Air Force Para Jumper,"—he smiled at Tanya—"and a soldier from the Australian SAS who had nothing better to do," Lacey chuckled, looking at Craig. "From what I understand, both of you have training in advanced trauma life support?"

When they both nodded, Lacey said, "Excellent."

* * * * *

Lieutenant Colonel Lacey allowed thirty minutes for a full kit check, preparation of gear, a quick weapon cleaning, and ammunition check prior to mission launch. Tanya rifled through her medical pack, checking quantities and annotating which stores were depleted and needed restocking. The small British hospital aboard the carrier was helpful, giving her what she needed without argument, which was a refreshing change. Usually she resorted to begging and borrowing to ascertain stores, particularly when working with foreign nations. Twice she had been forced to steal, although she hated having to do it. With ten minutes to go, her medic pack was fully restocked. Swinging it over one shoulder, carrying her helmet and weapon in the other hand, she followed Craig up a narrow, steep, metal ladder, through a hatch, and along a constricted corridor. Twice, sailors were forced to wedge themselves against the wall in order to let them pass.

"Thanks," nodded Craig to a sailor.

Half way up the next Spartan, metal ladder, Tanya paused as she felt the familiar, dull thud shudder through the ship's structure as the catapult on the flight deck above did its ceaseless duty.

Craig could hear the muffled, incessant noise of the flight line above as aircraft were departing or landing and knew they were close. Pushing through one last door, they were on the outer perimeter of the ship, a waist high barrier being the only thing barring them from the open ocean far beneath them. The assault of fresh salt air was nice and Tanya paused to take a deep breath. The noise from the flight deck thrummed, whined, and growled loudly; an indication hearing protection be worn or run the risk of tinnitus twenty-four seven.

Craig placed the hearing protection into his ear canals before strapping on his helmet, waiting for Tanya to do the same. When she gave a smile, thumbs up, and a wink, he smiled back before moving on up the final ladder that would lead them out onto the carrier's upper deck.

A Wildcat helicopter was churning and burning nearby; one loadmaster stood beside the aircraft, waiting patiently. When he saw them, he gestured for them to approach and board. Tanya and Craig walked briskly across the deck towards the waiting chopper. Helmet on, dark visor down, and carbon fibre facial shield protecting the maxilla area of his face, the loadmaster simply nodded to them. Any other communication short of radio or hand signals was impossible given the engine noise. The pair climbed aboard, noticing the Royal Marines were already seated and waiting, although one of them seemed to be fighting a losing battle with his seatbelt. The crisis was resolved when the second loadmaster approached the Marine and slapped his hands away, deftly pulling the seatbelt loose and handing it back to the now sheepish Marine. His comrades were watching him in silent amusement, one of them chuckling while slapping his forehead with the palm of his hand.

Minutes later, with all on board, the Wildcat raked itself into the sky, and accelerated away from the carrier. Within moments, ocean ended and land began as a thin section of beach whipped by beneath them. Forty feet sounded high. King Kong was fifty feet tall and was a veritable giant, but at two hundred and fifty kilometres per hour and with some trees reaching thirty feet out of the forest canopy, it felt low to Tanya. She swallowed, remaining silent, watching hues of green blur beneath them as they scudded impossibly low across the Australian landscape.

She grunted as they banked violently to the right. She hoped and prayed nothing had malfunctioned and they were not about to smash through the forest to the rock hard ground below. Death would be instant at least. Usually Tanya felt quite comfortable flying, particularly in choppers. Realisation dawned on her just how much the recent crash had affected her. Clutching her rifle, she felt the clamminess of her hands and felt her heart hammering. She looked across at Craig and felt immediate relief as he smiled and winked at her. Forming an 'o' with his index finger and thumb he signalled everything would be okay. Taking a deep breath, she relaxed a little.

Word soon spread from soldier to soldier that the evasive manoeuvre had been carried out to avoid a section of forest in which troops were currently in contact with the enemy. Pilots preferred not to fly above a firefight for obvious reasons. In a long sweeping turn, they came back on course and continued towards target. Movement caught her attention and she saw the closest loadmaster holding up three fingers. Three minutes. She was looking forward to departing the chopper. Glancing down, she ensured the safety catch was engaged on her weapon, magazine properly engaged with no chance of falling out. Running a hand quickly over the medic pack clasped between her feet, she confirmed all pouches, pockets, and zips were fully closed. Tanya already knew they were, but it was a force of habit.

Clearing a section of forest by mere feet, the chopper descended quickly into the woodland towards a natural clearing. Bringing the nose of the aircraft up, the helicopter flared, rapidly bleeding off forward momentum. A moment later, they thudded onto the ground and the Royal Marines departed at full sprint, disappearing into the brown out caused by the powerful rotors.

Tanya leapt clear of the chopper, ignoring the sting upon her skin caused by flying dust, leaves, and twigs. Running clear, she found a small, natural depression in the earth and lay on her stomach to wait for the Wildcat's departure. Twisting, she looked behind and noticed

Craig had followed her. He was taking cover behind a mighty looking tree. Ascending, accelerating, and turning, the chopper clawed its way above the canopy and clattered away into the distance.

When the engine's noise had almost subsided, Tanya reached up slowly and pulled the hearing protection out of her ear cavities. Kneeling up, she pulled the weapon into her shoulder and watched as the Marines patrolled away from them into the forest. They moved well, covering their arcs, leaving plenty of space between them. As for the two heavily bearded men, they followed at a more sedate pace, stopping often to look or listen. Tanya felt comforted. Although she worked with all aspects of the United States military, she rarely worked with foreign soldiers. She had been apprehensive about deploying with the British, but she realised she need not have been.

Craig whistled softly to her and moved off after the rapidly disappearing group. Tanya nodded, shrugged the medic pack into place and stood, following. With practised ease, her eyes glided across the Australian scrub as she walked, ever watchful for threats.

Tanya noticed Craig deliberately maintained a fair distance from the Marines in front of them. She moved smoothly, watching her environment, but acutely aware of where she placed her feet and what lay immediately in front of them. Triggering a trip wire or stepping on a mine would kill her instantly and critically wound Craig. She then realized that he had taken a knee behind a tree and was staring intently off to the left. Tanya paused and crouched amongst the thigh high grass. Although following his gaze, she was not sure what he spotted, but when she looked back, Tanya noticed he was on the move again.

Minutes later, the Marines stopped and fell into a small defensive position while the commander consulted a map. Tanya reasoned they must have been close to the spot marked on the map back at Lacey's office. She knelt by a tree, leaned her weight against the trunk, and gently lowered the medic pack to the ground, feeling relief as the large muscles of her back were allowed to rest for a moment. While keeping a watchful eye on her surroundings, she was not oblivious to the birds around her either; she enjoyed listening to their strange calls. It was almost like another world; there were no birds in Washington State like the ones she could hear now. A little cheeky, black bird flitted amongst the branches above her head, darting close to her, wagging its tail feathers at her before flitting away again. She smiled at it.

Signalling the direction they needed to take, the commander stood and led his men into the forest. Again, Craig waited until they had gained some distance before following at a sedate, yet deliberate, pace, stopping often and thoroughly analysing the scrub around him. Pausing, he gestured Tanya to approach and then pointed at the ground. As she neared, Tanya saw a pile of spent bullet cartridges. They were military spec; a firefight had taken place here. Glancing around, she saw more scattered all over the forest floor and knew in her heart they were close. Moving on, they noticed the Royal Marines had halted once more. They had seen evidence of the fight as well as they quietly attempted to make radio contact with the patrol they were searching for. Given they had failed to make radio contact post engagement with the enemy, it was unlikely the Royal Marines would be successful in their bid, but they had to at least try. Letting them know a friendly patrol was also in the area might help avoid a blue on blue.

For five minutes they attempted, without success, to raise the missing patrol before moving on. The bullet cartridges became more numerous and scattered amongst them were larger, 7.62mm cartridges. Probably enemy rounds, guessed Tanya. Following the mounting piles cartridges, other tell-tale signs became evident—faint boot prints in the ground, snapped branches where a soldier had barged past—either fighting towards his enemy or attempting to break contact and withdraw from the area—and remnants of abandoned gear.

It was then they smelled the aroma with which Tanya had grown all too familiar; rotting flesh. Granted, it may have been a dead kangaroo, but the sheer overwhelming stink suggested that—whatever it was—there were several of them. The Marines exchanged foreboding glances with one another before pushing on towards the sickening odour.

Tanya noticed the birds were absent from the immediate area of forest. There was nothing but sheer, ominous silence, as if the forest itself knew something terrible had taken place.

Quietly moving through the scrub towards them came the pair of heavily bearded soldiers, one of them used the 'come here' hand signal to Tanya and Craig, then repeating the signal to the commander of the nearby Marines, before taking a knee and waiting. The second man knelt facing the opposite direction.

"We found 'em," whispered the British soldier, shaking his head sadly. "All dead. Not much you can do I'm afraid," he said, looking at Tanya.

The Marine commander looked down at the leaf-littered ground and silently snarled, shaking his head.

Tanya nodded. "Take me to them," she whispered back.

Pursing his lips, he nodded, stood, and walked quietly through the forest. After almost two minutes of slow patrolling, they reached the scene of the battle. The Royal Marine Commandos went into all-round defence, exchanging haunted glances with one another. One of them was dry retching, covering mouth with his bush hat to try to stifle the noise.

The smell was repugnant; so strong, Tanya could taste it. Deliberately, she inhaled a deep breath of the putrid odour, exhaled, and then inhaled another long breath, refusing to allow herself to vomit. She continued breathing slow and deep for some time, forcing her sense of smell into olfactory fatigue. Eventually the nausea passed as she slowly became desensitised to the stench. When she was ready, she moved amongst the deceased, stopping here, crouching there, always checking, observing, carefully allowing her eyes to move slowly across the scene and wilfully blocking any emotional response—and therefore attachment—to the mass of corpses. It would not be the first time an allied soldier had mistaken the approaching friendlies as enemy and been discovered hiding amongst the dead, in a last bid effort to avoid being captured.

It had been an incredible battle, realised Craig. A platoon size number of Royal Marines lay dead in an all-round defence position where they fell. But surrounding them were three, maybe four, times the number in enemy corpses. The Marines' position had been overrun by sheer weight of numbers, but they had fought incredibly well, right to the last man. Assuming the surviving enemy soldiers had since departed the area, the original size of the Indonesian force must have been anywhere from five to ten times the size of the Marine platoon.

As he scanned the bodies, ground, shrubs, and branches for possible booby traps, mines, or trip wires, he noticed that one of the dead enemy soldiers was lying well away from the others. Frowning, he slowly moved towards the corpse, trying his best to blank out the putrid stink that was throwing his guts into turmoil. The Indonesian soldier lay on his back, a terrible, deep laceration travelling from beneath his right ear to the front of his throat explaining how he had died. Around him, staining the leaf-litter black, were the litres of dried, life-blood that had initially flooded out of the wound, causing his fast and silent death.

Quietly scanning the area, he noticed boot prints leading away to the west. As he followed them, he discovered they became hidden amongst a multitude of other boot prints and dog paw prints. Kneeling, he studied the initial boot prints leading away from the dead enemy; they were British, he was sure of it. The other boot prints that joined the original set were quite different treads and matched the boot pattern on the many dead Indonesians nearby. A hunter force; there was a Royal Marine somewhere out there on the run.

Looking around, he caught the eye of one of the British Special Forces soldiers, who was watching him with interest.

When the remaining soldiers were made aware of the find, information was passed back to Marine Command located aboard the aircraft carrier. Orders came back to mark the position where the battle had taken place and exfiltrate the area. A larger force and more choppers would then be deployed to recover the British dead.

Inside two hours and they were back on deck of the HMS Illustrious. Tanya, Craig, and the Royal Marine officer were sat before Major General White, the overall commander of the Royal Marine contingent deployed to the Australian conflict.

"So we found them," White nodded. "That's something, I suppose." White was middle-aged man of average height, bald and plump. He adjusted his spectacles so they sat higher up on his nose. "Terribly sad," he said, looking forlornly at the recently printed photographs captured by the pair of British Special Forces. He breathed a heavy sigh. "The body retrieval mission has been organised, four Chinooks and two Apaches for top cover. They'll be departing first thing tomorrow morning."

Apart from a gentle ticking emanating from a clock hung on the wall of the office nearby, the room was silent as White continued to flip through the photos, tutting and shaking his head.

"Excuse me, sir," the Marine officer said, interrupting White's perusal of the images.

"Hmm?"

"I still got a Marine out there on the run; we need to get out there and find him!"

White paused and looked over the rim of his glasses at the officer. "Lieutenant Macalister, I am not going to waste further Marines and expensive resources, like helicopters, to find one man. For all we know, he is probably dead!"

Craig sat dumbfounded, unable to believe what he was hearing. By the way Tanya tensed in her seat, he guessed she felt the same.

"Come… again?" spoke Lieutenant Macalister slowly, exasperation evident in his voice.

"Lieutenant Macalister, you have my final answer! We will retrieve our men, but as for the missing Marine, that is, if there even is a missing Marine,"—he glanced at Craig a moment, silently insinuating that the Australian may have made a mistake—"there will be no rescue mission."

"With all due respect, sir," Macalister said quietly, anger edging into his tone. "I'm going back out there to get my fucking marine!"

White looked up sharply before standing. "You will do no such bloody thing! Do I make myself clear, Macalister?" he shouted. "I catch you—or any of your Marines—going out there on some mad rescue mission, I'll charge the lot of you! What's more, I'll strip you of your rank!" White's face was red, a vein threatening to burst through the skin of his forehead. "Are we clear?" the major general asked through clenched teeth.

"Sir," replied Macalister, the anger in his voice not lost on his superior. Standing, he turned and left White's office without another word, slamming the door behind him.

"Well, what are you still doing here?" White demanded of Craig and Tanya.

"Fuck yourself," Tanya spoke, standing and leaving.

"What did you just say to me?" demanded the officer, but Tanya ignored him.

Craig stared with disgust at the officer, shook his head, and followed Tanya out, leaving the door wide open.

"Close the bloody door!" roared White.

Craig ignored him, speeding up to catch up with Macalister.

"Hey, mate!" he called. Macalister stopped, turning.

"I'll find him, mate," said Craig, placing a hand on Macalister's shoulder. "You get your soldiers home. That's enough for you to worry about at the moment."

"What?" Tanya asked, turning to Craig. "You can't go out there by yourself!"

Craig smiled at her. "That's my job," he replied. "Besides, I just get in your way."

"That's a load of horse shit and you know it," said Tanya.

"I'd sure appreciate it," replied Macalister. "I know my men certainly would." The marine officer jerked his thumb over his shoulder in the direction of Major General White's office. "The boss doesn't need to know about it. What a fuckin' knob jockey… seriously." Anger was still evident in Macalister's eyes.

* * * * *

After they had eaten dinner, Craig sat with Tanya in a vacant briefing room.

"I could come with you," she said softly.

He smiled and shook his head. "I'd love you to, but these fellas need your skills here. They're in and out of missions all the time; they need someone on hand if they have wounded."

She looked at the floor and nodded.

"Won't take long; his tracks are pretty clear, they'll be easy to follow."

"I hope so," she replied, fidgeting with her hands. Craig had never seen her so unsure of herself. For the first time, he was seeing her real side, gone was the confident, self-assured façade.

"What are you going to do after all this is over?" Tanya asked, holding Craig's steady gaze.

He chuckled. "Shit, that came from left field!" He thought about the question for a moment. "You know, I have no idea. I'll probably stay on in the regiment a few more years. Depends."

"On what?" she asked.

He shrugged. "Depends how this all ends I s'pose. It may never end. We could still be flushing out remnants of the bastards from the forests decades from now." He fell silent, watching her. "What are your plans?"

"I'm thinking I might stick around. I've grown fond of Australia."

"I was hoping you'd say that," he grinned.

She laughed and winked at him.

Grasping the opportunity, he leaned forward and kissed her gently. She did not withdraw from him, but kissed him back, tenderly to begin with then with mounting passion. He pulled her onto his lap and softly kissed her neck, slowly working his way down until he was at the collar of her uniform. Throwing her head back, she groaned softly.

Standing, he carried her to the door. "Bear with me," he said, flicking the lock. She laughed, but the noise was cut off and replaced with a sigh as he continued where he left off. They made love despite the occasional thump of the steam catapult high above them and the powerful rumble of the ship's engines far below them.

* * * * *

"How's the cereal?" Tanya asked at breakfast the following morning.

"Boring," he responded, grinning.

"Thanks for the romantic evening," she said quietly, squeezing his hand.

"It was romantic wasn't it?" he said. "They can keep their sunsets and walks on the beach. Give me a briefing room on an aircraft carrier in the middle of a war any day!"

"Definitely a memorable experience!" she smiled, winking.

"Excuse me, sir, ma'am," said a sailor, stopping beside Craig, looking at them both.

"I'm bloody sure I've been through this with you before," he said, looking up at the man who could not have been any more than twenty years old. "Call me Craig, I work for a living, mate, remember?"

"Sorry, sir—Craig I mean!"

"Sir Craig? Shit mate, you've just promoted me to a knight!"

When the sailor fell silent, unsure how to proceed, Craig put him out of his misery. "What's up, mate?"

"Lieutenant Macalister has asked for you both to attend a briefing in briefing room seven, deck two, in five minutes."

"Thanks, mate, we'll be there."

"Okay, Craig."

"Stop!" said Craig with authority, halting the sailor in his tracks. "What did you just call me?"

"Sorry, sir!" he said, panic beginning to enter his voice. "I meant to call you sir!"

Craig stood, laughing. "You poor bastard, you should see your face!" He slapped the young sailor on the shoulder. "I'm only joking! Thanks for letting us know."

The sailor nodded and departed, looking quite unsure of himself.

"That was a cruel thing to do," Tanya admonished him.

"True," Craig said over his shoulder as they headed towards the exit. "Bloody funny though!"

* * * * *

Within thirty minutes the meeting had concluded and they were airborne, flying fast and low, scooting at sea level. The refreshing smell of ocean air was soon replaced by the sharper aroma of the Australian native forest as they ripped past at treetop level. Tanya sat quietly, staring out the open door of the Blackhawk at a distant flock of birds taking to wing as they evacuated a tall gumtree. It was a cloudless sky, the midday sun beating down with remorseless power. Traversing down a deep valley, they were cast in shadow as mighty mountains towered either side of the helicopters. There were three Chinooks, one Blackhawk, and an Apache tasked on the mission. Flying close together ensured the door gunners of the utility aircraft could combine their firepower to overwhelm any gunfire they might encounter from the ground.

Tanya felt Craig shift in the seat beside her and smiled across at him. He had ensured his pack was complete with gear to last him at least two weeks in the field. At just over forty kilos in weight, it would be an arduous journey for him. But as was his way; he had simply grinned and told her it was his job. His chest rig weighed in at ten kilos and he would, of course, carry his weapon as well. She did not envy him and knew she would miss him terribly. They had been through a lot together and had been inseparable until this moment. Between missions, she would feel lost without him, as though a piece of her were missing. As if reading her mind, she felt his hand on her leg. He squeezed her knee affectionately and winked at her as if to say, "It'll be all right, you'll see".

She patted his hand, but could not help the wave of sadness that enveloped her, but she refused to cry. Instead, she checked her weapon, instinctively examining that the safety catch was engaged and magazine was attached securely; she knew the weapon had already been cocked so it was already in action condition. Running her eyes over her chest webbing, she ensured all the pouches were fastened. She focused her mind on the coming mission and what was expected of her, noticing the sadness had passed and she felt much better for it.

Craig was looking out at the forest sliding by beneath them, his dark eyes raking the ground when it could be seen, searching for enemy, friendlies, or landmarks. It was hard for Tanya to know what for certain, but he was focused. Gone was the softness to his face, his eyes glittered with fierce determination.

She felt the helicopter slow and descend violently. Flaring at close to a forty-five degree angle, the chopper decelerated briskly before levelling out and landing on the ground with a smart thump. Before she could think to say anything, Craig patted her on the leg, smiled, and gave thumbs up. Then, amongst the dust thrown skyward by the rotor wash, Craig disappeared.

Chapter 9

"Yesterday, during question time in the House of Commons, Shadow Minister Terry Thrane is thrown out after shouting, 'just bring our bloody troops home!'." - *Daily Mirror (UK)*

They sat silently around the dinner table listening to Finn's recollection of recent events. If what he was saying held any truth, Finn's troop had patrolled straight into not only an ambush by an enemy of superior number, but, Mick suspected, a possible enemy stronghold. Jade was watching the Royal Marine with wide, innocent eyes, her dinner forgotten.

Mick nudged her gently and pointed at her plate. "Finish your dinner, love," he said quietly, and then asked, "No one else survived?"

Finn simply shook his head, although it was obvious to see the incident had left him shaken and, as Mick well knew, would remain with him for the rest of his life.

"Do you reckon we should go out and bury them?" asked Ben.

If the location Finn specified was accurate, then the area upon which the firefight occurred was less than ten kilometres from the Hi Barra homestead. Mick had hoped that with the withdrawal of the majority of Indonesian military and several nations now taking the fight to what he thought was a beleaguered enemy force, he could concentrate on life back on the farm.

But Finn's arrival had smashed that idea. It was possible, even likely, that enemy troops were all around them and much closer than first realised. It was probably only through sheer luck they had not stumbled onto the Hi Barra homestead itself. Holding off a small enemy patrol with the help of Craig and Matty had been one thing, but this was something entirely different and decidedly more sinister.

"Don't be bloody stupid!" Mick replied gruffly, glaring at Ben. "We wouldn't last more than a few minutes if we go out there alone!"

"All right old man, all right," said Ben holding out his hands, "calm your farm. Jesus."

"Cheers for the offer," said Finn, nodding at Ben. "But our blokes will be out looking for them by now. HQ will have noticed my troops' failure to check in by the specified time for a sitrep. They'll give us twelve hour's grace to make contact then HQ will try to make contact themselves. Failing that, they'll launch a search mission to my troops' last known location."

Finn sniffed and became ridged for a moment as he struggled with his emotions. "They'll have found them by now," he said softly. Clearing his throat, he pushed his plate away. "Thanks for the hoof'n scran."

"You're welcome," replied Katie, smiling. Then, in a tone that was not so much question as it was an order, she asked her daughter, "Jade, honey, will you please finish your dinner?"

Jade was sitting looking up at Finn, holding a long forgotten fork in her little hand. On the fork was skewered a small piece of sausage.

"It'll get cold," added Ben.

Jade looked back at her plate and began eating again. "It's not cold!" she giggled. Within minutes, she had almost cleared her plate.

"Mister Finn?" she asked, tugging on the sleeve of a shirt Mick had loaned him.

The Marine looked down at her.

"Sorry 'bout your friends," she said, her eyes speaking nothing but honesty.

"Thanks, sweetheart," he croaked. He nodded, eyes welling with tears. "Excuse me," he said, departing the table and walking outside.

The family left him alone to his own thoughts as they washed up the plates, cutlery, and cups. Mick was drying up and ensured he was drying items almost as quickly as Ben was washing them. Katie watched the two men; arms crossed and smiling, she shook her head. Everything the two did together turned into a competition, in one way or another. The night before, as Ben was drying up, he 'accidentally' pulled the plug out of the sink as Mick was reaching for a stack of plates.

"Oh whoops, sorry, mate," he had said in mock innocence. Jade had doubled up with laughter, thinking it was the height of hilarity.

Even Mick could not help but chuckle.

Within minutes, they had finished the chore. With everything placed away, tea towels drying on the long handle attached to the door of the oven and the soft chatter of Jade as she played with her dolls at the far end of the house, Ben felt content.

Whilst Katie and Mick departed to check on Jade, Ben walked outside, the refreshing night air enveloping him as he closed the front door behind him. Finn was standing away from the house, arms crossed, looking up at the night sky. As his eyes slowly became accustomed to the darkness, he noticed light from a three-quarter moon illuminated the area well. Certainly not a night to go out on patrol into enemy territory. Ben swore silently. We're probably in enemy territory right now, he thought sardonically. Trotting down the steps of the veranda, he walked slowly out to join Finn.

"How many were there in your platoon?" Ben asked. He learned quickly from Mick not to tiptoe around issues, but to tackle them head on. Pretending that Finn somehow had not survived a truly horrific experience would not help the situation.

Finn rubbed his eyes, sniffed, and wiped his nose with his hand. "Troop. We call it a troop. Forty-two of us all up. There was a load more enemy though; we must have been outnumbered near ten to one if I had to guess."

"Shit," Ben muttered.

"We must have killed nearly half of them," Finn said in a distant voice as he looked back up at the night sky, his eyes sliding across the stars. "It just weren't enough." He shook his head, took a deep breath and let it out slowly. "Weren't enough."

"I wish there was something I could say, mate, but I got nothing." Ben shrugged, feeling awkward.

"Cheers, Ben, appreciate your honesty. My troop should have been retrieved by now. At least they'll get a proper burial; it's the least they deserve."

"At least their families can say goodbye too 'em, mate, instead of hoping against hope for years on end. I've heard of that happening before. It's fuck'n shithouse, mate, don't get me wrong, but at least they can rest in peace."

Finn nodded. "I'm fuck'n hangin' out," he muttered, rubbing his eyes. When he realised Ben was staring at him in confusion, he grinned. "I'm tired," explained Finn. "I keep forgetting you lot aren't familiar with bootneck lingo."

* * * * *

Kookaburras laughed in piercing voices, welcoming the dawn as shards of pink speared across the eastern sky and illuminated the sparse clouds, making them glow salmon. Eventually the sun peeked over the horizon, slowly defeating night and throwing a blanket of light and warmth across the land. Before the sun could rise fully above the treetops, Mick was up, padding quietly around the house so as not to wake anyone else. Filling a glass of water, he self-administered his morning medications. There weren't many, only three small tablets—one for blood pressure, an Aspirin, and another to keep his cholesterol down. He took them religiously. Mick did have another medication, a nitro-glycerine spray that went under his tongue, but that was only when he had chest pain. He had not used it in years.

Stretching, he rubbed his face and yawned. After making himself a coffee, he walked outside and sat on the veranda, looking out at the distant forest. Sipping the warm drink, he closed his eyes, savouring the taste. The first brew of the day was always the best.

A mob of kangaroos, nothing more than tiny blobs amongst the knee-high grass of a distant paddock, ate their morning fill. One of them, a large animal, probably an older buck, was alerted to something. Whether it was something it saw or heard, Mick could not be sure. Pausing with the cup of coffee half way to his lips, Mick watched the animal. It stood tall on its hind legs, looking towards the forest, ears forward, fight or flight instinct engaged. The entire mob was now up on their hind legs, all looking in the same direction.

Mick sipped his brew, thinking it might have been nothing more than a fox returning to its den after a successful night of hunting. The gunshots came in quick succession. Mick almost dropped his cup on the wooden floor.

"Fuck me!" he swore, recovering from the initial shock.

The kangaroos were in full flight, bounding fast away from the shots. Although the homestead itself was not immediately in danger, Mick knew whoever was shooting was on his land. With mounting anger, he knew the direction from which the continuing shots resounded was originating from the five hundred acre paddock into which Ben and he had mustered the cattle. For close to three weeks the four of them had enjoyed a quiet existence at Hi Barra. Some days it was difficult to imagine a war was still being waged out there.

The piercing shots had been an unwelcome reminder that all was still not well.

Finn was the first to appear, dressed in clothes borrowed from Mick and holding his rifle in one hand. Mick saw that his eyes spoke two things; one was fear, the other was anger. Finn had a score to settle, and Mick knew the young Royal Marine would be an asset if things went south.

"Are we on?" Finn asked, approaching Mick.

The older man shrugged, finishing his coffee with one last gulp before placing the cup down beside him. "Not sure, mate. I'm goin' to wait until whoever it is finishes and then I'm goin' to take a squiz."

"What are they firing at?"

"My bloody cattle probably!" replied Mick, anger once more welling up.

The family sat and listened to the gunfire or almost two hours before it finally faded away. Mick was remiss to investigate the area until the shots had ceased in case they happened upon a much larger enemy force.

Katie had wanted to go with them, but knew she could not rely on Jade to be quiet the entire time, so chose to stay at home with the little girl.

Since the paddock from where the shots had been issuing was less than two kilometres away, they decided to walk in, rather than risk engine noise, which might bring unwanted attention. They walked slowly, spread well out and watching the environment around them. Mick led the way, Ben in the middle, and Finn taking tail-end-charlie. Mick noticed immediately he would have no problems with Finn; he was a good lad and from what he had seen thus far, a switched-on soldier.

The group patrolled off the road and into the foliage, their slow movement reducing their noise. A flock of birds, startled by the sudden newcomer, took flight from in front of Mick's feet, twittering to each other as they cleared the trees and headed away from the area. Mick did not flinch physically, but internally he had jumped five feet in the air. With elevated heart rate and adrenaline pouring into his system, he took a deep breath and moved on.

Birds of all species flooded the forest with music, adding to the chorus of insects. Hearing a soft whistle from behind, the old farmer paused and turned. Finn was gesturing towards some broken foliage in the near distance and indicated he would investigate. Mick nodded and took a knee, Ben slowly following suit. Within minutes, the Royal Marine crouched beside Mick.

"There's been a lot of movement through this area," the young soldier whispered. "I only noticed the broken branches from a distance, but up close, foot traffic has created a track. Must be some kind of route they use between locations."

"Shit," Mick mouthed, it was worse than he expected. He had known there were a few Indonesians in and around his property, but he thought, or perhaps hoped, it was no more than one rogue platoon. This new discovery spoke of something quite different, however.

"Definitely good to lay an ambush later," whispered Finn.

Mick nodded, liking the way the younger man thought.

The three men moved on, slowly edging away from the enemy track and deeper into the forest adding a further twenty minutes to their journey. However, Mick would prefer to arrive late than not at all.

Finally, just over an hour later, they crouched along the edge of the tree line and looked out at the massive, wide-open paddock. Cattle were grazing in the distance. To the casual onlooker, nothing appeared to be amiss. However, Mick knew at a glance that at least one quarter of his herd was gone. Tyre tracks criss-crossed the ground where heavy vehicles had been driven back and forth for days, maybe weeks, probably collecting the bodies once the cattle had been shot.

Ben did not have to look at Mick to know the farmer was furious. He was angry for Mick. When it was all over, Ben knew it would be a great struggle to bring the farm back up to scratch and start turning a profit, especially with the rapid decline in the herd. The property had been steadily losing cattle ever since the invasion had occurred. Ben knew it would also eat at the older man to know he was unwillingly responsible for supplying rations to the enemy.

Taking a deep breath and letting it out slowly, Mick nodded and shrugged, obviously weighing up some kind of internal debate raging within. After a moment, he signalled they should return to the homestead.

Later that same afternoon, the family—including Finn—sat out on the veranda, looking out at the afternoon sun slowly sinking towards the west.

"There's not a lot we can do about the cattle, unfortunately," admitted Mick. "We've moved them from the bottom paddock up to the closest one. Best we could do."

"Worked for a while," added Ben.

"A couple o' weeks anyway," said Mick, sighing. Katie watched her father at his wits end, and a look descend upon his face she had never before seen. He genuinely did not know what else to do.

"We could cut the fences and set them lose," she suggested. "They'd stick as a herd to an extent, but it'd be a hell of lot harder for them to track down and shoot, especially when they're not standing out in an open paddock like sitting ducks."

Silence descended on the group. But Mick was staring at his daughter a hint of a smile playing at the edges of his mouth.

"You bloody beauty! You're a genius, sweetheart!" Mick broke out in an infectious laugh.

Jade giggled. "You bloody beauty!" she squealed, mimicking her grandfather, punching the air and dancing around. "You bloody beauty!"

The cattle were all ear marked with Property Identification Codes (PIC) issued by the Department of Primary Industry to identify from which property the animals originated. When the Indonesians eventually were defeated, the strewn out cattle would be easily identifiable to the locals—especially other farmers. Bringing them home may become a long drawn out affair, but at least he would have some stock with which to work when the invasion ended.

"Good thinking, love," Ben said, smiling at Katie.

"Up here for thinking," she tapped her forehead grinning.

"Definitely got your brains from your mum," Ben smirked, but Mick was too pleased to bite at the comment.

"First thing tomorrow morning then," Mick said. "We'll free 'em first thing tomorrow morning."

* * * * *

With the exception of Jade, too young to leave at home by herself, all were armed. Mick, Ben, and Katie with bolt-action rifles, and Finn with his L85A2 automatic assault rifle. Katie and Jade rode the quad bike, Jade sitting behind, hugging up against her mother. Mick rode the mare, which Ben had learned was called Daisy.

"Really?" he had asked with raised eyebrows when Mick told him.

"Don't blame me, Jade named her."

"What? Daisy's a good name!" said Jade, frowning and planting little fists on her hips.

"Yes, it's a great name, you little munchkin!" said Ben.

"You bloody beauty!" giggled Jade, dancing around in a circle.

"All right, that's enough swearing, young lady," Katie admonished, tapping her daughter's head. "Come on, let's go get the quad."

"Yes, Mum," Jade said. "Bye," she said to Finn as she followed her mother towards the distant farm shed.

"Finn's coming with us, sweetie," said Katie as she walked. "He'll be with Ben in the Ute."

"Oh," she said, nodding her head vigorously as she trotted to catch up with her mother, snatching her hand and clasping onto it before breaking into a skip.

Driving the Ute at the head of the small convoy, Ben concentrated on travelling no faster than forty kilometres per hour. He did not want Daisy, trotting behind, to tire out too quickly. The journey was much faster than it had been earlier in the day. Opening the main gate and ensuring to leave it wide, they moved into the paddock. The cattle had moved a small distance from their previous location, but not by far. Cantering up beside the Ute, Mick leaned down.

"I'll go cut the fence on the far side, Katie's taking care of this side," he said, gesturing towards the quad accelerating towards the fence line. "You fellas stay here and keep watch. You spot any of those fuckers lurking about, you know what to do." His eyes bored into Ben.

The younger man nodded and smiled. "Don't worry, mate, we've got your back."

Mick turned Daisy and cantered away.

Ben allowed the engine to idle, the smell of gun oil emanating from the weapons wafted around the cabin. He allowed his hand to drop to the butt stock of the rifle, his fingers touching the cold wood helping him relax.

"Good idea this," observed Finn, nodding towards Katie who had now cut through all the strands of barb in one section and had pulled the wire clear to create a large gap in the fence line.

"Yeah, she's a smart girl," smiled Ben, watching her.

Mick, who had much further to travel, had only recently arrived at his area of fence to begin work. But he moved fast. Within minutes, one section was down and the cattle were watching both Katie and Mick with interest. One or two were walking closer to have a better look. Soon they would have free reign of the entire area; tens of thousands of acres.

"Once they know they can get out, they'll be in heaven," said Ben as more cattle followed the courageous few now standing close to Katie.

"Won't know where to start," chuckled Finn.

Katie whirled and yelled something at Jade. The girl ran to the quad and climbed aboard, waiting for her mother, who was not far behind.

"What the hell?" said Ben.

She turned the four-wheeled motorbike away from the fence and came roaring towards the Ute. Ben noticed she looked panicked.

"We got company," she said as the quad came to an abrupt halt beside the driver's side window.

"You sure?" asked Ben, sweeping his eyes across the paddock but seeing nothing.

"I heard engines in the distance."

As if to confirm Katie's statement, Mick was in full gallop towards them, a light streak of dust following the thunder of Daisy's hooves.

"They're coming in from the far gate," said Katie. "They won't arrive for another couple of minutes, but they're on the way."

"I'm scared, Mummy," said Jade, cuddling into her mother's back.

"It's okay sweetie," Katie reached behind to rub her daughter's back. "It's okay, we'll be fine."

"Go," said Ben. "We'll stay back with Mick, you head back to the house."

Katie nodded. "Take care, babe," she said.

"You too," Ben said, and then she was gone, accelerating away towards the gate through which they had entered.

With another several hundred metres still to travel, Mick pushed the horse hard. But in the distance behind him appeared a convoy of three Indonesian Unimogs. They came to a skidding halt, soldiers dismounting from the rear and shooting at Mick. Dirt kicked up as bullets hammered into the dirt near Daisy's hooves, ricocheting past Mick with loud whines. Finn pushed the door wide and went to ground behind the rear tyre of the Ute, providing covering fire. Ben returned fire from the driver's seat. Two Indonesians were down, one writhing on the ground in pain. A third joined them as Finn's bullets thudded into his chest.

Several loud cracks nearby indicated the enemy were now aiming at the Ute. Rounds burst through the windscreen, hammering into the empty passenger seat. With both fear and adrenalin coursing through his system, Ben leaned out the open window.

"Moving!" he yelled.

In short order, Finn had relocated onto the flat bed tray of the Ute, pushing his back against the cabin and sitting cross-legged. Pushing elbows into the crease of his legs near his knees, Finn created as stable a firing platform as possible given the situation. He continued to fire rapid, single shots at the enemy. The rounds were well aimed, either streaking through the air near Indonesian soldiers, forcing them to keep their heads down, or slamming into flesh and bone.

"Good work, keep it up!" roared Mick as he galloped past, Daisy breathing loud and rapidly as she began to fatigue. "Keep going, girl!"

"Hold on, mate!" Ben called to Finn in the back.

He brought the Ute around, his rifle now sitting silent on the empty seat beside him as he concentrated on driving. Incessant rifle cracks continued from the rear of the Ute where Finn was wreaking sheer bloody hell on the Indonesian soldiers. Thirteen were now scattered across the paddock, eight of them dead. Meanwhile, the Unimogs had parked up, allowing the soldiers to fight ahead of their position.

Bullets thudded into the Ute, ricocheting off the thick steel tray, stitching the ground nearby or smashing through the thin metal of the cabin. Ben, unwounded and thanking his lucky stars, threw a brief glimpse over his shoulder, relief washing over him as he saw Finn was still in the fight. When Australia regained some semblance of normality, Ben reminded himself he must buy a lottery ticket.

Daisy had slowed to a walk, her rump slick with blood. She had taken a bullet in the hindquarter. Not an immediate life-threatening wound, but enough to slow her to a limping walk. Mick had dismounted and was walking beside her, coaxing her on. Every so often, he went to a knee and fired a few shots at the Indonesians before catching up to Daisy and encouraging her on. Ben realised it was a losing battle; the Indonesian soldiers were rapidly closing the distance.

Finn's gunfire stopped and was followed by a shout of "magazine". Ben whipped around in his seat to see the Royal Marine was reloading.

"Back in!"

Within seconds, the weapon opened up with devastating effect. Half the Indonesian force was now wounded, dying, or dead.

But Ben realised it was not enough; He knew Mick would never abandon Daisy to some unknown fate at the hands of the Indonesians. Finn was an exceptional soldier, but outnumbered as they were, it was only a matter of time before they were overrun.

"We're sitting ducks, Finn!" Ben yelled as more rounds thudded into the vehicle.

"No shit!" roared Finn.

In what could only be described as a moment of insanity, Ben decided he would provide a distraction in order for Mick to escape. After giving Finn the option of dismounting the Ute and joining Mick—which the Royal Marine declined—Ben shouted, "Hold on, mate!"

He brought the Ute around so that he was now driving towards the Indonesians. Seconds later, Finn was standing up in the tray of the vehicle with his elbows leaning on the cabin's roof; facing forward, he continued firing at the enemy.

Accelerating to more than one hundred kilometres per hour, Ben steered towards the left flank of the Indonesian advance. The enemy were fully focused on the vehicle, allowing Mick some reprieve. Bullets hissed, cracked, and buzzed past the Ute, but a fast moving target was difficult to hit.

Once the vehicle was in line with the flank of the Indonesian extended line, Ben turned and stamped on the accelerator. The closest soldier panicked as he realised, too late, he was about to be run over. The man was half way to his feet when the Ute struck him at almost seventy kilometres per hour. His head exploded against the bull-bar, spraying blood and gore across the bonnet while a fine pink mist settled on the windscreen.

Keeping the accelerator flat to the floor, the Ute continued to pick up speed as it smashed into the next enemy soldier before he too disappeared beneath the vehicle. Bullets shattered the windscreen, tiny fragments of glass lacerating Ben's face. He ducked low behind the vehicle's dash, a dull thump and slight bounce indicating another Indonesian had gone under the tyres. Less than ten seconds later, Ben sat up in the driver's seat. Rapidly approaching the fence line of the paddock, he braked hard, hoping Finn had a good grip in the back.

Turning in a tight circle, he surveyed the damage. Most of the Indonesian soldiers were dead; some lay in macabre postures, legs and arms splayed out at impossible angles. Several were lying still, groaning or screaming, claret leaking from various points of their body. With the likelihood of gross internal trauma, death would claim them quickly. Two, however, were at full sprint towards the distant Unimogs. Single rapid shots from the rear of the Ute dropped them both in quick succession. The Indonesian vehicles had fired to life and were rapidly accelerating away from the scene of carnage.

Ben felt sick, his hands shaking and nausea floating around his stomach. Opening the driver's side door, he leaned out and vomited. As the young man tried to regain his composure, Finn dismounted the Ute and was striding amongst the dead enemy, ripping weapons and ammunition from their bodies. As for the dying enemy, he left them to their agony. One of his brothers had been imprisoned following his tour to Afghanistan after he shot a dying enemy combatant. The man had been critically wounded during a firefight and was dying a slow and agonising death. In reality, he had put the man out of his misery. But the Ministry of Defence took a rather different approach, finding the Royal Marine guilty of war crimes and putting him in prison for the term of his natural life.

With this in mind, Finn ripped the weapons from the dying enemy soldiers. One of them was screaming in pain, blood seeping from his mouth, nose, and ears. When he had an armful of automatic rifles, he strode back to the Ute and dropped them into the tray. By this time, Ben had regained his composure.

Within the space of ten minutes, they gathered a veritable weapon's cache, including automatic rifles, ammunition, grenades, and maps of the area—one of which highlighted exactly where the main Indonesian base was located in the immediate vicinity. Ben discovered a rocket launcher carried by one soldier, and a landmine carried in a small backpack carried by another. He voiced how lucky they had been by driving over the Indonesian without setting off the mine, but as Finn pointed out, the weapon had not been armed. One wounded soldier had already passed away from his wounds, but the remaining few continued to suffer in agony as their life slowly seeped away.

The Unimogs had long departed the area, their drivers having panicked at the vicious counter-attack. More than likely, they would be back, but next time in larger numbers. The men climbed into the Ute and Ben drove from the scene of carnage.

As they left the paddock heading towards the homestead, Ben managed to have a good look around and noticed the cattle had long since departed the area. More than likely, the opening moments of the firefight had scattered them through the downed fence. Inevitably, some would still be hunted and killed to satisfy the hunger of the Indonesian soldiers. It would, however, no longer be like shooting fish in a barrel; the cattle were free to roam across tens of thousands of acres of forest, roads, and grassland.

They pulled in next to the homestead to see Mick only just having arrived himself, escorting the wounded Daisy. With a better, less rushed look, Ben saw the horse had taken a bullet in the right rump. No doubt the wound was painful for the animal, but by the look of it, no major arteries were damaged.

"Good work back there," Mick called to the two men. "Saved my arse."

"How is she?" asked Katie, coming out of the house to look Daisy over, Jade by her side.

"Sore, but she'll live," said Mick, passing a hand down Daisy's flank.

He washed the wound with clean water and let it dry in the sun before rubbing an antiseptic ointment on the area. The cream served two purposes, to kill germs and bacteria working their way into the wound and to provide a physical barrier against flies and other insects attracted by blood.

Leading Daisy around to a small, rarely used paddock near the house, Mick fed her with some Lucerne and closed her in so she could not wander. Mick called it the hospital paddock and had not used it for some years. Daisy would need to be closely watched and cared for over the next few weeks as she healed.

Ideally, the bullet needed to come out, but until Australia regained her feet and veterinary services with specialised surgery came back online, the wound would have to heal as is.

The Ute was emptied, the weapons carried onto the veranda where they could be sorted, inspected, cleaned, oiled, and made ready for combat. Next time the Indonesians came calling, they were in for a nasty surprise.

Chapter 10

Major General White, overall commander of the Royal Marine contingent, sat in his office aboard the HMS Illustrious staring at the large map of Queensland attached to the wall opposite his desk. Small, red pins were pushed into the map where Royal Marine patrols had been involved in firefights against Indonesian forces. The markers clustered together in a narrow band that stretched from Greenvale down to Roma. The allies owned the coast, and on a national scale had destroyed the Indonesian resistance. Queensland, however, remained the last stronghold of diehard Indonesian soldiers. They controlled a portion of the high ground of the Great Dividing Range and were fighting hard to keep it. From reports he had read, briefings he sat through, and conversations with Royal Marines fresh from the field, White knew the enemy would never surrender. They would not give in or walk away; never would they throw down their weapons and stumble out of the forests with their hands up, begging for mercy. No, they would fight until they were killed or died as a result of the harsh Queensland elements. White knew it would not be an easy fight. The allies would win, of that there was no doubt, but at what price? How many more of Her Majesty's troops would need to lay their lives down to secure victory? He leaned back in his chair, placed his glasses down on the desk, closed his eyes, and sighed.

Gently tapping a pen against the wooden surface of the desk, White sat solemnly, deep in thought. He continued to stare at the map of Queensland as if it might offer a solution of its own. After a moment, White picked up his glasses, placed them back on his face, and leaned forward, an angry glint entering his eyes.

"I'm going to fucking kill you all," he spoke softly to the map of Queensland. Picking up the phone nearby he dialled a number. "My office, five minutes" was all he said before hanging up.

* * * * *

Less than an hour after she restocked her medical pack, another casualty evacuation call came in and Tanya's heart began thumping. Normally cool under stress, Tanya could not help thinking she may well be on her way to pick up Craig, wounded or dying. With shaking hands and a sick feeling in her stomach, she shouldered the pack, grasped her weapon, and strode through the rabbit warren that was the lower deck of the carrier. Briskly ascending ladders, dodging sailors along the narrow passageways, and stepping through doorways designed to be sealed watertight should the carrier begin sinking, she eventually made her way up to the flight deck where the helicopter tasked with casualty evacuation had just commenced its start-up procedure. Within a couple of minutes, the rotors were beginning to turn and all were on board. In less than ten minutes, the chopper had bumped down on the dry, hard packed ground of a paddock where a group of Royal Marines waited in all round defence position. A short time later, the casualty was lifted on board and Tanya was able to start work on the wounded soldier. Although focused on her task, Craig was in the back of her mind.

* * * * *

"Sir, you can't be serious?" one officer exclaimed. "There are still Australian civilians out there scattered throughout the forests."

"How the hell do you know that?" asked Major General White.

Five officers sat before White--three from the British Ministry of Defence and two from the United States Air Force.

"Because my soldiers have come across some in the field, secured them, and brought them back here. Back to safety."

"I've heard reports of Australian resistance fighters too, sir," added a second officer.

The others were nodding.

119

"How many B-52s do we have at our disposal?" White asked, turning to the most senior of the USAAF officers.

Colonel Ramirez, assistant to the second-in-command of the Global Strike Command out of Barksdale, Louisiana, leaned back in his chair and sighed. "We can have one hundred on line inside a week."

"Where?"

Ramirez folded his powerful arms across his chest. "They'd be flying from Guam initially, then deploying around Australia to already secured air bases. They'd then begin rolling missions from those bases."

"Can we make that happen as of now?"

"Certainly," responded Ramirez hesitantly. "But it's not advisable."

"Oh? And why is that?"

"For the same reasons these gentlemen highlighted previously," replied Ramirez, gesturing towards the officers sat beside him. "The B-52 is not a precision strike weapon, regardless of what CNN would have you believe. It will defeat the enemy, definitely, but in the process it will wipe out hundreds---if not thousands---of innocent Australian lives."

White remained silent for a long time as he looked from one man to another before his eyes came to rest upon the map of Queensland behind the officers.

"One hundred and seven," said White, eyes still glued to the map of Queensland.

"Sir?"

"That's how many Royal Marines have died so far in the line of duty." He gritted his teeth and added, "Under my watch."

Silence enveloped the room.

"Two hundred and eighty one," said White, his eyes refocusing to bore into Ramirez. "That's how many British personnel from Army, Navy, and Air Force have died thus far in this conflict."

Colonel Ramirez held his hands out before him. "Listen, sir, I understand where you're coming from."

"Do you?" responded White. "Do you really? Because these men and women were relying on me to bring them home safely. Now, as I speak, many of them are being buried in the cold earth of their hometowns."

Ramirez's eyes hardened. "You think you're the only one who's lost people?" he asked quietly.

White returned the man's glare but remained silent.

"We've lost more than nine hundred!" Ramirez growled.

"This isn't a pissing contest, gentlemen," one of the officers said, cutting in on the altercation. "One person lost in the line of duty is one too many; let's at least agree on that much."

"True," nodded Ramirez, relaxing.

"Well, let's bloody end it. We won't need to worry about further loss of life then!" White said, slamming his hand down on the desk.

"We are ending it. It just takes time," said one officer.

"Rubbish!" snarled White. "We could end it next week with the B-52s."

Colonel Ramirez leaned back in his chair, a thoughtful look passing across his face. He crossed his arms, scratching his chin. "You know, we could have ended the war in Iraq inside six weeks. There was similar discussion then as to why we shouldn't just end it. If we'd ended it quickly, we would have killed hundreds of times more civilians than were already killed during that conflict. The countries of the entire Middle East would have been baying for our blood. It's not as easy as bombing the crap outta everything."

"Who's going to be baying for our blood here? New Zealand perhaps? Antarctica?" White smirked.

"If this went ahead and thousands of our Australian friends were killed during the process, could you live with yourself afterwards?" asked Ramirez. "Could you ever sleep peacefully again?"

White spread his hands. "Of course."

"Sir, with all due respect, you're either lying or we're all far better men than you," Ramirez replied, gesturing to his peers beside him.

White sneered.

Save the ticking of a clock on a nearby wall, silence again enveloped the briefing room.

"All right," said White, sighing. He leaned back in his chair, laced his fingers behind his head, and looked up at the ceiling. "I'll give you one month to win this."

"Sir," one of the officers interjected. "We need at least six months minimum to flush the Indonesian Army out of those forests and hills. If you can at least---"

"One month!" growled White, glaring at the officer. "We'll meet again in a month's time and then talk about the logistics of bringing the B-52s online."

* * * * *

"That's fifty feet... forty... thirty..." The loadmaster was leaning out the port side of the chopper, counting down the altitude to the ground for the pilot. Dust, swept up by the powerful rotors, enshrouded everything before it.

"No joy, no joy, no joy," the loadmaster spoke, confirming he had lost visual of the fast approaching ground due to the brown out. With a violent, jarring thump, the aircraft touched down and Tanya beat the small team of soldiers out the door, sprinting through the dust, a shamag and goggles protecting her mouth, nose, and eyes from the dust. She held her rifle across her chest; her master hand curled around the pistol grip, index finger touching the safety catch, ready to disengage it. She could hear the distant click and pop of gunfire as the small group made their way towards the TIC and their injured patient. Halting, they formed a small protective circle while the signaller contacted the nearby soldiers to notify them of their presence. The last thing Tanya wanted was to be shot by friendly fire. Now aware of their presence and the direction from which they would be approaching, Tanya and her security detail were clear to move forward.

They had advanced to the forward area where a platoon lay in depth. Although they were hidden by a small rise in the ground that offered protection, two more platoons were heard fighting forward in the near distance. Inside the circle of defence the depth platoon offered, laid the wounded soldier. He was groaning continuously, a combat first aider knelt beside him, deftly winding a bandage around a bright red, stained dressing. Tanya sprinted to him and knelt.

"What you got?" she asked, looking at the soldier.

The young man's eyes glinted with determination and fear. "Gunshot wound straight through his right elbow. Ma'am, I think the bullet's nicked an artery."

Tanya felt the wounded soldier's pulse. It was fast, much faster than it should be; combined with his pale skin and increased respiration rate, a quick assessment suggested the soldier was bleeding out. A tourniquet had already been applied proximal to the wound—the combat first aider had performed his duty well. Checking the exit wound, Tanya saw it had almost severed his arm in two at the elbow. Taking out a small cardboard splint from her medical pack, she bandaged it firmly in place to help stabilise the arm.

"Get a stretcher organised," she ordered her nearby security detail.

Moving to the other side of the wounded soldier, she cut off his shirt and undershirt, looking for further wounds. As she pulled the shirt from under him and threw it aside, she noticed 'A+' was marked on one of the uniform's sleeves. She made a quick note of the blood type and continued. With no further wounds found, she placed a cannula in a vein and prepared a bag of Hartman's solution to start running into the vein. After taking his blood pressure and finding, without surprise, that it was much lower than it should have been, she administered a dose of Ketamine. She then moved on to examine his lower body. Cutting off his pants, she checked and found no sign of any further wounds.

They lifted him gently off the ground. The soldier was still groaning, but more softly now.

As the security detail lifted the wounded man and departed in the direction they approached from, Tanya turned back to the combat first aider. He was still knelt down, staring at the patch of ground where his wounded mate had been lying moments before. She knelt before him, placed a hand on his shoulder, and gave a firm squeeze. He looked up at her. "You did a good job today, you hear?" she said. "You did well."

He nodded, but remained silent. She gave his shoulder one last squeeze then turned to follow the others.

Within minutes they were airborne again, ascending and accelerating from the area, flying low and fast. In the centre of the cabin, plugged in to the aircraft's main power, was a small refrigeration unit that held a select few units of blood. She found only one bag of A positive—enough for the journey back—and commenced the blood infusion immediately.

* * * * *

Tanya lay on her bed, hands behind her head, staring at the ceiling of the small cabin. Four decks below the flight deck, the constant thud and thump of the catapult was blissfully distant. She had showered, changed, and felt human again. The phone rang, making her jump. Here comes another mission, she thought.

"Tanya, what you got?"

"G'day, shit lips," the refreshing Australian accent said.

She broke into a wide smile. "Colonel Mal Tabb," said Tanya. "It's been a while."

"It has," he said.

She could hear popping in the background and smiled again as she realised Mal must have been idly popping bubble wrap that he had probably been keeping in his pocket.

"Where's lover boy? Been trying to contact him, but no luck. It's almost like he dropped off the planet," he chuckled.

He was not to know how hard his choice of words hit Tanya. She fought back tears for a moment, took a deep breath, and gathered herself.

"He's out on a mission," she said, her voice sounding more even and controlled than she felt.

"Oh, sorry, love," said Mal, his voice softening as he realised what he had said and the affect it must had caused to Tanya. "I'll try again in a week or so, I'm sure he'll be back by then."

"I hope so."

"Mark my words, Tanya, he'll be back. I'll give him one thing, he's a resilient bastard!"

"Yes, he is," she sniffed. "I'm sure he's fine."

"He'll be fine, love. Try not to worry too much. I know that's easier said than done," said Mal, more popping sounds erupting in the background.

Tanya chuckled. "You found more bubble wrap?"

"I'm never without it, Tanya, never without it. I can sniff it out anywhere. How you holding up there?"

"Fine, but busy, makes the time go by faster I guess."

"Yeah, I'm hearin' ya," said Mal. "Bloody busy this end too. Word is Queensland's the last stand of the Indonesian Army. They've been pushed inland, but still fighting hard. We've had a lot of trauma through. Lost a couple today, which is shithouse, but the vast majority have been salvageable. One lost his leg, a couple lost hands, and one poor prick lost both legs and an arm, but they're alive. That's the main thing, isn't it? That's why we do this. Those guys get to go home and see their families again."

"Never a truer word spoken," replied Tanya. In truth, she was only half listening to Mal. She was more aware of his Australian accent, which made her think of Craig and her hope against hope that he was safe.

"Listen, you take care, my love, and if you ever need to talk, you know my number, call me any time, day or night. Righto?" said Mal.

"Thanks Mal, I will. I'll let you know as soon as he comes back."

"Please do, Tanya, and I look forward to seeing you both again at the hospital soon."

"Look forward to it. Speak soon."

She ended the call and placed the mobile phone down on the tiny bedside table bolted to the floor.

Sighing, she lay back upon the bed. Where was Craig? Was he even still alive?

* * * * *

Craig lay within a natural hollow in the side of a creek bank. He had carefully dragged dead branches and bulrush weeds across the tiny entrance to provide camouflage. His uniform was soaking wet, mud and grit working its way between skin and uniform, ensuring he was never comfortable. But he had gone through the experience many times before. During selection, wading through creeks and navigating up mountains stretching far into the sky above, dirt and grit always guaranteed it rubbed his skin red raw—particularly in his groin and in his armpit areas. In reinforcement training, they had been dropped into the Western Australian desert with a hessian sack as their only source of clothing and a small survival kit. Training with the British Special Boat Service saw Craig and his patrol swim five kilometres into the beachhead before force-marching fifty kilometres inland to their target. Lying still inside a small opening in a creek bank was easy; it was the company-sized patrol of Indonesian soldiers strolling alongside the opposite bank which had forced him into hiding that was difficult.

He heard them in the distance long before he saw them, giving him enough time to find concealment. They moved well and with good spacing, ever watchful while patrolling their arcs, although walking along the edge of an obvious ambush site was poor soldiering. Still, these Indonesian soldiers were a far cry from the complacent, lazy, and arrogant soldiers he had come across at the beginning of the invasion. They had either learned from the stiff resistance offered them initially by the Australians—and later by the coalition, or these soldiers had always been present, but were overshadowed by the less professional ones who had long ago fled before the coalition's onslaught.

Up until being forced into hiding, Craig had been making good progress on tracking the lone Royal Marine Commando. The remnants of his boot marks suggested he had crossed the creek close to where Craig was hiding. He only hoped the numerous Indonesian soldiers traipsing across the opposite side had not destroyed what little remained of the sign left by the lone British soldier.

The Indonesians slowly halted as a command was passed down the line from the front. They took a knee, each soldier covering a different arc confirming that all sections of forest around them were covered by at least two soldiers ready to return fire should the need arise. Craig gripped the pistol grip of his M-4 firmly, finding comfort in the cold grip. Touching the thumb of his right hand against the safety catch, he verified for the second time in as many minutes that it was disengaged.

Raking his eyes across the stationary soldiers less than thirty metres away, his eyes came to rest on one who was taking particular interest in the hastily scavenged camouflage Craig had dragged across the small entrance to the enclave in which he hid. In a half-foetal position, Craig brought the M-4 to his shoulder and slowly aimed the weapon at the soldier in question. If the Indonesian opened fire, it would be the last thing he ever did. There was a slim chance that if circumstance took a turn for the worse, few—if any—of the soldiers near the Indonesian in question would realise from where the kill shot had originated.

Eventually hand signals were passed down the line and the soldiers quietly climbed back to their feet and continued to patrol onward. More than likely, the patrol commander had stopped to review a map, or consulted his lead scouts to ascertain whether anything untoward had been spotted along their axis of advance. Several short, antagonizing minutes later, the Indonesians had disappeared into the forest. The crunch of the last few soldiers slowly faded to silence until all that kept Craig company was the sound of a soft breeze teasing the treetops.

It was already late in the afternoon, so he thought it best to remain where he was for the night. In the morning, he would be able to pick the trail back up and continue following the lone Royal Marine. The British soldier was in dangerous territory and may have already either been killed, or captured—Craig hoped that was not the case.

As the sun disappeared over the horizon and night swept over the land, a light drizzle began to fall. Craig moved into a slightly more comfortable position and relaxed, although he remained alert for many hours. When he began feeling tired, he allowed sleep to envelope him. He slept lightly; whether it be a nearby birdcall or the sudden snap of a dead branch as some animal wandered through the forest with its nose close to the leaf litter, hunting for food and oblivious to his presence, he woke to the slightest noise,.

In the early hours of the morning, the thundering roar of several fighter jets screaming over at treetop level made Craig jump and clutch his rifle, his eyes wide and heart thumping in his ears. Within seconds the deafening noise had subsided to a distant burr; moments later it was gone altogether. With the promise of dawn on the horizon, Craig gently moved aside the camouflage hiding the small entrance to the dugout in the side of the creek bed. He stopped often, listening for the tell-tale noise of approaching soldiers. When nothing but the sound of the natural forest met his ears, he continued to quietly push the branches aside until he was able to push himself out of his hide.

Suppressing a groan as stiff muscles rebelled, he climbed to his feet and stretched. Moving back up onto the top of the bank, he backtracked until he came across the Royal Marine's boot prints. The day before, he had been standing in the same place about to follow where the soldier had crossed when the sound of patrolling soldiers had forced Craig to find the nearest hiding spot. He waded across the creek—ignoring the cool water as it chilled his body, climbed out the other side, scrambled up the opposite bank, and paused to find the British soldier's track. They were difficult to spot at first, because the enemy patrol had destroyed some of the prints when they had moved through. Craig, however, regained the track and began following it, making sure he was also aware of his surroundings. Walking into an enemy patrol was not high on his bucket list.

He noticed the British soldier had at least three Indonesian soldiers and two dogs following him at all times. Whether they actually caught him remained to be seen. Craig moved at a sedate four or five kilometres per hour through the bush, careful of his footing, watching his surroundings, and keeping a close eye on the footprints he followed. At times, the boot prints disappeared amongst the leaf litter and particularly hard or rocky ground, but if he meticulously followed in the direction of travel left by previous prints, more often than not, he was able to pick the track up further. Only twice was he forced to backtrack to rediscover the prints and then move on over rocky terrain where the prints had disappeared.

The smells of the Australian bush ebbed and flowed around him with the gentle breeze. Aromas of eucalypt, tea tree, rotting leaves, blooming flowers, and native grasses blended and together formed a silent voice that spoke a single word—"home".

Cradling the M-4 across his chest, Craig knelt beside a boot print. Looking around, he noticed a small, dry creek bed in the distance. Rising, he walked slowly towards the feature, well aware that it served well as a possible firing lane for an enemy gunner. Stopping short of the creek, his alert eyes swept over the massive root system of a long fallen tree. What interested him most though, were the scuffmarks and boot prints around one side of the root system as if someone may have crawled amongst it to seek shelter or concealment.

He approached the dry creek on his guts, crawling forward to the edge and carefully checked both directions in case some enemy gun team had set up shop ready to mow down any unsuspecting person crossing the creek. Craig knew it was unlikely, but the slim possibility was enough for him to exercise caution. When he was satisfied the creek was clear, he slide over the edge and walked across the dry bed to the opposite side, stopping at the mighty root system. At this range, he could see hand prints as well. Looking in through the natural cage structure the roots provided, he could see where someone, probably the Royal Marine, had been lying. He must have stopped here to rest. The scramble of hands, boots, and knee prints suggested he had left the area in a great hurry, possibly in a panic, as if the hunters were gaining on their quarry.

Craig moved on, patrolling quietly through the scrub, pausing often to watch or listen. Once, he was forced to push himself amongst a thick shrub, kneeling down and silently watching a small

Indonesian patrol walk past not fifty metres from him. Unaware of his presence, they departed the area as briskly as they arrived, although Craig remained, watching and listening for a second patrol. A mud wasp buzzed near his face, methodically inspecting its nest. Being stung was all he needed. Regardless of how much it might have hurt, he would need to maintain the discipline to remain silent and still—or at least move away from the shrub slowly. Luckily, the mud wasps were not particularly aggressive and he counted himself lucky it had not been a paper wasp nest.

With no sign of a second Indonesian patrol, Craig stepped quietly out of the shrub and continued on his way, M-4 clasped across his chest, butt resting gently against his right shoulder and barrel pointed towards the ground. Keeping the butt stock against his shoulder made bringing the weapon to bear easier and faster. Some soldiers patrolled with the stock of the rifle between their elbow and body, meaning if they needed to take a sight picture fast, there was a possibility of a delay bringing the weapon to bear, as the butt stock knocked into webbing straps or elbow.

Several hours passed without incident, although in that time, he climbed over several barbed wire fences, indicating he was at least within a few kilometres of a few houses. That in itself meant nothing, however; the dwellings could just as easily be occupied by Indonesian soldiers, as they could be with Australian families. It was worth skirting around the edges of the homes. If they appeared vacated, only then would he approach with caution to look for the British soldier and possible sources of extra food or water. He paused to watch a mob of kangaroos bounding in the distance. He slowly knelt, his eyes raking the area to identify the source of the kangaroos' fear, but with nothing obvious, he carried on.

Craig paused as the stink enveloped him. Rotting flesh. More than one corpse. He quietly made his way towards the stench. Pushing his way through a close stand of dense bush, he saw the long dead kangaroo. Its body had been scattered as if wild dogs had gorged themselves. He moved closer and found a deceased dog on the far side of the roo. It had received a powerful, traumatic blow to the side of its head, ending its life instantly. But as he inspected the leather chest harness clasped around the bloated corpse, Craig realised it was not just any dog; it was a military dog. Glancing around the area, he noticed three human corpses in close proximity to each other and his heart fell. Walking to them, he knelt, fighting to keep the nausea at bay. None of them wore the uniform of a British soldier. The story the scene before him portrayed suggested that up until this point, the Royal Marine still lived. He smiled sardonically. The hunter force had finally found their quarry… and died as a result.

It took some time before Craig finally found the Royal Marine's prints out of the area. He identified a large pine snapped off at near ground level as the rudimentary shelter in which the soldier had been holed up in until the altercation. An hour later, and still strong on the trail, Craig began realising the terrain began to feel familiar. He crossed a dry creek covered in smooth pebbles. He remembered he, Matty, Mick, and Ben had crashed in such a creek following an Indonesian ambush. Increasing his speed, he brushed past trees, side stepped spider webs, and eased through thick shrubs.

A half hour later, he knelt on the edge of an open paddock, a grin painted across his face. In the near distance, on top of a small flat feature, lay the black, burned out remains of an eight-wheeled Indonesian communications vehicle; the same vehicle he and Matty had destroyed with the help of Mick and Ben. The Royal Marine Commando had survived and had sought shelter in the nearest house he could find and had miraculously found Mick!

Smiling, Craig pushed himself to his feet and began patrolling the last few kilometres towards the Bent Wood Cullen Bone homestead; his home away from home.

Chapter 11

"Rumours prevail of a mass bombing mission headed for Australia. A large number of B-52s were allegedly filmed on the move in Barksdale Air Force Base, Louisiana. The man who states he filmed more than twenty B-52s flying in formation towards the coast, reports his camera was confiscated by Military Police." – *The Daily Reveille (US)*

Major Gilang Simanjuntak sat on a small log in the makeshift shelter from which the senior officers planned their operations. The shelter was some fifteen metres long and seven metres wide. As far as temporary shelters were concerned, it was well built. The roof, lined with camouflage ground sheets and tarpaulins, was waterproof against all but the heaviest of rain. Situated in the middle of a high feature, they had good views in all directions.

Under his command had been almost six hundred Indonesian soldiers; although battle and the incessant Australian climate had killed over one hundred to date—three from snakebites alone. There were fifty similar outposts in extended line along the length of inland Queensland, for a total of thirty thousand soldiers prepared to fight and ready to die if necessary. Although the Indonesian fighter jets had been withdrawn, leaving them short of an important air asset, they still had a limited number of transport and attack helicopters at their disposal.

Indonesia was desperate for the wealth of space and resources Australia had to offer and Gilang was unwavering in his single-mindedness to be the victor, even if the politicians in Jakarta could not appreciate his vision. The officer grunted and spat, shaking his head.

The vast majority of the Indonesian military had withdrawn almost two months before, and stoic though he was, Gilang felt helpless at how far they had fallen during that short time. He had enjoyed his relaxed position as a transport officer. Apart from the capture of the Australian soldier—Spud had been his name, if Gilang was not mistaken—nothing much exciting had occurred.. It still irked him how the man had escaped in the hands of that mad-looking Australian-Indonesian soldier.

He ground his teeth together and put it from his mind, remembering instead the day the might of the Indonesian military had fled, with tucked tail, from Australia. At the time, he was ordered to withdraw, but of course, he refused, accusing his hierarchy of cowardice. The war was being won, regardless of the enemy reinforcements. Send more enemy and we will continue to kill them had been the opinion of Gilang and the vast majority of Indonesians who chose to stay. But now he was not so sure.

With dwindling supplies, short on ammunition, and limited radio communications between similar outposts up and down inland Queensland, it was difficult to maintain cohesion in order to conduct large-scale operations involving thousands of soldiers working towards the same objective.

However, through the use of horse mounted messengers riding from outpost to outpost, some semblance of comms was able to be maintained. They had been able to advance towards the coast for a time, but fighter bombers and fresh soldiers had pushed them back at every turn. For the most part, his soldiers had faced the British— Royal Marines, if he was not mistaken. They were exceptional soldiers, he granted grudgingly.

Sighing, he stood and departed the rudimentary building; time to make the rounds and show his face to his soldiers. He usually liked to make similar rounds at least three or four times per week. The walk down to lower ground was much easier than the return journey, however, the worn track and steps chiselled into hard clay, or chipped into stone made it that much better.

Within minutes, he was striding between the encampments of his soldiers; a myriad of waterproof sheets stretched between trees or corners pegged to the ground with small branches standing in the centre to provide a pyramid type shelter. Several of them were higher than one metre from the ground and Gilang spoke quietly to those in question, asking them to lower their shelter. During the day, the temporary shelters were dropped to the ground and packed away, only being raised again at sunset. Even this far inland, chances should never be taken. They were facing a first-class enemy. An enemy recon unit could easily work out the exact location and strength of Gilang's unit simply by counting the number of shelters. Dropping the waterproof sheets to the ground at dawn and packing them away resolved the problem.

But as evening began to settle in, Gilang's soldiers were preparing for a much deserved hot meal and then sleep. The major squatted in front of one shelter, the occupant lying flat on his back, hands behind his head, rifle and webbing upon the ground beside him.

"All good here?" Gilang spoke.

"If that's you again, Nando, I'll skin you alive! I was sleeping!"

"Sorry for waking you," said Gilang. "It is not Nando."

The soldier glanced up and saw Gilang's face in the dying light. He sat up sharply.

"Sorry, sir. No disrespect intended."

Gilang chuckled. "None taken. How are you holding up?"

"Good, sir, looking forward to winning this war so I can move into my own home!" the soldier replied with a grin.

"That's the attitude, young man," said the major tapping the soldier's boot. "Get some rest." He stood and moved on, stopping every now and then to briefly talk to one or several soldiers. For the most part their morale was high. The soldiers under Gilang's command showed a steely resolve that was absent from the forces which had been withdrawn two months before.

After making his rounds amongst the camp proper, he made his way towards the cook fires some two or three kilometres away. The fires had been deliberately moved away from the position in case enemy fast air or recon patrols were moving through or near the area. Naked flames were easy to spot at night; enemy patrols and aircraft were likely to call in the position for closer observation or investigation.

The cook fires were moved once per week. Last week they were located south of the position; currently they were west, and next week Gilang would have them relocated north.

For the past month, the dinner meal had consisted of roast kangaroo, a relatively tasty meat, but with a terrible aftertaste. In recent days, however, cattle had been discovered on a nearby farm and morale had soared as beef was served with each evening meal.

The long trail to the cook fires was scattered with small groups of sentries, all keeping a silent watch on their surrounds. Most of them whispered a challenge to the major, then a brief apology after he identified himself. Others remained silent, used to Gilang's routine each evening and knowing that, more than likely, the person walking along the trail approaching from the direction of the main Indonesian position was either Major Simanjuntak or a fellow soldier.

A dry twig snapped underfoot with a loud crack. He stopped for a moment to flick it off the trail with a boot. Each morning the trail was quietly cleared of any branches and twigs that had fallen to the ground overnight from the towering trees around them. He had witnessed one massive branch, thicker than a man's body, snap from the upper limbs of a mighty gum tree, seemingly for no reason. It had crashed to the ground with a powerful thump. Apparently, this was a common occurrence and he had heard rumours that many Australians, particularly those from rural areas, sometimes referred to gum trees as 'Widow Makers'—now he knew why.

Half an hour later he was standing near one of the cook fires, walking amongst the soldiers. A few of them were keeping a close eye on the fire, feeding fresh wood into the blaze. The carcass of a cow, skewered with a thick piece of metal, was held in place above the fire by the metal framework of a Unimog's rear tray, cut from the vehicle for just such a purpose. Welded to one end of the metal pipe was a large cogwheel, around which was a chain similar to a bike chain but much thicker. The chain led down to another cog attached to a small petrol motor. It was this motor that was started at short intervals whenever the mighty carcass needed turning.

The smell wafting around the bush was intoxicating. Gilang's mouth watered as he watched the meat sizzle, spit, and pop. Oil and fat dripped from the lowest point of the carcass into the fire where the flames consumed it with a hiss.

"Tomorrow will be a big day," a voice spoke from beside him.

Gilang turned to look at the face of one of his sergeants. His eyes were alert and intelligent, but carried a cruel glint. He tried to remember the man's name, but failed. It was on the tip of his tongue. The soldier stood beside the major, staring into the fire, mesmerised by the flames as they weaved and danced. Pandu! That was his name.

"Yes, Pandu, an important day indeed. I trust you and your men are ready?"

His eyes showed surprise, then respect for Gilang for taking the time to learn the names of the soldiers under his command, but only for a fleeting instant before the cruel glint returned.

"We were ready weeks ago! Those bastards have been hunting for us for almost a month now. Only a matter of time before they find our position and call in support." He snorted and spat into the fire.

Gilang felt anger warm him. Was Pandu questioning his authority?

"And would you have done it any differently?" he asked the sergeant, allowing a touch of anger to enter his voice.

That surprised look returned. "No, sir, of course not!" he replied turning to look at Gilang for the first time. No disrespect intended, sir."

Didn't think so, he thought.

"None taken, Pandu. None taken," he replied.

"It will be good to be rid of them once and for all."

"All in good time," said Gilang. "It may take several days before we find them."

"The sooner, the better," snarled Pandu, clenching a fist and punching his palm.

Gilang nodded, but remained silent. He had faced Australian soldiers before. If memory served him correctly, apart from a few minor skirmishes with civilian guerrilla fighters, Pandu had not. The Australian soldier was versatile and cunning beyond belief. The Indonesian officer knew that at least a platoon strength number of Australian soldiers were on the hunt for his position and had been for more than a month. Twice, brief contacts had ensued before the Australians realised they were grossly outnumbered and conducted a fighting withdrawal out of the area. The first contact left seven of Gilang's men dead. The second left eleven to be buried.

Neither time had Pandu been involved. Yesterday, the major ordered a small recon patrol out to observe in order to find the Australian position. They had returned less than half an hour ago, carrying a dying comrade amongst them. Although they had pinpointed the Australian position, on their way out of the area they made contact with a section sized enemy patrol protecting the area.

At the time, dark had been closing fast and Gilang was remiss to send his soldiers out in the night. First thing in the morning, as dawn was breaking, they would make their move and hope the Australians had not relocated to a new position in the meantime.

Moving a platoon-sized number to a new location was easy, quiet, and fast. Uprooting a battalion-sized group was a much more difficult task. It was noisy and slow, with all sorts of logistical nightmares thrown in. It was time to hunt the Australians down and eradicate them once and for all.

"Patience, Sergeant. As I said, all in good time."

When the beast had finally been cooked, the carcass was dragged carefully from the fire by soldiers wearing thick, heat resistant gloves. Then it was carved, the cuts of meat placed in large plastic trunks, which, once full, were carried away by four soldiers—two on each end. When the sixth trunk had been filled and the carving complete, Gilang began making his way back towards the main position.

The dinner meal was another logistical nightmare and Gilang only took his meal once he was sure the five hundred or so men under his command were eating.

Smiling his thanks, he accepted the meal placed into the foldable metal container he carried in his pack. Once again, the meat tasted exceptional. With their resupply line now non-existent, the meal consisted of little else apart from meat. On occasion, they may be treated with a garnish of bush plums or boiled roots, but they were few and far between. Even then, Gilang suspected the treat had only been served to the officers alone.

Major Simanjuntak sat with his back against a tree and ate his meal, listening to the junior officers talking amongst themselves nearby. As he ate, he considered the possibility that tomorrow he may well die.

* * * * *

Jimmy, who Spud had made number one scout, led the platoon through the forest. They moved slow, quiet, and alert. The Aboriginal soldier walked lithely across the leaf littered ground, instinctively aware of his footing. Stepping over branches, gently brushing aside dry twigs with a boot before proceeding, he was next to silent.

It was the smell that brought him to a stop. Without looking back at the soldiers behind him, he held up a thumb pointed to the ground. Knowing the platoon had disappeared from sight as they slowly dropped to their guts, making ready to fight if required, he moved forward at a half crouch.

The smell wreaked like raw sewage; definitely human defecation. Bringing his rifle firmly into his shoulder, Jimmy patrolled slowly, finger resting gently on the trigger. Often he stopped and dropped gently to a knee, listening and watching. When he was satisfied no sound or movement around him was produced by possible enemy soldiers, he smoothly stood and continued.

Finally, he knelt beside the latrine, trying to block out the smell.

Filthy fuckers could have filled their dunny in, thought Jimmy, shaking his head. The Indonesian position, probably of platoon strength if Jimmy was not mistaken, had for some reason needed to clear the area quickly. It might have simply been poor soldiering, but Jimmy did not think so. The lion's share of Indonesian military had tucked tail and run once the coalition of countries came to Australia's aid. But the soldiers who remained, refusing to give up the fight, were an entirely different kettle of fish. They were driven, motivated, well-trained, and for the most part, fearless. Estimates from various intelligence units pinpointed the enemy number in Queensland anywhere from ten thousand to fifty thousand.

Spud's platoon had now seen themselves through close to twenty firefights, having to call for resupply ten times. Usually provided by helicopter, although on one occasion, the resupply had arrived via a convoy of Humvees that had been tasked with resupplying several units working in the same area as Spud's platoon.

Although they had been requested to return to base for debrief and a short break before redeploying, Spud had refused. During one particular heavy engagement with the enemy, he was positive he had seen Major Simanjuntak, the Indonesian officer who had held him prisoner so long ago. He wanted revenge. He wanted to kill him. He and many of the soldiers under Spud's command placed Kane's death squarely on Simanjuntak's shoulders. Spud was confident the Indonesian officer would either be killed, or he would die trying.

Sweeping his eyes once more over the area to ensure there was no enemy activity he had overlooked, Jimmy stood and carefully made his way back to report to Spud. He reached the platoon commander and knelt beside him.

"Enemy latrine; pretty fresh, mate," whispered Jimmy.

"How fresh?"

"Well, I didn't fuckin' taste it if that's what you mean,"---Jimmy grinned---"but they bugged out less than forty-eight hours ago."

Spud nodded. "Wonder what spooked 'em," he whispered.

Jimmy shrugged. "Dunno boss, but we're closin' on 'em."

Spud nodded. "We'll box 'round," he whispered.

Jimmy gave him a thumbs up and moved away. Spud rose, signalling the platoon to stand and advance. Jimmy patrolled carefully around the old Indonesian position. There was a slim possibility that booby traps or mines, such as trip wire initiated Claymores, were still in place; particularly if the enemy had withdrawn at short notice. Spud wanted to steer well clear of the area to avoid the possibility.

As he patrolled, Jimmy constantly swept his eyes across the forest, dividing the area in front of him into distant, middle, and near. The distant forest was the area at the limit of his vision; near was the area directly before him, including being aware of his feet and where he was about to step. Middle was somewhere between the two points. Patrolling in such a way was fatiguing and by the end of the day, he was usually bone tired.

Within half an hour, the former Indonesian position and, thankfully, the smell was behind them. As the hours passed and the sun began to drop towards the western horizon, there seemed to be greater evidence of Indonesian activity in the area---small tracks leading through the area, boot prints, and the remains of several large fires.

Jimmy quietly dug into the depths of the ashes with a stick, withdrew it, and felt the tip with the back of his hand. Bone cold. The fires had not been burning in some days. He found the remains of large bones, more than likely of bovine origin. Must have been cook fires.

Leading away from the fires' remains was a large track, almost three feet in width, suggesting a heavy amount of foot traffic. Odds were, the track led to the main enemy position, unless they had moved on again.

The aboriginal soldier backed out of the area, never turning his back on the track before him. Minutes later, he knelt beside Spud and informed him of the find and his thoughts on where it might possibly lead.

"Well, then," whispered Spud, smiling with chilling grimness, "let's harbour up here for the night. In the morning, we follow the track."

*****

Major Gilang Simanjuntak took a deep breath of fresh air, stretching and yawning simultaneously. With the sun about to break over the horizon, he crawled out of his sleeping bag and packed it away. Cleaning his rifle, he quickly ate breakfast, prayed quietly and then readied himself for the morning's briefing.

As the first glimpse of the sun peaked over the forest in the east, Gilang stood surrounded by officers, sergeants, and a few corporals who were in charge of their relevant platoons.

"Today is the day we rid ourselves of the Australians for good," said Gilang. "We have the upper hand here, we know the terrain. I want our force split into five groups. I want four section sized patrols to act as listening posts. They will patrol north, south, east, and west respectively. Have them move no more than two hundred metres from this position. The main force will remain here ready to move at a moment's notice. Any questions?"

He remained silent for almost twenty seconds. When no questions were forthcoming, he continued. "If a listening post detects enemy in the area, one soldier---I repeat---one soldier is to return to this position to inform us. The main force will then proceed to engage. Are we all clear?"

Nodding, a few grunts, a brief exchange between a couple of officers at the rear of the group acknowledged the major's orders.

"Good," said Gilang. "Let's make it happen. I shall accompany the listening post patrolling south."

"Sir," one officer spoke. "Are you sure that's a good idea? You will be vulnerable. If something goes wrong out there, a section sized patrol could be overrun by a much larger force."

Gilang looked at the officer, a tall man by the name of Aditya, an average officer, but lazy according to reports Gilang recalled. "If I'm commanding my soldiers to step into danger, is it not appropriate that I put myself in the same amount of danger?"

"Not necessarily," replied the officer. He chuckled. "I shall send lesser men to do my bidding while I remain here."

"Lesser men?" said Gilang, taking a step forward so he was less than an arm's length from Aditya.

"Do you think so little of the men under your command?" he asked, anger entering his voice.

"No, sir," Aditya responded, a flash of fear entering his eyes. "It's just that... well, you might be in great danger, sir."

"So?" he asked, shrugging. "May I remind you this is a war, Aditya? And in a war, there are certain elements of risk. I am sending my soldiers out into danger. Some of them may well die today. I may well die." He pointed a finger at the officer's chest. "You may well die, Aditya."

The officer shifted uncomfortably and nodded. "Understood, sir."

"I hope so," said Gilang, eying his subordinate. "I hope so." With a brisk flick of his wrist, he dismissed Aditya to join his peers already walking back to their soldiers.

* * * * *

Almost twenty minutes later, Gilang patrolled south. The eight soldiers with him were spread out around him. Three in single file to his right, another three in single file to his left, one in front of him serving as lead scout, and one behind protecting their rear. The open file formation patrolled through the forest parallel to the wide track leading south. Walking down the track itself was simply asking for trouble, especially as day was breaking and the knowledge that an enemy patrol was somewhere in their vicinity. Moving slowly, they were next to silent; the lead scout, with his weapon pulled into his shoulder and safety catch disengaged, moved smoothly in a half crouch.

They were all dispersed a minimum of ten metres from each other, patrolling their arcs and maintaining regular eye contact in case a hand signal needed passing along.

When they had covered two hundred metres, Gilang called a halt and ordered all round defence. The soldiers crept out in a small circle facing out, before slowly lowering themselves into the prone position. They would hold their location in silence for the day. A boring job, but like the other three listening posts covering the remaining points of the compass, it was important. Gilang checked his watch, slowly brushed a beetle from his cheek and waited.

* * * * *

As day break threatened in the east, Spud and Jimmy moved north, parallel to the track. Spud had considered taking the platoon in its entirety, but decided a small recon patrol might be a better idea initially. Two men could move through the scrub more easily and much quieter than thirty.

The laugh of Kookaburras intermingled with the bickering of cockatoos echoed in the near distance. Jimmy took a deep breath of fresh morning air as he carefully stepped over a dry branch. He felt at home in the bush, almost as if the earth was calling to him. He knelt by a freshly snapped sapling and quietly studied it. Looking at the ground, he saw kangaroo tracks and knew the sapling was damaged by an animal rather than a man. Standing fluidly, he moved on.

Hearing a soft clicking behind him, he glanced back to look at Spud. The soldier was kneeling, indicating something off to the far right. Jimmy slowly knelt and looked towards where Spud was pointing. In the distance, a thick shrub was moving. With a breeze absent, it could mean something – or someone – was moving. Remaining silent and frozen, Jimmy watched, his alert, dark eyes, boring into the area around the shrub. Slowly bringing his rifle into his shoulder, he stared down the scope, finger teasing the trigger.

Suddenly a kangaroo stood bolt upright, as if it had detected some kind of threat. Jimmy removed his finger from the trigger, although now interested in what had caused the kangaroo to startle. He slid his eyes across the scrub around the animal. It was possible the animal may have smelled them, but at a distance of almost one hundred metres and no breeze, he doubted it.

Relaxing, the kangaroo crouched back to the ground to graze. Slowly turning back to Spud, Jimmy gave a thumbs up, grinned, and then stood, gently moving forward. They made slow progress, always ensuring they were within at least fifty metres of the track. Even after several hundred metres, the track was just as wide and heavily trodden as it had been when they started. It was definitely a main route of some kind.

The rising sun cast light intermittently through the forest canopy. It looked quite beautiful in a way, but Jimmy was uncomfortable. The Norforce soldier could not be sure whether it was the brightening light of daybreak or the sudden silence of the forest, but something had him on edge. Something at the back of his head was causing him to proceed with extreme caution. Trusting his instinct, he slowed to a halt and took a knee. Without looking behind at Spud, he signalled to stop and drop down.

Pulling the rifle into his shoulder, he stared down the battle sights on top of the scope and nestled index finger onto trigger. The safety catch had already been disengaged prior to the commencement of the patrol. Even the tiny click of a safety catch being flicked off might be enough to alert a nearby enemy to their presence; the reason they preferred patrolling in a ready condition.

Lethargically sweeping the forest around him, he moved from right to left. Like most people, Jimmy read books from left to right; moving his eyes in the opposite direction was foreign to the optic area of his brain, forcing it to take in far more detail than were it moving in a direction to which it was accustomed.

Half way through his sweep, he paused, heart rate increasing, adrenaline skyrocketing, his breath deafening in his ears. Nestled in the battle sights was an Indonesian soldier lying prone no more than seventy metres from him. Looking beyond the soldier, he saw a further three enemy soldiers. Although he was unable to spot more, Jimmy was sure others would be close by and hidden from view.

He swore silently. Taking his non-master hand off the Steyr's fore-grip, he signalled thumbs down to Spud behind him, never taking his eyes of the silent enemy before him. Neither force moved. The two Australians remained frozen in place, unable to advance or withdraw for fear of causing too much noise. The Indonesians unaware of the tiny enemy patrol, but all it would take was for a soldier to glance in Jimmy's direction and it was on for young and old.

Fifteen minutes later and no indication of the would-be standoff ending, Jimmy signalled to withdraw. Holding his position, he waited as Spud moved back at a painstakingly slow pace. Five minutes later and a single, almost inaudible click signalled that Spud had taken up position and was providing cover for Jimmy.

Taking a good look at the ground around him before he moved, Jimmy was acutely aware of the location of small dry branches and twigs that may cause unwanted noise if he were to step on them. When he was sure of his foot placement, he moved in slow motion. Close to five minutes later, he had passed Spud and taken up position. Signalling for Spud to move, he could no longer see the Indonesian soldiers, although he pointed his weapon in the general direction where he thought they were located.

Spud, moving in a crouch, walked slowly, careful of his footing. With wide eyes of disbelief, Jimmy watched an Indonesian soldier slowly stand, only his head visible over a nearby shrub. He must have been relieving himself. As he urinated, he yawned silently and as luck would have it, glanced in Spud's direction. Eyes locking onto the Australian soldier's back, he froze before bringing his weapon to bear.

"Cover!" yelled Jimmy, firing several rounds in rapid succession. One bullet slammed into the throat of the enemy soldier, another drilling through his face and exiting in a splatter of blood and small chucks of brain matter.

Facing the enemy position, Spud dropped to the ground with his weapon pulled into his shoulder. The Indonesians, unsure of the exact location of their enemy, were shooting blind when they returned fire.

Pulling two smoke grenades out of a pouch, Jimmy threw one just in front of Spud before hefting the second much further in the general direction of the Indonesian position.

With purple and green smoke drifting through the forest, the pair made a fast withdrawal from the area.

Chapter 12

"The Ministry of Defence will not comment when asked about reports of a Royal Marine unit rumoured to be missing in action." - *Whitby Gazette (UK)*

Daisy was healing well. With each new day she grew stronger, although the wound needed cleaning and disinfecting morning and night. The wound was a healthy pink and closing well, with no sign of proud flesh forming. Mick fed her in the paddock, checked her water trough was full enough, and then headed back inside.

"Hello, Grandad," said Jade, walking out into the living room dressed in her pyjamas.

"Morning, chicken," he said, kneeling to hug her. "Want breakfast?" he asked, ruffling her hair.

She passed a hand through her hair, straightening it where Mick had messed it, although careful to make sure Mick did not see. "Yes please!" she said, skipping into the kitchen. "Can I help?"

"Sure you can. What do you feel like?"

"Bacon, eggs, baked beans, umm, let me think," said Jade, holding index finger to chin, looking at the ceiling, "and sausages!"

"Good choice, love," said Mick, aware their supply of food was diminishing. There was no bacon left, and the chickens had not been laying well lately. Baked beans was no problem, he and Ben had managed to scavenge a truckload of canned goods when they raided the supermarket. That felt like a lifetime ago, he reflected as he opened the doors of the pantry.

"Only joking, Grandad!" laughed Jade, jumping up on a stool. "I know we don't have any bacon or eggs. How about cornflakes?"

"Cornflakes! Now that I can do!"

Even the cornflakes were running thin. Only two boxes left. Twenty litres of long life milk remained. That might last them a fortnight, and then only if they were careful. Mick swore under his breath; soon all there would be to eat was steak. Mick knew he could live with that, but he was not so sure about the others.

"There you go, chicken," said Mick, pushing the bowl full of cornflakes towards his granddaughter. She thanked him and began eating. Humming to herself as she chewed, she studied the same piece of junk mail that had been sitting on the bench since the invasion.

Mick glanced at the pages as Jade flicked through the glossy paper. It was advertising specials at one of the large supermarkets in the closest large town. How easy things seemed back then. Just pop into the shop, buy your groceries for the fortnight, and drive home. Now, there was no such luck. Now all they had was empty shelves, long since rotten produce, or getting shot for the effort. Australia was a different place. First world problems were a pipe dream, a long lost wish. If only the worst problem one could face was their phone making some stupid noise to notify it was going flat, or being stopped at traffic lights for one minute too long.

"What you thinkin' about, Grandad?" Jade asked.

"Hmm?" he looked up at her, then smiled. "Oh nothing, love. Nothing at all. How's brekky?"

"Yummy thanks!" she beamed, shovelling another spoonful of cornflakes into her mouth.

Mick took his morning medication, rattling the boxes as he did every morning. As with each new day, he realised his medication was dwindling. He knew there was three weeks of medication left at best. Then what? He sighed, passed a hand over his face, and felt a gentle hand on his shoulder. Turning to look into the face of his daughter, he pulled her into a hug and held her tight.

"Morning, Dad," Katie said.

"Mornin' love."

"All right?" offered Finn to all and sundry as he walked over to the counter to begin making coffees.

"You gonna finish that?" asked Ben, sitting beside Jade.

"Maybe," she said, grinning.

"You better, or I'll polish it off!" Ben said, making a grab for the bowl.

Squealing, Jade pulled the half-finished bowl of cornflakes closer, giggling as Ben tickled her.

* * * * *

From memory, Craig determined he was within two kilometres of the Bent Wood Cullen Bone homestead. He walked quietly through the bush, steering well clear of the road which led towards Mick's home. Distant noise brought him to a halt. He took a knee and waited. In the distance, off to his right, was the definite noise of humans walking through the forest. He listened for voices to see if he could identify friend or foe, but heard nothing. The noise was growing closer; at least five, maybe more, Craig estimated, remaining frozen in place.

Several minutes later and he was watching the Indonesian patrol move through in single file. They were about one hundred metres away, patrolling well and keeping good distance. There was a definite difference between the soldiers who had stepped ashore during the initial invasion and those who chose to stay when Indonesia officially withdrew.

A crunch of leaf litter beside him sent Craig's stomach into his throat. Sweeping his eyes to the side, he saw in his peripheral vision two kangaroos standing on their haunches beside him. They had approached silently, that or he had been paying too much attention to the enemy patrol. The animals were watching the progress of the Indonesian soldiers, their ears forward, eyes intent and unblinking.

The enemy soldier bringing up tail-end-charlie stopped and stared at the roos.

Murphy's fuckin' law, thought Craig.

He was half-concealed behind a long fallen, moss-covered tree trunk, but his face, painted with camouflage, was visible just above the log. Thankfully, the Indonesian was more interested in the kangaroos than anything else.

The soldier suddenly lifted rifle to shoulder and fired several short bursts. One kangaroo dropped to the ground dead, the other burst into powerful bounds. Initially, it raced towards the soldier, then changed direction. The soldier fired several more bursts, a couple of bullets snapping through the air past Craig's head. He threw himself to the ground, hoping the movement did not attract the attention of the Indonesian.

Who taught you how to shoot, ya fuckin' nemmer? thought Craig, crawling away to take cover behind a large tree. The shooting soon stopped; he could just make out the Indonesians talking amongst themselves, and then the sound of movement as they departed the area. Or at least that was Craig's initial thought until they seemed to be coming closer. Much closer. In fact, in the space of several minutes, they were within twenty metres of his position.

Placing the rifle down, he unclipped one strap of his backpack and controlled the cumbersome weight as he placed the pack down upon the ground. Unclipping the top flap, he slowly took out a claymore and set it up directly in front of him. The detonator was already connected, so it was only a matter of pushing the legs of the weapon into the ground.

He should have been sixteen or so metres behind the claymore, but there was no time for that. Placing the 'clacker' in front of him, he picked up his rifle, pulled it into his shoulder, and waited.

Squatting down around the dead kangaroo, the soldiers were less than five metres from Craig. They were butchering the animal, placing cuts of meat into plastic bags. Still hidden behind the log, only one enemy soldier was within sight of Craig, and he had his back to the Australian soldier.

Good, he thought, sighing a silent breath of relief. Slowly moving his head to the side so that he was looking over his shoulder, he checked there was no one behind him. All clear. In slow motion, he looked back at the soldier in front of him. He was still squatted over the roo, cutting into it with a sharp knife.

Finally finished, the Indonesians stood. Three of them hefting plastic bags full of kangaroo meat over their shoulders. They were happily chatting to one another. Morale was probably soaring now they had something to eat for the evening meal. Craig assumed their supply lines were non-existent and had been forced to live off the land for quite some time. They began moving away, much to Craig's relief. They were soon out of sight, the noise of their progress through the forest becoming more distant by the second.

Missed me by a bee's dick, Craig thought, breaking into a grin, the whites of his teeth almost fluorescent against his dark camouflaged face. He waited, still and silent, for almost half an hour after the subtle noise of the Indonesian soldiers had dissipated just to be sure. Moving slow, he packed the claymore away, shrugged his pack back on, and in slow motion rose up. Glancing over the fallen log, he saw he was alone.

Scanning the forest around him, Craig ensured there was no threat, like a lone Indonesian taking a shit behind a tree. He grinned again and stood. Regaining his bearings, he began patrolling towards Mick's house once more. Less than two clicks to cover and he would arrive at his destination.

As the sun reached its zenith, Craig calculated he was approximately eight hundred metres from Bent Wood Cullen Bone. The going had been slow and difficult. Five times he had been forced into concealment as Indonesian patrols moved through his area. Most of the time they were only within distant earshot, but on one occasion, a large company-sized patrol had trudged through the forest within one hundred metres of him. Almost twenty minutes passed before they were clear of the area. It seemed enemy patrols were often patrolling near Craig and he knew deep down a large Indonesian stronghold must be situated near Mick's home. There was the possibility the Indonesians had taken control of Bent Wood. If this was the case, he would be required to exfiltrate the area in the direction he had approached before calling for dust off.

An hour later he was within three hundred metres of Mick's house. If memory served him, thick forest surrounded the house to within fifty metres. Stopping, he took a knee and shrugged the pack into a more comfortable position. Resting for a couple of minutes, he stood and looked into the face of an Indonesian scout walking towards him not fifty metres away. The scout's eyes widened like dinner plates, but before he could react, Craig brought his rifle to bear and fired twice. Readjusting his rifle and staring down the sights of the grenade launcher attached beneath the barrel of his rifle, he fired a grenade. The scout's body dropped heavily to the floor in an unmoving heap, while the grenade exploded amongst the soldiers behind him. The survivors broke left and right, going to ground in an extended line and returning fire.

Craig withdrew at a full sprint for twenty metres before going to ground, releasing his pack, and setting up the claymore as before. Standing up, he deliberately exposed his position to the enemy soldiers. Firing half a magazine, he ducked back to ground, slapped a fresh magazine into the weapon, and crawled away from his pack and claymore at a rapid rate. He moved parallel to the enemy's axis of advance. As he leopard-crawled, he fed out the cable leading to the claymore behind him. Paying out the last of the cable, he came to a stop and faced the enemy who were still firing and moving towards his previous position. When he was sure several of them were within ten metres of his pack, he depressed the clacker. The claymore fired with a mighty boom, sending seven hundred ball bearings at knee height screaming through the forest in an ever spreading arc. Several enemy were cut from their feet, screaming in agony. As the others composed themselves and began analysing what had taken place, Craig fired another grenade from his new position. It slammed into the ground and exploded with devastating effect.

Holding his fire, Craig, eyes glaring with intense purpose, watched his enemy from the safety of concealment. Many of them were wounded. A few of them were dead. The others were firing and continuing to move forward towards Craig's initial position.

Taking out a grenade from a pouch on his chest webbing, he pulled the pin and waited. When he was sure there were several soldiers rifling through his pack, he placed the rifle down. Holding the grenade in one hand, he released the safety lever under control with the other. Usually the safety lever flicked clear of the grenade with a metallic click as the grenade left the thrower's hand, but maintaining control of it ensured silence. The grenade's fuse was now ignited and would explode in approximately five to seven seconds.

Waiting a good three seconds, Craig leaned up and threw the grenade hard. Sailing through the air, it landed with a soft thud amongst the leaf litter. The Indonesian soldiers, flinching at the sudden nearby sound, turned to investigate and died as the grenade exploded in a deafening crescendo.

Craig picked up his rifle, quietly pulled it into his shoulder, and allowed his eyes to sweep the area. Apart from the moans, groans, and cries of the wounded or dying, the forest was silent, all bird life having long ago departed in terror. Movement caught Craig's eye, and he watched as an Indonesian soldier crept forward. Kneeling down beside a wounded comrade, he slung his weapon and provided first aid, whispering words of comfort to quiet the man.

The same soldier – obviously the designated medic – moved efficiently between the wounded providing first aid. Several of them had already passed away. The others received rudimentary treatment as befitted a lone medic surrounded by so many casualties. Craig allowed him to go about his business, watching him and yet remaining vigilant to any other flanking manoeuvre that might be attempted by the Indonesians. Confident his enemy either had no idea of his location or thought he may have withdrawn from the area completely, Craig was satisfied to remain where he was for the time being.

Ideally, he needed to withdraw from the area to place distance between himself and his enemy. He knew he was close enough to the Indonesians that, no matter how quiet he might be, at least one of them was bound to hear him. Had he been another fifty metres farther away, he may have been tempted to make a move.

With the sun beginning to sink towards the west, he remained still and silent. Night would offer him concealment and a way out of the area. It was not without risk, but the risk was diminished somewhat. Patiently, he watched the medic continue his work. When all his patients had been attended, he ordered a few soldiers to begin making stretchers. Many of the wounded were assisted out of the area, limping or hopping in the direction from which they had advanced, but there appeared to be three more seriously wounded who needed to be carried out.

Happy to let them proceed, Craig knew that over the coming days and weeks, one wounded soldier would hinder the freedom of movement of at least one, two, or---more likely---three other enemy soldiers. In itself, this would provide his enemy with a logistical and tactical nightmare.

As dusk settled upon the forest, some of the birdlife had returned---albeit with reservation, skittish to even the smallest noise. Craig remained like a statue, only his eyes moving as he watched the last of the enemy soldiers leave the area. They left his pack, although it had been opened and searched. His map, radio, GPS, and SOFLAM laser designator were all carried within his chest webbing. Unfortunately, the lion's share of food and water rations were carried in his pack, along with a second claymore, spare batteries for the radio, GPS, and SOFLAM, as well as other niceties. He could survive another forty-eight hours on his chest webbing alone, but then it would be time to consider living off the land.

He had lived off the land before, as part of training and once when the logistical element of a planned exercise had failed in an abysmal way. Survival was easy. It just took a lot of time, patience and energy conservation---none of which Craig could afford, given the present situation. But, being so close to Mick's house, unless the Indonesians had overrun the homestead, he need not worry about survival. Time would tell.

With a full bladder, Craig waited impatiently for night to fall, which seemed to take an age. Crickets chirped, several tired birds called softly from treetops, and insects and lizards scurried through the leaf litter, but there was no foreign sound. Nothing Craig heard suggested it was not normally in the forest at that time of evening. He pushed himself into a kneeling position and pissed into the bushes, breathing out as relief washed over him.

Standing, he stretched, suppressing a groan before moving in slow motion towards his pack. Alert to the fact the Indonesians may have connected a trip wire, pressure device, or some other imaginative booby-trap on or near his pack, he was cognizant of his footing. He was careful to feel the ground gently with his leading foot before placing his full weight upon it.

Twenty minutes passed before he reached the pack. Carefully kneeling, he closed the top flap and tightened the straps before lifting it over his head and easing it down upon his shoulders. Standing, he regained his bearings and began patrolling towards Bent Wood Cullen Bone.

An hour later the half-moon was rising, casting mediocre light upon the forest. Given it was still low in the sky meant the shadows thrown by the trees were long, often merging into each other and allowing him plenty of places to hide. Later on, as the moon rose higher into the sky and shortened the shadows, the moonlight would no longer favour Craig. He patrolled from shadow to shadow, often taking a knee to confirm his bearings or to pause, listen and look around.

Finally, with the moon rising, Craig knelt beside a large tree. One of the few remaining before the forest gave way to a large clearing--- at the centre of which sat the Bent Wood Cullen Bone Homestead.

Switching on the night vision capability attached to his rifle's scope, Craig brought the weapon up to his shoulder and stared down the scope, watching the house. Slowly sweeping the structure, he watched for movement. The windows appeared to be blacked out and he could not see nor hear movement issuing from within the dwelling. He needed to move closer. Stepping forward, he felt exposed as he entered open ground. The same feeling one might experience if they had dreamt about walking into a crowded shop and realising too late they had forgotten to wear pants. Craig grinned at the thought.

Much closer to the house, he took a knee and listened. He could hear faint movement from within the house. The rapid thump of small feet and then a high-pitched squeal, followed by laughter. It was Jade's voice. Craig smiled and relaxed. It appeared Mick and his family were home.

* * * * *

Jade squealed as Ben scooped her into his arms.

"Gotcha!" he said chuckling. "That was a good hiding place!"

He lifted her up, giggling and squirming, so she was lying across his shoulders.

Mick sat at the kitchen table with Katie. Finn, exhausted, had retired to bed early.

"I suppose we can't stay here forever, much as I'd like to," Mick said, his hands clasped together and resting on the table in front of him.

"Yeah, you're right, Dad, but I don't think you realise we need to leave sooner than you think."

"Ah, don't worry about me, love, I'll be right."

"Dad, you need a refill of your medications! You'll be lucky if you have a week's worth left."

Mick shrugged. "I'll be right, love," he repeated.

"No, you won't, Dad," Katie said sternly. "Me, Jade, and Ben are leaving in a couple of days and trust me, you'll be coming with us."

"And where are we going to go, Katie?" he asked.

"They have hospitals setup along the eastern seaboard. I mean... when Indonesia officially withdrew, we were okay here at Bent Wood. But they have been pushed inland to the point where we are going to be inundated soon. They'll kill us without a second thought, and I'll not let that happen to my daughter. We need to get out while we still can. Another week or two and it'll be too late. First, we need to get your meds, and second, we need to keep this family safe. Surely you can see that."

Mick sighed, looked down at the table, and nodded his head. "I suppose you're right."

There was a knock at the door, making Mick jump in his seat. He reached behind him and snatched up his rifle that was leaning against a wall.

152

"Avon calling!" called a familiar voice through the open window next to the front door.

"Who is it?" asked Mick, proceeding down the hallway towards the door, rifle pulled into his shoulder.

"Oi, Mick! Good to see you, mate!"

He relaxed.

Opening the door, he pushed it open to see a soldier in Australian uniform standing before him. He wore camouflage on his bearded face, his pack lying on the veranda beside him, M-4 assault rifle resting atop the pack.

The face looked familiar, like a long lost friend whom he had not seen in an age.

Realisation slowly passed over Mick. "Holy shit, it's Craig!" he yelled over his shoulder as he stepped out to meet the soldier.

"Good to see you, son," Mick said, ignoring the offered hand and pulling the younger man into a tight embrace. "Jesus Christ," Mick said, pushing Craig away at arm's length. "You fuckin' stink, mate. What, ya shit yourself?"

Craig burst out laughing. "Yeah, I think I did a couple of times."

Draping an arm over Craig's shoulder, Mick led him into his home.

Jade sprinted to the soldier and slammed into him, standing on his boots and hugging his legs. He lifted her up and hugged her. Wrinkling her nose, Jade remained silent about the smell and hugged him back, resting her head on his shoulder.

"How have you been, sweetheart?" asked Craig.

"Yeah, good," she replied, as if he had never been away.

* * * * *

After a shower and change of clothes, he felt refreshed. Sitting out on the veranda, Craig cleaned his weapon, helped by Jade who was sitting on his lap. The rest of the household sat close by listening to the young soldier as he spoke softly.

"There were a few close calls; one was just within a klick of here."

"Yeah, we struck trouble out in one of the paddocks the other day," confirmed Mick in a whisper.

Ben and Katie sat listening, holding hands.

"Yeah, well I reckon you might be sitting in a bit of a hot spot here, mate," said Craig, holding the barrel up against the moonlight for inspection. "Glad I found this fella though," he said jerking a thumb at Finn sitting nearby, silent.

The Royal Marine nodded. "Glad me mates have been found and taken care of. Their families deserve to know," he said with sobriety.

Craig nodded, putting the M-4 back together. Aware of Jade's presence, he left the magazine out of the weapon, keeping one full magazine in his pocket and the weapon with him at all times. Children were curious and had been known to play innocently with loaded firearms with fatal outcomes. Having a magazine in his pocket meant he could rapidly make the weapon ready to fire long before donning his chest rig, which he left inside the house near the front door.

Once settled, he pulled out the meagre contents of his pack. Although all the water, food, claymore, spare ammunition, and most of the batteries were missing, one battery he had deposited in a hidden pocket under the top flap of the pack remained. Luckily, it was the spare battery for his radio. Craig did not intend to hide the battery, it was simply a case of the pack being so full he had placed the battery in the zip pocket under the top flap to ensure it did not fall out.

Turning the radio on for the first time since departing the helicopter, he may not even need the spare battery. Double checking he was dialled onto the correct channel, he brought the radio to his mouth.

"Zero One Alpha, this is Delta Six One, over."

Almost thirty seconds of silence past. As Craig was about to speak into the radio again, static exploded from the radio's speaker, followed by, "Delta Six One, this is Zero One Alpha, go."

"Delta Six One, I have the package, I repeat, I have the package, over," he said, glancing at Finn.

"Roger, Zero One Alpha. Go with golf romeo, over."

They wanted a grid reference. "Fuck me," whispered Craig. Bringing the radio to his lips he said, "Delta Six One, wait out."

Pulling out his GPS he clicked a few buttons before bringing the radio back up to his mouth. "Delta Six One, golf romeo to follow, prepare to copy, over."

"Zero One Alpha, send, over."

"Delta Six One, golf romeo 1720 4720, read back, over."

"Zero One Alpha, I read back 1720 4720, acknowledge, over."

"Delta Six One, acknowledged. Anything further? Over."

"Roger, Zero One Alpha, major enemy camp believed to be located at golf romeo 1720 3900, acknowledge last, over."

"Delta Six One, yeah, fuckin' acknowledge that, over," Craig replied, unaware he had sworn, unease washing over him.

Jade clasped both hands over her mouth and giggled.

"Zero One Alpha, emergency evacuation your loc recommended. Mass Doom-One-One mission your loc imminent, acknowledge, over."

Craig exchanged a concerned glance with Mick. The older man knew the call sign from his Vietnam days. Although he controlled his external demeanour, sheer terror swilled around his gut. Doom-One-One was a carpet bomb run by several B-52 bombers. He had seen the aftermath of such a raid first hand. Not much had survived. A mass Doom-One-One mission? He hated to think what that entailed.

"Delta Six One, I acknowledge your last, out."

"Christ, we can't stay here," said Mick. "We're gonna have to make for the coast."

"Why?" asked Jade.

Mick did not reply, instead he looked out at the forest in the near distance. If they did not move, and soon, they were all dead.

Chapter 13

```
"The Department of Defense confirms a Blackhawk
helicopter has been shot down by ground fire. It
is not yet known if there are any survivors." -
LA Times (US)
```

The pair leapfrogged away from the Indonesian position rapidly. Gunfire exploded from the Indonesians, but still unsure where their adversary lay, the shots went wide. Only twice did bullets hiss and snap close to Jimmy. The Norforce soldier sprinted through the forest a short distance before taking cover behind a large Blue Gum.

"Yup!" he said in a voice only loud enough for Spud to hear.

Spud leapt to his feet and ran past Jimmy, taking a knee behind a fallen tree trunk.

"Go!"

Jimmy moved back past Spud, and so it went until they eventually linked back up with the waiting Australian platoon. Sweat beading on his skin and breathless, Spud sat in thought, then five minutes later signalled the platoon to move out away from the Indonesian position. They patrolled at a brisk pace, fast enough to chew through the kilometres, but slow enough to remain as close to silent as possible.

An hour later, Spud called a halt. Pulling out a map from his pocket, he confirmed their location, and then signalled Jimmy to him.

"Right, we're here," he said, pointing to an area on the map with a blade of grass. "Indos are here,"---he moved the blade of grass slightly west. "Seems to me they've setup on this feature,"---he pointed to an area on the map indicating a small hill. "We must have run into a listening post or clearing patrol."

Jimmy nodded.

"I reckon we circle all the way around, approach the hill from the opposite direction, and then hit 'em hard."

Deep in thought, Jimmy glared at the map then grinned, his teeth pearly white against his dark skin. "You're one fuckin' crazy bastard, ay?"

"Don't like it?"

Jimmy nodded. "Nah, mate, you got a good idea. We'll take 'em by surprise. Only thing is, we dunno how many of 'em there are."

"We don't have to hit 'em hard straight away. We could probably hold off for a bit and scout out their position."

"Yeah, Spud," said Jimmy, grinning once more. "I reckon I like that idea better. Find out what we're up against, then give 'em a floggin'."

Spud nodded, remaining silent as he considered the map. Ten minutes later, several of the senior platoon diggers were sat near a rudimentary mud map of Spud's making. He explained the situation, mission, how it was to be executed, and actions on enemy contact. Once he completed the briefing, he allowed time for each soldier to voice their questions or concerns. These experienced soldiers had served more than five years as riflemen. It would be folly for a commander to neglect their thoughts on such a situation. For the most part, they mirrored Jimmy's concerns. Scouting the enemy position from the near distance might not uncover all threats, or give them a detailed idea of actual enemy number. A full-blown assault under such circumstances might uncover nasty surprises they were unprepared for once they closed in on the enemy.

With the brief complete, the platoon moved out carefully through the Australian scrub, maintaining good distance from one another. Spud was taking no chances, ensuring they were three kilometres north of their original position before turning west. After covering a further three kilometres in a westerly direction, he confirmed on a map they were north-west of the feature atop of which the enemy had positioned themselves. With evening falling upon them, the platoon harboured up their defensive perimeter before commencing their evening routine; quietly clearing sleeping areas and eating. The men were split up into pairs, one soldier always remaining in the prone position, facing out with his weapon ready to fire. Once the other man had finished his routine, they swapped.

The platoon stood to as the sun slipped beneath the western horizon and remained so until night's blanket settled upon the land. Once they were stood down, most of the soldiers departed for bed. Three machine guns---faced out at the ten o'clock, two o'clock, and six o'clock positions respectively---remained manned by two men each. The platoon members would take turns rotating through the three guns during the night, keeping a careful watch over their sleeping brothers.

* * * * *

"Cease fire!" yelled Major Gilang Simanjuntak.

Most of them obeyed, but several soldiers continued shooting blindly into the scrub.

"Cease fire!"

Silence descended upon the forest. Gilang's soldiers remained vigilant; their alert, adrenaline-fuelled glares raking the foliage, searching for a threat.

He had once been advised never to order soldiers under one's command to do something one was unwilling to do himself. That in mind, Gilang caught the eye of his lead scout and ordered him to approach. Gilang prided himself on remembering the names of many of his non-commissioned officers and all of his senior non-commissioned officers, but had a terrible memory when it came to the privates. He wracked his brain but could not remember the young man's name. The scout moved quietly through the shrubs and long grass in a half crouch. Eventually he knelt beside Gilang, waiting for an order.

"You and I will fall back and gather the main force."

The scout, a short, lithe but strong looking man, nodded. "Yes, sir."

"Then we'll hunt the Australians down," said Gilang, clenching a fist. He jerked a thumb. "Lead the way."

The scout nodded, rising into a half crouch and moved off smoothly. Gilang ensured he maintained plenty of distance between himself and the soldier, aware of his arcs, including his six. With only two soldiers in the patrol, Gilang knew he did not have the luxury of knowing there were friendly soldiers spread out around him to protect the flanks.

Twenty minutes later, soldiers guarding the outer edge of the main position challenged them. Holding weapons above their head, the two soldiers halted and identified themselves before being allowed to proceed. Eventually they were within the perimetre of the main position proper and Gilang found himself looking into the cruel face of Sgt Pandu.

"We heard the fight," Pandu said before Gilang could speak. "Any losses?"

Gilang nodded. "One man. Ready the soldiers... we move in two minutes."

Pandu nodded. "We are ready now, sir; lead the way."

* * * * *

Jimmy led the platoon through the forest, refreshing early morning light spearing through the canopy. His dark, alert eyes missed nothing; sweeping across the forest, flicking from shrub to clumps of grass, resting for a second on the low hanging branch of a nearby tree, which had partially snapped. Convinced the damage to the branch was not fresh, he allowed his eyes to continue their relentless movement, flitting and gliding across his immediate environment searching for enemy or signs of recent enemy presence, trip wires, booby traps, mines. Number one scout was usually an unenviable position of any platoon; it required a lot of concentration and a calm mind. He loved the job though, especially coming from an unconventional unit such as Norforce trained in close surveillance.

Gunshots exploded from the forest in a deafening wall of sound.

"Ambush left!" shouted a voice, almost inaudible over the cacophony.

The platoon reacted instantly, going to ground and returning fire. Soldiers sprinted in short bounds before hitting the ground.

"One and two sections up front!" roared Spud. "Three section in depth!"

As a member of one section, Jimmy glanced across at his number two scout, Bear. The soldier fired several shots then yelled, "Go!"

Jimmy pushed himself to his feet, glad to hear Bear's weapon open up once more. He sprinted forward, managing two steps before a hiss and a crack near his head suggested he was pushing his luck. Slamming himself onto the ground, he brought the Steyr into his shoulder and fired. "Go!"

Catching sight of movement at his eleven o'clock, Jimmy saw an enemy soldier had risen up to take a sight picture. Jimmy brought his weapon to bear and fired several rounds in quick succession. The enemy soldier dropped behind a shrub, but Jimmy was not sure whether he hit him or not. Firing another few rounds for good measure, he heard Bear crashing through the forest before slamming onto the ground with a grunt and opening fire.

Looking along the line of one section, he caught the glance of his section commander who signalled him to halt. Realising he and Bear had crept forward of the axis of advance, Jimmy gave thumbs up.

"Hold!" he yelled across at Bear.

"Right-o!" he replied, and less than a minute later, the scouts were back in line.

"Scouts!" came the section commander's shout, all but drowned out by the firefight.

"Go!" roared Bear, his rate of fire intensifying as Jimmy took a deep breath, stood, and sprinted forward.

Pushing through a six-foot clump of grass, Jimmy looked straight at an enemy soldier lying at his feet. Reacting before he could think, he fired point-blank into his head. Going to ground behind the dead body, Jimmy yelled, "one dead!"

The words were repeated along the line of the platoon. Within minutes, more enemy dead were announced up and down the Australian line of assault as they began to overrun the Indonesian position. Another ten minutes, the Indonesian dead were searched and Spud's platoon had reorganised, checked their ammunition status, and redistributed rounds where needed. Cordite's aroma drifted through the forest, strong enough in some places that Jimmy could taste it.

* * * * *

Gilang sprinted through the forest towards the distant firefight. He could hear his soldiers barging through the forest behind him, some of them hissing at him to slow down. Although he knew it was a polite way of saying, "quiet the fuck down!", the major was tired of losing soldiers. He knew the Australians were loitering around the area probing the position and now he knew exactly where they were located. He wanted to catch them and advance to contact before they could once more melt away into the forest.

"Sir!" growled a familiar voice.

Gilang turned and saw Pandu, but gone was the cruel glint. Genuine concern now shone from his eyes. "Sir, slow down! We'll be heard for miles."

Gilang ignored him, anger warming him. Pandu's hand clamped down on his shoulder. "Sir!"

He shrugged the hand loose. "Do not touch me!" snarled Gilang. "It's time to finish this once and for all!"

The firefight, minutes before sounding like the harmless popping of kids playing with cap guns in the distance, had taken on a decidedly different noise. Gilang was closing the distance; the gunfight, loud and foreboding, echoed through the forest. He swore he could even hear distant shouting and screaming amongst the conglomeration of noise. Then as soon as it started, the fight was over, the last two gunshots seeming to echoing through the canopy for an eternity.

* * * * *

Picking up and beginning to patrol away from the area, the platoon heard the sound of people running through the forest towards them. A lot of people. As Jimmy turned towards noise and took a knee, he estimated it to be more than a hundred…far more; maybe even up to three hundred. Concern washed over him as his index finger moved to gently brush against his weapon's trigger.

Spud signalled for a deliberate ambush and the platoon moved quickly and quietly into position facing the approaching threat. Spud was located roughly in the centre of the platoon, which had now spread back out into an extended line facing the rapidly approaching enemy.

Jimmy liked Spud, thought he was a great soldier and good commander, but did not like this decision. Badly outnumbered, even the best-trained troops in the world could be overrun by a rabble. Although, he certainly did not see the Indonesian soldiers as a rabble, which made the situation even worse. He would have preferred to patrol out of the area and remain silent and hidden than force a fight. A fight, which they may not be able to win.

* * * * *

Gilang cursed as he ran headlong into a spider's web. He stopped to rub the sticky web from his face. Pandu stopped beside him, weapon slung, hands resting on knees, and sweat beading on his forehead.

"Sir, please reconsider!" Pandu panted. "We should advance quietly, not announce our number and position. You know this!"

He whirled to face the man. "Don't tell me what I know, Sergeant!" he snarled. "Are you a coward?"

Fury glinted in Pandu's eyes, he clenched his jaw and remained silent for a moment. "No," he finally replied.

Gilang nodded and turned away. "Good!"

He leapt over a long dead tree trunk and accelerated into a fast jog.

"I'm just not stupid," Pandu said under his breath and made to follow his commander.

Gilang leapt over a clump of grass, dodged a mighty Ghost Gum, and flinched, skidding to a halt as the forest exploded with the noise of bullets hissing, cracking, and whizzing past his head. He dropped to the ground, breath coming in sharp rasps, sweat dripping from his nose.

Panic settled in the deepest depths of his gut, threatening to break free and envelope his entire being. He managed to control the powerful and frightening feeling, but barely.

"And what now, sir!" roared Pandu, who had dropped to the ground nearby, leopard crawling up so he was in line with the major.

"Get the men up in extended line, take the fight to the enemy!"

To the sergeant's credit, he realised it was neither the time nor place to fight about who was right or wrong.

Gilang leaned up, pulled rifle into shoulder, and released a short burst at a thick shrub from within which he thought he had seen several muzzle flashes. The air around him came to life as hot lead ripped past, thudding into the ground, slamming into tree trunks, or cutting saplings in two.

Pandu was roaring commands beside him as more soldiers began joining the fight. His ears ringing, Gilang could not make out the sergeant's exact words, only that he was controlling the soldiers with incredible skill. The Indonesian force immediately mounted a counter-attack and were pushing towards the Australians. Soon, the numerically superior Indonesian force drowned out the Australian gunfire. Gilang---legs weak from either fatigue or fear, he was unsure which---pushed himself to his feet. Sprinting forward several steps, he threw himself to the ground, a bullet passing so close to his cheek he could feel its heat. Gilang knew his troops would soon overrun the enemy position.

✶ ✶ ✶ ✶ ✶

"Withdraw! Withdraw!" the command was passed up and down the length of the extended line.

"About fuck'n time!" shouted Jimmy.

"Go!" he yelled at Bear, firing several rounds at an Indonesian sprinting towards him. The enemy dropped from sight, but Jimmy didn't know if he had hit him or not.

"Yup!" he barely heard Bear's voice over the near deafening symphony of violence. Pulling a smoke grenade from a pouch in his webbing, he ripped out the pin and heaved it hard. When red smoke began drifting across the Australian axis of withdrawal, Jimmy knelt, fired several shots, and then sprinted back, going to ground near Bear.

An Indonesian burst through a dense shrub straight into Jimmy's sights. He fired twice before the weapon went silent. Smoothly disengaging the empty magazine, he dropped it down the front of his shirt, slapped in a fresh one, charged the weapon, and fired a few more rounds.

"Go!" he yelled, throwing his second last smoke grenade and following it with a well-placed bullet that dropped an enemy soldier to the ground. No doubt he'd hit that one.

Bear jumped to his feet and sprinted back.

Jimmy craned his neck and saw the rest of his section were drifting off to the right---or more accurately, he and Bear were drifting to the left.

Once back in line with his comrade, he yelled, "Next bound, push right!"

Bear looked at him quizzically, before holding a cupped hand up to his ear.

"Push right! Push right!"

A nod and thumbs up. "Fuckin' heard me that time, ay?" Jimmy muttered to himself, grinning.

✶ ✶ ✶ ✶ ✶

Later that evening, the platoon was resting, only fifty percent of the soldiers standing to, whilst the rest slept or at least attempted. Spud had placed the platoon in all round more than five kilometres from the ambush site. Although the deliberate ambush had resulted in at least twenty confirmed enemy kills, Jimmy still considered it a poor decision, not to mention a needless waste of precious ammunition. The Australians withdrew from the firefight with one casualty, a soldier with a badly sprained ankle. How they had not taken far heavier casualties was beyond Jimmy. He put it down to blind luck.

"I swear I saw that fucker," whispered Spud.

Jimmy's dark eyes observed the man, his face faintly silhouetted against the dark forest by a sliver of moon.

"Who ya on about, brother?"

"Simonjunk or whatever his fuckin' name is. Could pick his face out of a crowd any day." He tapped his temple. "Got his ugly mug burned permanently up here."

"That why you wanted to ambush 'em? Make sure he was there, ay?"

"Yeah, partly at least."

Anger flooded through Jimmy. "Spud, ya fuckin' dick 'ead!" he hissed. "You could've got us all killed! In fact, you're lucky we got away without loss. If they hadn't broken contact and continued following up instead, we'd be fucked, brother. Fucked! You know that, don't ya?"

"Yeah, but I saw the little fucker!"

"I don't give a flying turd, mate. You put your entire platoon in danger, just for your own personal war, ya know what I mean? You start thinkin' angry, you start fightin' angry, and if you start fightin' angry, our soldiers start dyin'. Got it?" Jimmy leaned towards Spud, his eyes glaring. "Dunno 'bout you, but I'm not ready to die just yet, ay?"

"Yeah, you're right," muttered Spud.

"Course I'm right, brother, I'm always bloody right!" he grinned and slapped the man on his shoulder.

"I'll find the little prick myself and bring him back here." Spud made to stand up, but Jimmy held him down.

"Are you bat shit crazy?"

Spud ignored him, shrugged the hand off and stood, followed quickly by Jimmy.

"Listen you big, ugly headed bastard, you ain't going out there by yourself!" Jimmy whispered.

Spud turned to him. "You're right, Jimmy. I put all our lives in danger today. Bloody stupid thing to do, especially so badly outnumbered. I'm gunna go and grab that little rat bastard and drag his arse back here. Then we can head home to resupply."

Jimmy remained silent, watching the soldier depart.

He stopped and turned to his comrade. "Oh and, Jimmy? If I ain't back by first light tomorrow morning, I ain't comin' back."

The Aboriginal soldier remained silent, but he shook his head. You'll come back one way or another, brother. We'll come and find ya.

Racked with guilt, Jimmy regretted airing his concern about the ambush, but it needed to be said. Spud had spent plenty of time in recon platoon and could take care of himself, especially when operating by himself, but that did not detract from the heavy blanket of guilt settling upon Jimmy.

* * * * *

Spud knelt by the main gun of one section and briefed the two soldiers on watch where he was going and to expect him back some time before dawn. He did not, however, explain why. As professional soldiers, he expected them to challenge him upon his return, but in light of recent events, he did not want to take the risk that one or both might have itchy trigger fingers.

"I'll see ya soon," he whispered, patting the nearest on the shoulder.

"Yeah, no worries, mate. Watch your back out there."

"Always."

He stood, suppressing a groan as he did; it felt like he'd pulled a muscle in his leg during the firefight earlier that day. He advanced slowly, acutely aware of his foot placement, exploiting shadows cast by trees, saplings, and shrubs. Where possible, he moved to the low ground to avoid being potentially silhouetted.

It would be all for nothing if even one of the Indonesians possessed night vision goggles, but old habits die hard. He stopped and took a knee, grimacing as his right thigh protested and sent pain shooting down his leg.

Pulling his shirt over his head and cupping a pen light in his hand, he allowed the light to fall upon the compass he wore on a piece of hutchie cord around his neck, the compass itself hidden within a cut down piece of sock.. Double checking he was still travelling in the correct direction, he switched the penlight off, put the compass away, and shrugged his shirt back into place.

Taking a breath, he pushed himself back to his feet and continued. As the night progressed and after many stops to check direction, Spud became confident he was close to where the ambush had taken place. It might have been his imagination, but he swore he still smelled the faint aroma of cordite.

Probably havin' a fuckin' stroke, he thought absently. A distant cracking noise caught his attention and he dropped to his knee, bringing weapon up, finger touching the trigger.

Come on then, have a go if you're gonna. Watching for movement, he slowly swept his immediate environment, ears alert to even the smallest sound that might be alien to an Australian forest nearing midnight. Picking the direction from where he thought the sound originated, he stood and moved slowly, brushing past branches, stepping over long dead, fallen trunks. He paused when he saw the distant orange flicker of flames. Another crack as fresh wood was consumed by the fire. As he crept closer, he was relieved to see it was not in fact a bushfire, but a prepared fire. His stomach growled loudly as the smell of roasting beef drifted through the forest.

Livin' like fuckin' kings. As he closed the distance, Spud realised there were at least forty or more Indonesian soldiers around the fire. Some stood talking quietly, others squatted or sat, watching the flames in silence. Before he moved any closer though, Spud knelt quietly in place and spent a long time scanning the area of forest around him, watching for sentries that may have been placed as protection.

When he was sure there was no sign of sentries, he crept closer until he felt the faint heat of the fire upon his face. Dropping into a crouch, he winced as his thigh began to cramp.

Not now, you bastard! He sat quietly on the forest floor and stretched his leg, suppressing a groan of relief as the muscle began to relax.

Laughter broke the silence, followed by some quiet chatter as the Indonesians began lining up behind one another facing the fire. Intrigued, Spud watched. A soldier wielding a large knife began carving the beast, placing slabs of meat on a platter held by another man close by. When enough roast beef had been placed onto the platter, it was handed to the first soldier in line. The man then trudged off into the darkness along a well-worn track that Spud realised probably led towards the main position.

The process moved with military precision, one after another, each soldier loaded down with a platter full of succulent roast beef. Spud moved slowly, being careful to remain as silent as possible, until he was in position next to the track that soldiers walked. Slinging his rifle, he pulled his bayonet clear and glared at each man walking past, trying to ignore the inviting smell of cooked beef.

Unfortunately, they were moving so quickly, Spud had no time to intercept a soldier before the next one was following. If he were spotted this close to the fire, the light would reveal his uniform and give him away.

A clatter of noise followed by shouting drew Spud's interest. He watched as a soldier, who had accidentally dropped a platter, received a full, open-palmed smack on the face.

You hit like a fuckin' bitch! Say it! Spud thought, smiling as the man who dropped the platter held his cheek and replied. He had no idea what the Indonesian soldier said, but Spud hoped that had been his reply. Now was his chance. As the men gathered near the fire and watched the proceedings, Spud smoothly stood and walked out onto the track directly behind the next platter carrying Indonesian. Hesitation stalled him, but the thought of Simanjuntak caused fury to soak into the last fibre of his being. Speeding up, he approached the soldier, reached out, placed a hand over his mouth, and then began stabbing the bayonet relentlessly into his neck. The soldier dropped his platter and fell to his knees. Snarling, Spud followed him, continuing to stab repeatedly, feeling warm blood splatter across his face, hands, and uniform.

When the Indonesian soldier stopped moving, Spud stood over him trying to regain his breath. Clasping the man by his boots, he hauled the corpse from the track and out of sight before returning to pick up the empty platter. Kneeling, he patted the ground until his hand touched a piece of lukewarm meat. He picked it up and walked away, stuffing the roast beef into his mouth and enjoying the taste. Ignoring the crunch of dirt in his mouth, he savoured the warm oil dribbling down his chin.

Fuck that tastes good! He slowed once he caught up with the next soldier in line, who was strolling without a care in the world and clueless as to what had happened behind him.

I'm coming for ya, you little prick… The image of Simanjuntak's face had haunted Spud for too long.

Chapter 14

"In a twelve hour gunfight, one of our SAS patrols have fought their way out of a valley at the base of the Great Dividing Range in Western Queensland, Australia. Colonel Steve Coburn says the patrol, surrounded and heavily outnumbered, fought their way clear with the help of air support. The patrol suffered one casualty, with the signaller spraining his ankle." - *Daily New Zealand News (NZ)*

It had taken them the best part of a day to organise themselves and plan how they were going to evacuate. In particular, logistical elements like food and water supply for six people, ammunition supply, spare diesel and petrol, sleeping gear and so on.

"Yeah, Mick, hoofin'," said Finn, sitting in the rear tray of the Ute.

The older man paused, looking at the Royal Marine. "What?"

"All good," chuckled Finn. "Hoofin' just means good. I'll teach you to talk bootie yet."

Mick looked confused, then shook his head. "Not even gonna ask, mate, as long as you're happy there."

Finn grinned, settled down behind the cab of the vehicle, facing rearward. The supplies were packed around him in such a way that a cleared space in the shape of a 'T' was left for him. Finn, sitting where the horizontal and vertical lines of the 'T' met, facing the rear. This allowed him an unhindered fire lane towards the six o'clock position as well as clear lines of sight to left and right. He laid the assault rifle across his lap and waited for the others to mount up.

Katie climbed into the driver's seat, while Ben sat in the passenger's seat, and Jade wedged in between them.

"This isn't very comfortable," she complained.

"Best it's going to get I'm afraid, munchkin," Ben replied.

The Ute's engine roared into life, a dark cloud of diesel fumes blasting from the exhaust for a few seconds. With Mick driving, he and Craig would ride double on the four-wheeler. The older man had installed a make-shift rifle holster for his trusty old .303 rifle onto the front handlebars, allowing the weapon to face forward. He'd chosen a holster that boasted a zip running its length, meaning he could unzip and lift the weapon straight up, rather than having to pull the weapon back until the barrel cleared the mouth of the holster. Mick had decided it would probably be especially handy if he needed to gain access to the weapon at short notice.

Craig sat behind him, an improvised strap wrapped around him at his hips and tied down to each side of the four-wheeler, allowing the soldier to sit as far back as possible from Mick so that he could bring his weapon to bear with both hands if needed and not fear falling from the vehicle if they were mobile---at least, that was Craig's hope. He pulled the strap tight and felt it pull him down firm onto the motorbike.

So far, so good, he thought as the ignition turned over and the engine came to life beneath him.

The four-wheeler would lead the way, meaning they would have firepower facing forward and, with Finn sitting in the rear tray of the Ute, firepower facing rearward. It may not be much, but it was better than none at all.

"Ready?" Mick said over his shoulder.

Craig tightened the grip on his M-4. "Yeah, mate, whenever you're ready."

They moved off down the driveway, passing Daisy on the way. Mick had released her from the hospital paddock after rubbing cream onto her well-healed wound one last time. He had given her some gentle words, a couple of carrots, and then left her to her own devices. Daisy had freedom of movement for hundreds of acres. If she felt threatened, she would be able to gallop away in any direction until she felt safe.

"See ya soon, girl!" Mick called to the horse as Daisy, chewing on a thick clump of grass, stood watching the vehicles pass.

Mick steered the motorbike down Bent Wood Cullen Bone's long, dirt driveway, taking his time and avoiding ruts and washouts. When they were approaching the end of the driveway, they stopped and Craig stepped off, signalling for them to wait. He quietly moved off the driveway into the scrub. Kneeling at edge of the forest before it gave way to the road, he took time to look in all directions for enemy vehicle checkpoints and listening for potential enemy traffic. When he was satisfied there was no immediate threat, he moved back.

"Yeah, all good, mate," he said to Mick, hopping back on the motorbike and tightening the strap around his waist.

"Good to know."

They turned out onto the main road and headed east. Accelerating the four-wheeler to what Mick estimated to be almost ninety kilometres an hour, he kept a sharp eye on the bitumen road upon which they travelled. Craig had briefed him on the tell-tale signs of an IED. He watched for wires leading up to or even across the road, freshly turned earth that suggested digging had taken place recently, and any obvious obstacle partially blocking the road and forcing them to deviate off the hard stand. Conscious of all these things, he pushed the motorbike fast enough to make some good distance, but slow enough he could bring it to a stop quickly.

Katie, also aware of the situation, kept a one hundred metre distance from the four-wheeler. Craig had explained the distance would allow them to stop safely without fear of crashing into the four-wheeler if Mick braked suddenly. On a more sobering note, it also meant that should Mick misjudge or miss one of those tell-tale signs and an IED was initiated, with luck, the Ute would remain unaffected by the explosion.

Mick kept to what had once been the middle of the road. The road was badly damaged, much of the bitumen on each side having been ripped up or damaged by tracked vehicles. In some cases, the imprint of their tracks was still evident in the bitumen. Convoys of hundreds, perhaps even thousands, of heavy trucks had caused most of the damage, leaving the centre of the highway being the only place not truly affected by overuse.

Before the invasion, there were often dead kangaroos along the edges of the highway when Mick drove into town each fortnight. Interestingly, he had not seen one yet. It was good to feel the wind ripping through his hair again. He might be leaving his home behind, but they were heading to safety. It would only be a matter of time before he was allowed to return. Given the situation, Mick knew it was for the best. He felt guilty about the cattle and Daisy; he just hoped the stock came through the carpet-bombing unscathed. If there were some way to take them all with him, he would have done it.

"Prime candidate for an ambush, mate. Stay sharp," Craig shouted in Mick's ear.

Slowing and dropping down a gear, Mick approached a hairpin bend in the road. The bullet-riddled yellow road sign suggested a speed of forty kilometres per hour. Nothing untoward on or near the road suggested anything suspicious.

Accelerating out of the bend, he swerved to miss three Indonesian vehicles moving at a high rate of speed in the opposite direction.

* * * * *

Spud maintained pace with the soldier in front of him, often casting glances over his shoulder to check the Indonesian who had been punished for dropping his platter had not caught up to them. He checked for the fifth time in as many minutes and was again relieved that there was an ample gap between himself and the soldier who should have been immediately behind him.

He came to a sudden halt before running into the stationary man in front of him. Spud's hand dropped to the sheathed bayonet at his waist in case any suspicion was beginning to be cast in his direction. But through the dull, limited light thrown by the moon, Spud was able to see the long line of platter carrying Indonesian soldiers also halted, waiting patiently as the line slowly began creeping forward.

The human convoy must have arrived at the entrance to the main position and were possibly being counted in. Before long, the humbled soldier who would probably never hold another plate in his life without some kind of flashback would catch up to them. Time to make his move, or it would be too late.

Spud quietly melted into the scrub, the long line of Indonesian soldiers disappearing from sight. He stopped, crouched, and placed the empty platter upon the forest floor before unslinging his assault rifle and continuing parallel to the unseen queue of Indonesian, platter-carrying soldiers.

Several times, he was forced to pause after accidentally stepping on a dry branch or losing his footing, causing him to scramble through the leaf little and saplings to maintain his balance. He hoped the Indo soldiers had grown accustomed to the noises expected in an Australian scrub at night. If they were, they would think nothing of a rustle in the bushes or the crack of a long dead bough. The forests might be abundant with life during the day, but at night, their nocturnal brethren took over the reins. With possums, wombats, rodents, kangaroos, wild pigs, owls, and the occasional wild dog roaming freely through the forests, a disturbance of the undergrowth could be any number of things. So close to their main position, Spud hoped an enemy soldier might not be one of the things on their minds.

When he was sure no one was the wiser of his presence, Spud continued, acutely aware of his footing. The scrub seemed to take on a more sinister feel at night; tall, elegant pines becoming angry old men. Brilliant, powerful eucalyptus metamorphosing into great demons glaring down, the innocent breeze sliding between their leaves becoming their hissing jeers and curses. But surrounded by both darkness and Australian scrub, Spud was at home.

Moving down into a small creek bed, he took a knee and looked around, listening for any foreign noise. He heard soft talking nearby and what he thought might have been the flash of a torch. But given that he was so close to the main position and despite his instincts screaming to lay still or withdraw, he moved towards the source.

Pushing through a thick grevillea, he watched the platters being placed on a long makeshift table created from thick trunks, or at least that was the impression it left Spud with as the torch was switched on before being turned off almost as fast. A soldier used the light to ensure platters were being placed neatly beside one another.

Spud slung his weapon and pushed his way carefully out into the clearing behind a gaggle of enemy soldiers standing close to the table and waiting impatiently for the order to eat. After what seemed like an eternity, their wait finally ended and the ravenous soldiers surged forward to commence dinner. Spud walked between soldiers, the darkness hiding his face. He remained silent as he walked, quietly scanning for Simanjuntak but without success. It remained almost impossible with such low light.

The platters were scoured clean within five minutes and, with dinner finished, stacked neatly before being carried away for cleaning. A quiet voice began speaking and Spud noticed the Indonesian soldiers crowding in to listen. Spud followed them. He had no idea what the speaker was saying, but he recognised the voice. The familiar tones were burned for eternity into his cerebral cortex. It was Simanjuntak!

Only a sliver of moon cast light upon the clearing and it wasn't enough to make out Simanjuntak's face, but he edged closer to the speaker. When the brief ended, the Indonesian soldiers moved off in all directions, probably heading to watch duty or bed. Spud kept the dark grey silhouette of Simanjuntak's retreating form in sight. It was difficult; twice he walked straight into Indonesian soldiers, who seemed to tell him off in harsh, foreign words.

"Maaf, pak," Spud muttered as he brushed past one man. In English it translated to sorry, sir, and were the only Indonesian words he knew. He kept his voice deliberately soft, so as to make it more difficult for the enemy soldiers to detect his accent.

Keeping Simanjuntak in sight was difficult in the poor light, but with burning determination, Spud was not going to let him escape. One way or another, this thing was going to end.

If I die, so be it, the Australian thought soberly.

Finally, the Indonesian officer ducked under the low entrance of a makeshift shelter. He stopped outside the yawning, black mouth of the entrance, straining to hear voices that might indicate the enemy officer was not alone. But silence met him.

Unsheathing his bayonet, Spud ducked under the low entrance and stumbled into the simply constructed dwelling. Simanjuntak's voice spoke, probably demanding what he wanted.

"Surprise, motherfucker!" Spud said softly, switching on a pen light and shining it straight into Simanjuntak face.

The Indonesian officer squinted against the sudden glare and without hesitation, Spud struck the enemy officer three vicious blows to the temporal region with the pommel of his bayonet. The enemy soldier dropped silently to the ground. He wasted no time in dragging the unconscious man out of the shelter before lifting him up into a fireman's carry and striding away into the Australian scrub.

With the evening meal finished and five hundred odd soldiers preparing for bed, as quiet as they attempted to be, there was noise. Soldiers unzipping sleeping bags, or men quietly walking out from their position to take a piss, a whispered conversation, or suppressed laughter at some shared joke. So the noise Spud made as he carefully negotiated the Australian bush was not unexpected and none of the Indonesian soldiers were the wiser as to capture of their commander.

Spud managed to keep up the steady pace for ten minutes before he was forced to dump the unconscious man, without ceremony, upon the leaf litter. Catching his breath, he waited for his body to regain strength before lifting the man up onto the opposite shoulder and carried on. He stopped often to look and listen for a potential follow up, but with the dead weight on his shoulders, the thunder of his heart, and rasping breath in his ears, it was impossible to hear anything.

He knew it was simply a matter of exfiltrating from the area as rapidly as possible. Concentrating on his footing, Spud walked carefully up a shallow creek bed. A misplaced step might cause a sprained ankle, or worse. He could not afford any kind of injury, not if he wanted to escape the area undetected.

The Australian knelt and let the unconscious Indonesian slide from his shoulder. Taking a long drink from a water bottle, he wiped his brow and pulled out his compass to ensure he was still travelling in the correct direction.

When he was sure he was headed the right way, Spud held in a groan as he lifted to Indonesian back into a fireman's carry.

"Heavy fucker for a small bloke," he muttered. Remembering why he was doing this at all fuelled him with anger, tired muscles gaining a second wind as he walked at a pace sedate enough to ensure he could regather his feet if he tripped or lost balance, but fast enough to intersect the Australian position within the next hour.

* * * * *

Gilang came to with a groan, a thundering headache sending splitting pain through his skull. Still groggy, he realised he had been sleeping in an awkward position. He tried to reposition himself and was met with a harsh voice, speaking in English, to keep still.

As he ascended from the depths and awareness began reasserting itself, he realised he was being carried over a man's shoulder. Reaching up, he tentatively touched his temple and felt it slick with blood.

"Where am I?" he asked in English.

He was met with a chuckle, then silence as the man carrying him continued on.

Gilang asked again, wincing as the man's shoulder dug painfully into his pelvis.

"Shut your mouth," the man responded.

Fair enough.

He winced again, trying to ignore the pain.

"I can walk. It'd be easier for both of us."

"No!"

"Please, I am in great pain," said Gilang. It wasn't quite the truth, but nor was it a complete lie.

"All right mate," said the voice, dumping Gilang down, where he fell to his knees. "But you try anything, anything, and I'll fuckin' kill ya. Got it? Now stay in front of me!"

Gilang climbed to his feet. "Yes, no problem. But what do you want with me?"

"Oh, you'll see," said the voice. Gilang could detect the smile in the words. "You'll see."

* * * * *

Roaring past, the Indonesian vehicles braked hard, the last truck locking up, tyres screeching in protest, smoke drifting around the wheel wells.

"Harry von turbo pigs!" Finn got up and slammed his open hand upon the roof of the Ute's cabin.

The enemy vehicles were turning around and, although somewhat awkwardly it would not be long before they picked speed back up and gave chase.

"What?" Ben yelled out the window.

Finn leaned over the side of the Ute facing the cabin. "I said speed the fuck up! They're giving chase!"

A curve in the road hid the Indonesian vehicles from view, but the last Finn saw, they had all turned around and were building up speed, dark diesel fumes blasting from their exhausts. Increasing speed and moving to the opposite side of the road, they came alongside the quadbike.

"Can you go any faster, mate?" Finn heard Ben yell across at Mick.

"Whatta ya want, blood? No! This is as fast as she goes. Why?"

"Those Indonesian trucks are turnin' around and giving chase!"

"Course they bloody are!" Mick roared back, shaking his head.

Finn allowed his index finger to touch the trigger, eyes watching the road rip past. His assault rifle was the only weapon facing rearward, so it would be up to him to hold off the Indonesian trucks.

176

On the upside, only the first truck in the convoy could fire upon them, and only the passenger could open fire.

"Oi, Ben, me old son, which side of the road they drive on in Indonesia?" Finn yelled.

"No idea!" came the reply.

Finn heard Katie yell something, followed by Ben's voice. "Left, I think!"

"Right!" said Finn.

"No, left!" shouted Ben.

Finn turned around to see the wide grin. "Dickhead!" he yelled.

So if they drove on the left, the driver would be seated on the right side of the vehicle. Slot him and it might make things difficult for the vehicles travelling behind. Finn settled back into position and watched to the rear of them. The road behind them was still clear, although the Royal Marine had no doubt it would not be long before the enemy vehicles came into view. They passed burned out vehicles and diverted around massive craters in the road where air strikes had hit seemingly invisible targets, until Finn saw several Indonesian armoured vehicles lying in various states of destruction within a blackened area of forest where a bushfire had commenced as a result.

He'd almost forgotten about the Indonesian follow up when around a distant bend in the road appeared the enemy vehicles.

"Here they come!" Finn shouted.

"Yeah, okay," came the reply, followed by several beeps, probably to let the guys on the quadbike in front know it would soon be on, although Finn did not want to turn around to check; he felt more comfortable keeping a close eye on the approaching enemy.

Finn felt the Ute negotiate a sharp bend in the road and quickly grabbed a hold of a ratchet strap holding the supplies in place. It felt as if the vehicle would tip. The brakes came on hard and he grunted as he was thrown into the back of the cabin.

"What the fuck you doin'?" roared Finn.

He felt the Ute turn off the road onto a bumpy dirt track, and then turn again until they were hidden amongst thick forest.

"Out!" he heard Craig's voice as the Australian soldier sprinted past, weapon held tight, eyes alert. He headed back towards the road, keeping to the forest where he would remain hidden.

Finn disembarked and ran after him, realising the tiny convoy had negotiated around a tight bend in the road before leaving the hard stand and driving down a tiny dirt track until they had turned off into thick scrub and out of view from passing traffic.

As far as the Indonesians were concerned, their prey had driven around a bend in the road and would be none the wiser that the Australians had gone to ground when they themselves came around the hairpin bend in the road.

"What's the plan, racing snake?" Finn said, coming alongside Craig.

"Stay down, stay quiet," whispered Craig, taking a knee behind a thick iron bark.

The others approached at a brisk walk, Jade held tightly in Katie's arms. Finn thought the little girl looked afraid; although, to her credit, she remained silent, downturned mouth clamped shut, huddling into her mother's chest.

Finn caught her eye. He grinned and winked at her, watching her face soften although she did not smile. The engines grew louder as the enemy vehicles approached the tight bend. Repositioning himself behind a pine, Finn listened as the first vehicle began gearing down, he brought weapon into shoulder and stared over the top of the optic sight. Through the thick forest, he only caught the slightest visual of the Unimogs as it accelerated out of the turn, working rapidly up through the gears and increasing speed. The second and third were not far behind and before long, the engines were growing distant, finally being drowned out by the calls of birds perched high above the silent group.

Finn stood and ran across to Craig in a crouch. "Now they're ahead of us."

"Yeah, mate, exactly. We know where they are, but they have no idea where we are. If we'd continued on we might have run into more ahead of us, like a vehicle checkpoint for instance. We would have been bracketed in with nowhere to go."

Finn silently nodded in agreement.

The group remained in place for close to half an hour, waiting, watching, and occasionally talking in hushed voices. When they were about ready to mount up and commence moving again, Finn held up his hand and called for silence. The group froze in place.

The Royal Marine cursed silently, hoping he had been hearing things, but as Craig's piercing gaze bored into him, he realised he had not. The Indonesian vehicles were driving back towards them, much slower this time---they were still hunting. Although the engines remained in the far distance, they were gradually growing in volume.

"I'm goin' to jack up and thin out," said Finn, tapping Craig's arm.

"What's the plan?" the Australian soldier asked. He'd worked with Royal Marines in the past and knew their language.

"Draw 'em away, leave their vehicles parked up, that way you can hijack one," Finn said.

Craig nodded. "How you gonna get back?"

"Hadn't thought that far," said Finn, grinning.

"Once we nab the vehicle, we'll follow you up," said Craig. "It'll look to them like one of their vehicles is just moving up in support."

"Cluster fuck," muttered Finn.

Craig chuckled and nodded. "I'm hearin' ya, mate. All we got to go on at short notice though."

"You ready?" Finn asked, standing.

Craig grinned.

The Royal Marine ran along the dirt track and out onto the bitumen road. Finn stood in the middle of the road, part way around the hairpin bend. The enemy vehicles were loud, indicating they were not far away. They growled and grumbled at a sedate pace, obviously paying particular attention to the forest each side of the road. Their dogged determination spoke volumes about their discipline.

Ignoring his nerves, he found his mind sliding back to Mike. His mate had first been shot in the leg, causing him to scream in agony during the intense firefight. The section had patrolled into an ambush, were surrounded, and vastly outnumbered. A second round slammed into Mike's chest, silencing him. Mike's body lay prone, forehead resting on the leaf litter, left arm splayed out, and right hand clasping his rifle. As long as Finn lived, he'd never forget the way his mate had died. He was aware of his heartbeat thundering in his ears as he relived the terrible moment.

Movement in front of him caught his attention and he watched the first Unimogs drive around the bend towards him.

"Get a fuckin' hold of yourself!" he snarled, dropping to a knee and bringing his weapon up into his shoulder.

The vehicle rapidly decelerated, a hiss of air brakes bringing it to a sudden stop. Finn took the opportunity and squeezed the trigger, his first two bullets slamming through the windscreen and shattering the driver's skull. Adjusting his aim, he killed the passenger, stood, and began walking backwards, taking a deep breath as adrenaline poured through his system.

Finn could see soldiers jumping down onto the bitumen from the back of the mog. They began running up either side of the vehicle towards him.

"Too late for an egg butty?" he roared, firing several shots from the hip before sprinting off into the bush. The return fire was intense, several rounds pinging off the bitumen behind him. He dodged past a copse of trees, jumped over a dead trunk, pushed through a shrub, and stumbled down a dry creek bed. Raising his weapon above his head, he fired several more rounds.

The return fire had diminished to single, intermittent shots. Finn once again was on the run, only this time---strangely enough---he was enjoying the experience.

* * * * *

Craig indicated for Ben, Katie, and Jade to mount up on the Ute. Looking at Mick, he tapped the top of his head and the old Vietnam veteran instinctively moved towards him. He knelt down beside the young soldier, looking at him quizzically.

"Stay here, mate, but be ready to move," whispered Craig.

Mick nodded.

Craig moved through the forest slow and quiet. When the road came into view through the thick scrub, he stopped, knelt, and appraised the situation. It appeared the troops had disembarked from the vehicles and given chase to Finn, but the drivers were still with the vehicles. Two were standing near the last mog, whilst the remaining pair were near the front vehicle, one opening the passenger side door and jumping up onto the sidestep to peer into the cabin. He shouted something to his comrade behind him.

Craig moved through the last section of forest, walked out onto the road, and brought his M-4 to bear. The silenced weapon spoke four times. With the drivers dead, he quickly moved to clear the vehicles. When he was sure there were no more enemy soldiers in or around the Unimogs, he shouted for Katie to start the Ute and drive out onto the road.

"Mick, with me!"

The older man moved into view, his trusty old 303 rifle pulled into his shoulder. He whistled when he saw the carnage.

As they clambered up into the cabin of the rear vehicle, the forest exploded with automatic and machine gun fire. Craig started the Unimog's engine and made a U-turn. Holding his hand on the horn, the sound echoed around the immediate area, indicating to Finn they were ready to depart and to make his way back to the road... that was if the Royal Marine was not already dead.

Chapter 15

Spud placed the muzzle of his weapon into Simanjuntak's back and pushed the Indonesian onward.

"Get goin'," he said.

"Please, my legs hurt," replied Simanjuntak as he stumbled over a large rock protruding from the forest floor.

Spud knew the man was playing for time, hoping his soldiers realised he had been captured, but Spud knew his men would not become aware until well after daybreak.

"I don't give a flying fuck about your legs," said Spud, digging the muzzle into the soldier's back. "You can either speed up, or I'm gonna keep digging this weapon into you."

"I'll try."

"You'll do bloody more than try!" hissed Spud, driving the muzzle into Simanjuntak's back once more.

"All right, all right," conceded the Indonesian, increasing his pace.

"Better."

They walked in silence for close to ten minutes before Spud checked his watch.

03:53.

Just over an hour left before daybreak. Finally, he saw the large branch he had leaned against a tree when he had commenced this mission. It marked where he needed to depart the track to make for the Australian position. Spud pushed the Indonesian into the scrub and told him to stop. Taking out his compass, Spud checked direction. When he was sure, he steered Simanjuntak in the correct direction and shoved him forward.

"Hurry up!" snarled Spud.

"But there's no track to follow here," hissed the Indonesian.

"You place one fuckin' foot in front of the other. It's called walking! Remember?" replied the Australian soldier. "Now get your arse in gear!"

Every five minutes they stopped so Spud was able to re-check the compass before carrying on.

"Halt! Who goes there?" hissed a voice in front of them.

Spud felt relief. Finally, they were back in friendly territory.

"Spud, plus one," replied Spud.

"Blue," said the soldier.

A code was devised every few days. In this instance it was 'Blue Web'. Should someone approach the Australian position and had no idea what the code was, more than likely they would be shot--- especially given current circumstances.

"Web," hissed Spud.

"Advance and be recognised, brother," came Jimmy's voice.

He shoved Simanjuntak forward, the Indonesian stumbling over a branch and almost face planting into the ground. When he had regained his balance, Spud shoved him forward again, for good measure. Through the gloom appeared the main gun position. One soldier standing, weapon trained on the pair, the second soldier sitting behind the machine gun, although Spud wasn't aware of the second man until he was almost on top of him.

"Welcome back, mate," whispered Jimmy, slapping Spud on the shoulder as he walked through.

"Good to be back, trust me."

"Don't doubt it, mate," said Jimmy. "Hold up."

The pair stopped while the soldier slung his weapon and moved over to Simanjuntak. "Hands behind your back, fella," said Jimmy, grasping the prisoner's wrists and pulling his arms behind his back roughly. He zip-tied Simanjuntak's hands behind his back tightly before passing an empty sand bag to Spud. "Bag him when you get settled."

Spud nodded, took the empty sand bag, and pushed the Indonesian onward, aiming him towards the centre of the Australian position. When they were in what Spud estimated to be the centre of the area, he forced Simanjuntak to sit.

"Welcome home, fucker," snarled Spud as he pulled the empty sand bag over the Indonesian's head.

* * * * *

"When are the first B-52s expected to arrive?" asked Major General White.

Colonel Ramirez, hands folded and resting on the desk before him, held the Major General's steady gaze. "The first twenty-five departed Guam at zero six hundred hours this morning."

White glanced at his watch.

11:28.

"The flight's about four hours," said Colonel Ramirez, "so all things going well, they should have landed in Cairns, refuelled, and bombed up by now. The second squadron of twenty-five departed Hawaii around the same time the first took off from Guam. That's a seven and a half hour flight, so they won't land in Guam until at least thirteen thirty hours. The third squadron departed Barksdale at the same time, heading for Hawaii; they'll have arrived by now. Anyway, needless to say, at this time tomorrow all one hundred aircraft will be in country and ready for mission commencement."

"Sounds like a logistics nightmare," said White.

"To say the least," smiled Ramirez. "I'll be glad when they've all arrived"

White nodded. "I agree, it's about time we ended this once and for all."

"I still have at least one Marine out there missing in action," said the Royal Marine officer.

Lacey, was that his name? White thought to himself as he appraised the commander of the Royal Marines in Australia. There's always one troublemaker. "Well, that's a risk I'm willing to take," replied White.

"I'm bloody not!" roared the officer, slamming a fist on the table.

"Watch your tone," growled White.

The officer ignored him. "One soldier killed by friendly fire is mission failure as far as I'm concerned," he snarled.

"Come on, that's a bit of an over-reaction," said White.

"Is it? If that soldier out there was your son, would you reconsider your decision?"

White shrugged. "Probably."

"There you have it," replied the officer curtly.

"Look, to be honest, I don't remember your name," said White. "But I'll give you forty-eight hours before bombing starts. That way

184

your man has more time to show his face. Although in all honesty, if he hasn't turned up by now, he probably never will. Also, it'll give the B-52 crews time to rest up before the mission commences."

"I'm Lieutenant Colonel Lacey, sir, and thank you. It's better than nothing."

"Good, that's settled then. You're all dismissed; except you, Lacey, you remain behind," said White.

The other officers cleared Major General White's office, the last quietly closing the door behind him.

White leaned forward and spoke through clenched teeth. "If you ever speak to me like that in front of other officers again, I'll have you charged! Is that fucking clear?"

Lacey shrugged. "I'd rather have a charge over my head than the death of a good soldier on my conscience. You make any more stupid decisions like that again that put the lives of my people in jeopardy, you can guarantee I won't be so polite next time. So, you feel free to charge me, but bear this in mind, sir; your reputation means less to me than the lives of even one of my soldiers."

Before White could reply, Lacey strode out of the office and slammed the door behind him.

* * * * *

Spud allowed Jimmy to take the patrol commander position. He kept Simanjuntak close to him, hands still zip-tied behind his back and a sock acting as a gag clamped between the Indonesian's teeth. Simanjuntak was still able to cry out, but the sock would muffle the noise and also stop him from forming words. Rudimentary, but effective.

The platoon patrolled in open file, negotiating through the scrub at a sedate pace, heading back towards the coast. Spud knew morale was picking up. With their mission complete, it would not be long before they were able to eat a decent meal, enjoy a warm shower, and a long, well-earned sleep. As for Simanjuntak, he remained mostly silent throughout the day, only making a sound to indicate he was thirsty.

"See, we're not fucking barbarians," said Spud, allowing Simanjuntak several gulps from his water bottle before pulling the sock back into place. "Unlike you fuckers," he added, shoving the Indonesian officer forward.

As the sun sank towards the horizon, the platoon had covered close to forty kilometres through relatively light vegetation. The farther east they travelled, the less likely they would intercept enemy patrols. Another eight days of similar patrolling and they would be amongst friendly soldiers. Even though they were moving at only approximately four kilometres per hour, it was the ten-hour long days that added exhaustion to the already fatigued soldiers. Spud wasn't sure they could keep up the same intensity for that duration. It was a thin line between covering distance effectively and managing fatigue---not to mention injury susceptibility. By the end of the third day, the kilometres had dropped to twenty for the day.

"We keep pushing like this, we're gonna start pickin' up injuries, ya know?" Jimmy mentioned to Spud one evening.

"Yeah, I know, mate," whispered Spud in reply. "By my reckoning, we've covered close to a hundred clicks so far. Pretty damn good going."

"Better than good, mate," said Jimmy grinning.

Spud nodded. "I think we can probably have a crack at comms, see if we can't get an extraction; if not, at least a resup."

The platoon's signaller had been instructed to have the radio switched off the last few weeks as the hunt continued for Simanjuntak. Spud had his reasons; foremost being they would be well out of range of any friendly comms. Secondly, if they did use their comms, they might have been instructed to carry out a mission deviating from the capture of the Indonesian officer.

Spud believed the mission to find Simanjuntak had served a greater purpose in disrupting operations of the enemy in their immediate vicinity as well as denying them freedom of movement.

✱ ✱ ✱ ✱ ✱

Just after dawn, Seppy, the signaller and the platoon's youngest member, set up a horizontal long-wire antenna strung between two trees. The platoon remained in all round defence as Seppy whispered into his headset. Because of the headset, Spud was unable to hear the responses from the other call sign, but it was clear Seppy was in contact with a friendly unit somewhere. Spud had instructed the young soldier to request exfil or resupply. He thought he heard Seppy ask for exfil and when that was obviously refused, he asked for resupply. There was a long pause before Seppy slowly pulled the headset off and sat looking at the ground.

"Fuck's wrong with you, son?" asked Spud, tapping the soldier. "Ya havin' a fuckin' stroke?"

Seppy looked round at Spud. "Nah, mate," he replied, face sombre, eyes full of concern. "The entire area of inland Queensland is currently a no-fly zone. We're not getting an exfil or resupply."

"Why's it a no-fly zone?" asked Spud, an uncomfortable feeling beginning to spread through him.

"Mass doom-one-one mission inbound. They're going to level this entire area of Queensland."

"What about us?" asked Spud. "What? They're just going to blast us from existence as well?"

"Yup," said Seppy. "Unless we get our arses in gear and cover two hundred kilometres in less than twenty-four hours."

"Not possible, not on foot anyway." Spud swore softly and looked around, eyes thoughtful. "We need a bloody vehicle." Spud tapped Seppy on the arm. "Thanks, mate," he muttered before moving away.

After consulting their map, Jimmy moved the platoon towards the closest road, and within an hour they were patrolling on bitumen. Half the platoon patrolled at the far extreme of one side of the road whilst the other half of the platoon walked the opposite side. Maintaining the outer edges of the road allowed them to move into the forest and take cover quickly should the need arise.

Spud felt naked patrolling on the road, it went against all basic infantry tactics and his mind screamed at him to melt away into forest. But if they were to locate a vehicle, they were more likely to find one on the road. Needs must come first, and although it was a great risk to be out in such open country and moving down a perfectly good fire lane, they needed to haul arse out of the area. Die in a firefight, or be blown apart by a carpet-bombing run; the choices were dismal. But as Spud shoved Simanjuntak forward, he knew the platoon would die as a result of one of them, and likely sooner than later. He looked up at the sky, searching for a formation of aircraft and listening for the tell-tale rumble of incoming jets at high altitude. To his relief, neither was apparent.

Only a matter of time, he thought.

*****

Finn heard the vehicle's horn and changed direction on the fly, dodging a large tree, his breath coming in ragged gasps. Most of the enemy were still blundering through the forest shouting amongst one another, clueless as to Finn's position, but a small group of five or six were close on his heels.

The forest exploded into life behind him; bullets snapped and whizzed past him, thudding into trees and slamming into the ground around his feet.

"Fuck!" Finn managed in between breaths. If he continued to run, they'd eventually get a bead on him and he knew it. Time to fight. With lungs burning and legs aching, the Royal Marine took a knee behind a tree, trying unsuccessfully to control his breathing. Almost immediately, the enemy soldiers came sprinting into view. Finn opened fire with single well-aimed shots. The first two soldiers dropped dead, but the remaining four, now aware of Finn's firing position, darted in different directions and took cover behind logs or trees.

Return fire commenced and Finn threw himself to the ground as rounds cut through the air around him. Only a matter of time and he'd be shot, or the remainder of the enemy force would catch up and overrun him.

Good odds, he thought sarcastically, opening a pouch and pulling his last grenade free. Craning his neck, he saw two muzzle flashes in relatively close proximity. Pulling the pin free, he threw the grenade and watched it land almost exactly where he intended. Dirt, rocks, and leaves were thrown skyward during the following explosion. Almost immediately, a blood-curdling scream rent the air. Finn grinned through clenched teeth. The return fire became more sporadic as the Indonesians called to their injured comrade. Finn took the opportunity and rose up to a kneeling position, spotting one soldier running in a half crouch across open terrain towards the wounded man. Finn dipped his head to focus through the weapon's scope and shot the soldier through the chest.

Several bullets cracked the air beside his cheek and he threw himself to the ground with a grunt. "Fuck me!" he yelled, crawling back behind the tree.

Rolling across the ground and through concealing thigh high grass, he rose again and spotted the remaining soldier, weapon still trained on Finn's last known position. Bringing his weapon to bear, he fired two shots in quick succession, both slamming into the chest of the Indonesian. The remaining force weren't far away, he could hear them negotiating through the scrub towards him. Soon they would have him surrounded. Time to move. Grunting, he regained his feet and sprinted towards another horn blast coming from the road in the near distance.

✳ ✳ ✳ ✳ ✳

"We're gonna have to go, mate!" Mick said, looking at Craig.

Craig held his hand on the horn one more time. "Come on, Finn!" he said, ignoring the older man for the time being.

"Craig!" urged Mick.

"Yeah, I know, Mick. I know, mate. Doesn't look good. Sounded like he put up a good fight though." Craig swore, shook his head, and slid the Unimog into gear. He signalled for Katie, driving the Ute ahead of them, to move off. Easing his foot off the clutch, the truck began rolling along the road behind the Ute.

"I'm sorry, mate," Mick said, rolling his window down and looking out at the forest into which Finn had recently disappeared.

Craig wasn't sure the Vietnam vet was talking to him or Finn, so he remained silent, changing up the gears as the truck began gaining speed.

Mick's peripheral vision caught movement amongst the forest and he leaned out the window to look back at the scrub and silently urging Finn to appear. Come on, mate. Come on!

There! A figure running through the forest towards them; although he could not see whether it was friend or foe. Without taking his eyes off the area of forest, Mick slapped Craig on the shoulder.

"Hold up, son!" he shouted. "Bloody hold up!"

Craig slammed on the brakes the same time Finn exploded from the forest and out onto the road. The Royal Marine was short of breath, red face slick with rivulets of sweat.

"Onya son, get up here!" shouted Mick through a broad grin. He opened the door, jumped down, ran around to the back of the vehicle, and unlocked the tailgate, allowing it to swing down. Breathless, Finn stopped short of the truck and fired several short bursts into the tyres of the pair of remaining vehicles. Grabbing hold of the Unimog, he climbed up onto the rear tray, sat on the bench, and leaned back, trying to regain his breath.

Mick closed the tailgate, locked it in place and ran back to the front of the vehicle, signalling Katie, who had also stopped, to continue as he climbed up into the cab with Craig. The Unimog accelerated again. With Craig working through the gears, the vehicle gained speed. Mick glanced in the large wing mirror and leaned forward, squinting to make sure what he was seeing wasn't some illusion.

"Oh fuck, mate, go, go!" he yelled. It was no illusion. He watched as Indonesian soldiers came pouring out of the forest onto the road behind them. The enemy soldiers opened fire almost at the same time, bringing the air around the Unimog to life with bullets. Rounds ricocheted off the bitumen with loud whines, others cracked beside Mick's head as he ducked low in the seat.

"Can't this fuckin' crate go any faster?" he roared.

Craig changed up into the highest gear and pushed accelerator to floor as the Unimog nudged 100 km/h. Unlike the Australian Unimogs, these weren't speed limited to 80 km/h.

"That's as fast as she's goin'!" replied Craig, watching the Ute in front of them pulling away as it continued to accelerate.

Mick heard a brief burst of return fire from Finn in the back, followed by several thuds as enemy rounds slammed into the truck's body. One bullet passed in between Craig and Mick, hammering a small hole in the windscreen.

"Shit!" Mick yelled, glaring at the tiny hole around which tiny webs of cracked glass had advanced. *If they hit a tyre, we're shit outta luck*, Mick thought.

As the truck rapidly opened the distance, the incoming fire became more inaccurate before ceasing altogether. Mick relaxed slightly, although he knew the enemy would give chase. On the upside, however, both enemy vehicles bore the brunt of Finn's rifle and even if they chose to ignore the damage, they would never be able to match the speed at which Craig pushed the Unimog.

Even if they changed the damages tyres with spares, they would only be able to travel at a similar speed, therefore gaining no ground on Craig's truck. Mick smiled and leaned back in his seat. They were safe.

But what Mick didn't know was that during the contact, several bullets had pierced the fuel tank, allowing diesel to persistently leak. Although the holes were only small, the Unimog would be out of fuel in less than fifty kilometres.

*****

The patrol dragged on throughout the day. Refusing to rest, they pushed on through the blistering midday heat, stopping only once for a five minute break. To his credit, Simanjuntak did not complain or show any pain if he were in any. But then again, Spud knew the enemy officer would have suffered arduous situations himself as the Indonesian forces were pushed ever westward by the allies.

Walking up beside the Indonesian, he grabbed the sock, long ago saturated with Simanjuntak's saliva, and pulled it free of his mouth.

"Drink," said Spud, shoving a water bottle at the officer. He grabbed the man's head, pulled it back, and tipped water into his mouth. Simanjuntak coughed, but held his lips closed, refusing to allow any of the precious liquid to spill.

"Thank you," he said, nodding.

Spud did not reply as he pulled the sock back up into place.

The endless patrol continued with no sign of enemy activity, although the damaged bitumen road told the events of recent days. Heavy vehicles and tracked armour had fled west; some unfortunates unsuccessful in their plight still littered the sides of the highway. What was left of one burned out, blackened truck lay on its side in the centre of the road; the deceased driver, skin burned from his skull, seemed to grin knowingly at them as they past. The crater, which caused the demise of both truck and driver, was at least four feet wide.

Probably a five hundred pounder, Mick thought, glancing at the crater. The driver would have been dead long before he burned to a crisp. That was a good thing at least. They might be the enemy, but Spud hated to think a man suffered slowly before he died, no matter which side he fought on.

As afternoon turned to evening, the patrol continued. Each soldier knew how imperative it was to travel as far east as possible.

The patrol would continue long into the night if Spud had anything to do with it. He knew Jimmy felt the same way. Evening melted into night and still the soft sound of boot falls continued to gently thud along the bitumen as the platoon headed ever eastward.

*****

The Unimog was on empty, forcing them to pull over. There were two twenty-five litre jerry cans of diesel strapped in the back.

"The tanks were nearly full when we set off," said Craig, scratching his head. "I wonder if the fuel tank's been hit?"

He jumped out and checked the first fuel tank, it was intact. Walking round to check the second fuel tank, he saw several bullet holes had peppered the metal. He cursed.

"Lucky it didn't explode!" said Ben, walking over to them.

Mick chuckled. "It's not bloody Hollywood, mate!"

"It's been a long time since I did my driver's course," said Craig. "But I'm pretty sure the mogs carry two sixty litre fuel tanks. So we've got enough fuel to almost fill one tank."

"How far'll that get us?" Mick asked, not sure he wanted to know the answer.

"If memory hasn't escaped me, I think they're good for about twenty litres per hundred clicks, although that's only a rough guide."

"So we can get almost three hundred kays with fifty litres. Thank Christ for that!" smiled Mick. "Let's get her fuelled up and be on our way."

"Sounds like a plan," said Craig, disappearing round the back of the Unimog and climbing up into the back to access the secured jerry cans. There was a shouted curse and Craig jumped back down empty handed.

"Both jerry cans have been hit," the soldier said. "They're empty."

"We can't stand around talkin' about it," said Mick more to himself than anyone else as he passed a hand over his face. "Let's all cram in the back of the Ute and keep going."

Craig shrugged, walking towards the waiting Ute. "It's about the only thing we can do," he agreed.

"How much fuel's left in this thing, love?" Mick asked of his daughter as he climbed up onto the Ute's tray with a grunt.

"We've got quarter of a tank left," she replied.

192

"Fuck me," whispered Mick. "All right, love, let's get going. We'll go as far as we can."

Katie set off, gently working her way up the gears until they were travelling at a sedate ninety kilometres per hour; fast enough to cover distance in the most fuel efficient way.

Craig turned on his radio and double-checked he had dialled onto the correct channel. Time to break radio silence. He brought the hand piece to his mouth and began speaking, fear and hope swirling within him, fighting each other for dominance. After all this, after all they had been through, was this how it ended? Killed by a friendly bomb? It was beginning to seem more likely as the minutes ticked by.

* * * * *

Tanya sat looking out to sea, deep in thought. She had been based at Redcliffe for the last week, deployed along with six Blackhawk aircraft tasked on med-evac. She focused on the distant, tiny silhouette of the USS Ronald Reagan. Usually the sky on any given day was full of aircraft flying at varying altitudes and directions, some on return to the carrier after a mission, others about to conduct gun runs or bombing runs in close support of ground troops in combat. But it was now eerily silent, nothing could be heard but the ocean intermingled with the constant growl of diesel generators in the distance providing power for the Air Transportable Hospital.

Usually she could look forward to up to eight or nine med-evac missions per day to keep her busy, making the days pass at blistering speed. Today, again, was quiet. All ground troops had been withdrawn back to the coast in preparation for the Doom One-One mission commencing that day. Flying had been cancelled and all aircraft strictly forbidden to enter the airspace designated to the B-52s, which was the entirety of inland Queensland.

She heard the pops before she heard the footsteps. Tanya smiled.

"Hi, Mal," she said without turning around. He'd long ago broken her habit of calling him 'sir'.

"Fuckin' good ears you got on ya. They ain't painted on, that's for sure," said Mal Tabb. His hands in his pockets, continuing to pop the small roll of bubble-wrap he had stashed there.

"Any word?" she asked, looking up at the Australian officer.

He didn't need to ask what she was referring to. "No, nothing yet. I'm sorry," he replied. They probably never would. Craig was either dead or very soon would be. But Tanya held hope against hope, refusing to believe that was ever possible. Craig was larger than life, and she knew she would be lost without him.

"I wonder where he is?" she asked softly, not for the first time that day.

Mal popped another few bubbles but remained silent, staring out towards the thin line where ocean met sky.

"Sir? Sir!" a voice shouted.

Mal swore. "Fuck's sake. What is it now, you cock-womble?" he asked, turning to the rapidly approaching private.

"We've had radio contact with a group of people out in the middle of the no-fly zone! Higher think it might be a med-evac!"

Mal exchanged glances with Tanya, seeing the hope in her eyes. She leapt to her feet and grabbed the private's shoulders. "Where?" she asked, shaking him.

"I'll show you the grid reference," he said, turning and running back towards the ATH, closely followed by Tanya.

"Now hang on, you window-licking racing snakes!" shouted Mal breaking into a slow jog for the first time in twelve months. They ignored him. They disappeared in amongst the ATH making for the communications centre. Breathless, Mal slowed to a walk. Could it be Craig? Mal thought. He hoped so, although reality suggested it was more than likely something entirely unrelated.

A deep, thunderous noise enveloped Redcliffe, bringing Mal to a halt. Placing hands on hips, he looked up into the clear blue sky. High above the ATH and turning ominously towards the west flew more than thirty B-52 bombers in a loose formation.

"God help us all," he said softly, a cold chill passing down his spine.

"Hurry up!" screamed Tanya, jumping up and down. "It's Craig! It's Craig!"

Mal turned back towards her and began running again, this time as fast as his legs would carry him. As he ran, he watched Tanya slowly look skyward; focusing on what was the commencement of the Doom One-One offensive. She stood, rooted in place, hands dropping to her sides, mouth slightly open, refusing to believe what she was seeing. As Mal closed the distance, he could see her face clearly. Sadness washed over him as he looked into her eyes and witnessed the moment all her hopes and dreams died.

Chapter 16

"Good morning, you raging, ginger-fucking spunk bubble," Mal Tabb spoke into the phone. "Gotta favour to ask and fast... yup... yeah I saw 'em fly over, and that's not even half the bombers!"

Tanya sat nearby head in hands. With the no-fly zone enforced, there was little to no chance of mounting a rescue mission to save Craig and the others. She would be forced to wait and watch from a distance as he was blown to smithereens.

"Feel like going for a fly? There's a med-evac on," said Mal. Tanya looked up, watching the silent Australian officer as he listened to the voice on the other end of the line. She already knew the answer.

Mal slammed the phone down, shoved a hand into his pocket, and grabbed hold of the small roll of bubble wrap. Several small pops immediately followed.

"He'll do it," said Mal, turning to her.

She jumped to her feet and hugged the officer. "Oh, thank you so much!"

"He owed me a favour, so it's no trouble. But he and his crew have gotta get out from under their superiors' eyes without them noticing. That's the hard bit."

"Where will they fly from?" Tanya asked, shouldering her chest webbing into place and fastening it.

"One of these birds out on the flight line on the far side of the ATH. You're not thinking about going are you?"

"You bet I am!" she said, slinging her weapon and striding out of the door of the comms room.

"I'll have a receiving team prepared in case any of them are wounded or become injured during extraction."

Tanya stopped, holding the door open and turned back. "Mal, thanks again," she said, smiling.

"Go!" he shouted at her, ushering her out the door. "Go!"

She sprinted to the distant flight line and saw the aircrew already on board one Blackhawk, conducting start up checks. Moments later the engine slowly came to life and by the time Tanya jumped on board, legs aching and out of breath, the rotor had started turning.

She plugged her helmet into the communications jack.

"You sure you want to come along on this ride, young lady?" the pilot was looking back at her from the cockpit.

Young lady? Who the fuck you think you are?

"I'm Pararescue. You know what that means, buddy? Trust me, I've been in worse situations than this! We're wasting time here, now get us outta here!" she said, strapping herself in.

The pilot held his hands up. "All right, all right, no offence intended."

The Blackhawk lifted off briskly, tilting forward and accelerating hard. The B-52s had a good head start on them. Within minutes they were travelling close to three hundred kilometres per hour, but Tanya knew it was probably still not fast enough. The green, brown, and tan mash of forests and open fields slid by beneath them in a blur. Leaning forward in her seat, she looked up at the sky above, searching for any hint of the large formation of bombers, but they eluded her.

She grunted as her stomach felt like it dropped into her boots. The Blackhawk ascended violently to zip safely over power lines and a wide road before they descended to tree top level once more. She sat silently, listening to the chatter of the aircrew around her. The loadmasters---one on either side of the helicopter---kept an alert eye out their windows, watching for obstacles, other aircraft, or ground fire and constantly feeding information back to the pilot.

Try as she might, she could not locate the B-52s and hoped they had not commenced their bombing run. Other than the bomber crews, of course, no one knew where the first strike would hit. Which was part of the danger of flying under such conditions, but it was a risk she and the chopper crew were willing to take.

She wanted to do something, but other than sitting in her seat patiently, she knew there was nothing else she could do. So she sat, waited, and hoped.

* * * * *

The Ute made it another fifty kilometres before it ran out of fuel. They had not seen another vehicle or person in that time, so without a way to refuel or change vehicles, their only option was to continue on foot. Craig, Ben, and Finn stuffed as many extra provisions as possible into backpacks and bags to hopefully sustain them until they reached safety.

Mick walked ahead of the group, .303 rifle held firmly in his hands, and Craig brought up the rear, keeping an eye on their six, while the remainder walked in the centre. To her credit, Jade refused to be carried, instead walking beside Ben until she appeared to become tired. Ben then scooped her up, despite her argument, and carried her. Before long, the little girl fell asleep on his shoulder.

They stopped every hour for a five minute break, ensuring they drank a minimum of several mouthfuls of water. After four hours of walking and every person in the group sporting blisters---some worse than others, they felt like they had travelled nowhere. Craig called a halt and they sat amongst the forest on the edge of the road, sipping water and resting. Mick had pulled one boot off, stripped off his sock, and inspected a blister the size of his heel. It had burst, but was still tender.

"You'll live, old man," Ben said, slapping him on the back.

Mick glared at Ben. "Careful, son," he said.

"What? It's not like you'd be able to catch me," Ben said, standing and stretching. Letting out a groan he leaned down and slapped Mick on the shoulder once more. "Isn't that right, mate?"

Mick chuckled and shook his head, pulling the sock back on. "You're living dangerously, boy."

"Ben, you're a smart arse!" stated Jade.

"Excuse me, young lady?! Where did you hear that language?" reprimanded Katie.

Mick coughed and pulled the boot on. "No idea, love, no idea at all," he said quietly, winking at Jade.

"Should have known," said Katie, smiling. Faced with almost certain death, now was not the time to be disciplining her child. They might all be dead in another ten minutes.

"Time to move," said Craig, standing up and moving over to Mick. "You all right, mate?" he asked, touching the older man on the back.

"Yeah, Craig, I'm okay, mate," he replied standing up and accepting a helping hand from the young Australian soldier. They moved on, most of them sporting limps.

"Anyone got any song requests?" asked Craig.

"I hope you can sing better than me," muttered Mick, clenching his teeth against the pain as he strode on.

"Microwars by Kingswood," said Ben. "Love that band."

No one was expecting much, how well could a soldier sing? Although that thought lasted until Craig began singing. The man had an incredible talent. As they walked, Craig's powerful, impressive voice echoed around them effortlessly, moving from rock song to rock song. At one point, he picked Jade up and sang a children's song. The girl rested her head against his chest, listened, and smiled.

After close to half an hour, he stopped singing and drank a mouthful of water.

"Mate, I had no idea you could sing like that!" said Mick.

"Yeah, not many people do. I love crackin' out a song or three every now and then."

With the Doom One-One mission inbound and death more than likely, singing, talking, or walking down a road would put them in no greater danger than they already found themselves in. The songs had raised morale and taken the group's thoughts from the grim future.

It was the distant, thunderous roar that caused the morale to falter and then slide. Craig and Mick looked up simultaneously, silently searching the sky through squinted eyes. Katie scooped Jade into her arms and hugged the child tightly to her chest as fear washed over her.

"What's wrong, Mummy?" asked Jade, looking up into her mother's terror-filled eyes. "What's wrong?"

"Nothing, sweetie," replied Katie, swallowing back tears. "Nothing at all."

The B-52s were flying fast, approaching from the east.

* * * * *

From what Tanya gathered from the chatter between the air crew, the group had decamped a white utility vehicle and were fleeing down the road to the east. Unless she was mistaken, it was along this road they now flew above. How the rotor blades missed the trees on either side was beyond her. She caught glimpses of military vehicles strewn throughout the forest in various states of disarray and destruction. In one area, the forest was black for kilometres in every direction where a bush fire had commenced after the destruction of a small convoy.

Come on! How much longer? There's not enough time! The thoughts swirled in her mind as she stared up at the sky through the flicker of rotor blades, desperately searching for the B-52s and hoping the Blackhawk was winning the race.

* * * * *

The B-52s had banked towards the south, which would bring them sweeping straight over the group's heads. It was difficult to decipher distance when the bombers were at such high altitude, but as far as Craig could estimate, each aircraft was approximately one kilometre from the next. A massive killing ground some twenty to thirty kilometres across.

Craig burst into another song, once more his vocals flawless, but as the huge formation of bombers drew ever closer, their distant rumble began to drown out Craig's powerful voice. The ground began to vibrate gently.

"I'm scared, Mummy!" Jade cried, burying her face into Katie's chest.

"It's okay, sweetheart, it'll be over soon," she soothed the child, tears streaming down her face as she rubbed Jade's back. "It's okay."

* * * * *

"There!" The pilot's voice boomed over the intercom.

Tanya leaned forward in her seat to look through the front windscreen of the chopper, and perhaps four kilometres distant, walked a tiny group of people, looking smaller than ants. But at three hundred kilometres per hour, four kilometres wasn't far to travel.

"Bombs dropping! Bombs dropping!" roared one of the loadmasters.

* * * * *

The first explosion echoed off to the north with a dull thud, making the group jump. Another exploded to their north, much closer this time. Then almost as if on cue, a continuous barrage of explosions seemed to shatter the earth as bombs began falling in a line perhaps two kilometres to their north and coming closer to them by the second.

"Get into the forest!" shouted Craig. "Find some cover!"

Seeing Mick struggling, he ran beside him, placed a hand on the older man's back, and yelled, "Come on, mate! Go! Go!"

Craig then grabbed one of Mick's arms and slung it around his neck, supporting his weight and driving the older man forward. They were the last to leave the road.

"Get behind there!" roared Craig, pointing to a large fallen tree. Lichen had grown along the length of the trunk and it was probably half-rotten, but it was better than nothing.

Mick limped to it and lay face down, exhausted, but weapon still clamped firmly in his hands. He looked over and saw Finn lying behind a small boulder. The younger man winked at him and nodded his head.

The explosions were thunderous, their shockwaves rocking the ground. Mick could feel each explosion vibrate through the ground into his chest. Then, without warning, an even louder noise approached and a dark object flashed past above them. Mick pushed himself up and looked over the log to see the Blackhawk departing fast.

* * * * *

"Lost sight of them!" shouted one of the loadmasters.

No, no, no. Tanya kept her mouth clamped shut, but that single word swirled through her mind, causing both anger and fear to grow in the pit of her stomach.

"Too far, we've past them," said the other loadmaster.

201

The sound of the closing explosions could be heard clearly over the Blackhawk's engine and it wouldn't be long before the bombs were falling around them and adding the real danger of the helicopter being struck out of the sky.

Ascending violently, the chopper turned so hard it felt to Tanya like the pilot had turned a one-eighty on the spot.

"If we don't spot 'em on this pass, we're outta here," said the pilot.

Tanya looked down at the chopper's armoured floor and closed her eyes against the tears.

* * * * *

Craig spotted the helicopter too late and was sprinting out onto the road after it had already zipped over their heads. He stood in the middle of the road and waved his arms in the grim hope one of the crewmen might spot him, but the Blackhawk continued to become smaller and smaller, until it was a dark dot in the sky.

Allowing his hands to hang by his side, he remained planted to the spot, staring at the fast departing copter as the bombs grew closer by the second. Not long now and it would all be over. Then, as the last flicker of hope almost left, the Blackhawk banked so hard it almost seemed to fly upside down before sweeping back down to treetop level and moving towards him.

Craig grinned. Without taking his eyes from the approaching aircraft, he ripped open one of the pouches on his chest webbing and pulled free a smoke grenade. Turning, he threw it behind him, the grenade landing in the centre of the road, lying inanimate for a moment before hissing to life, and sending red smoke drifting across the forest. Turning back to the advancing bird, he waved his arms again, hoping the smoke behind helped silhouette him.

* * * * *

"There!" shouted the loadmaster.

Tanya looked up, hope destroying the darkness in her soul. The Blackhawk flared and began descending fast. Within seconds it had touched down onto the road. They were so close to the barrage of bombs, nothing could be heard over the noise of the explosions.

202

Tanya unstrapped herself and unplugged from the comms jack just after the pilot notified them they would wait no longer than thirty seconds. She jumped clear and sprinted around the Blackhawk to follow Craig, who jumped over a fallen log and disappeared into the scrub.

✶ ✶ ✶ ✶ ✶

"Go! Go! Get on the helo!" Craig shouted.

Katie and Ben were on their feet in a second, Jade in Ben's arms. Finn was running towards Mick, but Craig waved the Royal Marine off.

"I got him, mate, you get on." Craig pointed at the waiting Blackhawk.

"Come on, Mick. Let's go, mate," Craig said, helping the older man to his feet.

"Need a hand?" yelled a female voice.

A second later, Tanya was beside Mick, supporting his other side. Together the two lifted Mick and ran towards the helicopter, the Vietnam veteran protesting all the way. They unceremoniously dumped him in a sitting position onto the Blackhawk's floor. One of the loadmasters dragged him back, lifted him up, and dumped him onto a vacant seat then signalled for him to buckle up. The second loadmaster began briskly handing out hearing protection.

Tanya and Craig were barely on board before the bird ascended and accelerated with violence. The pilot turned hard and Tanya felt herself falling backwards out the open door. Panic ruled. As she began exiting the door, a firm hand clamped onto her arm and pulled her back in. Craig, clamping onto a hard point of the Blackhawk with his other hand, pulled her upright.

He pulled her to him and steered her to a seat before sitting himself. The Blackhawk flew south-east in a diagonal line away from the Doom One-One onslaught. Tanya clasped Craig's hand with both of hers and squeezed. He smiled at her and winked.

"All good," he mouthed at her.

She grinned, relief washing over her. She looked at the others. The older man looked exhausted, although certainly not beaten. His eyes, hard as flint, told her that much. He stared out the open door watching the forest rip by metres below them, an old bolt action rifle resting between his knees, barrel to the floor. Old soldier, Tanya guessed.

The young couple sat either side of a little girl whose eyes were red-rimmed. *The poor little thing must have been terrified*, Tanya thought, watching the girl who was staring up at the young man. The woman sat hunched forward, head in hands, while her partner clasped another bolt-action rifle in one hand, the other on the woman's back. He noticed the girl staring at him and grinned at her, ruffling her hair and leaning down to kiss her forehead.

Tanya smiled and looked away. The last man was definitely a soldier. He may have been clothed in civilian attire, but he watched the land pass by outside with an eagle-like glare that was so familiar to her. She noticed, on the floor clenched between his boots with the muzzle aimed out the open door, lay a British assault rifle, confirming her suspicion.

Looking back at Craig, she laughed as she watched him belting out a song, although she couldn't hear the words over the helicopter's engine. She'd only heard him sing on one occasion and knew just how talented he was.

Thankfully, the terrible, earth-shattering explosions were long behind them and it was not long before the helicopter reached the coast south of Brisbane. Banking to the north, they followed the coastline towards the ATH at Redcliffe showgrounds. Within five minutes they touched down and the chopper shut down.

The flight crew had a hard time departing the area as the small group accosted them, shaking their hands or hugging them, eternally grateful for saving their lives. Craig stood staring out towards the small silhouette of the USS Ronald Reagan anchored on the far side of Moreton Island, Matty's face clear in his mind.

"It's what we do, bud," replied the captain shrugging, almost wincing as Mick shook his hand.

Finally, after almost ten minutes, the crew managed to politely disentangle themselves from the group and headed back to their quarters.

Katie scooped Jade into her arms, hugging and kissing her relentlessly.

"Mum!" giggled Jade, trying to sound reprimanding, but failing dismally.

The group headed towards the ATH where people awaited them.

"Welcome back, arse clowns," said Mal Tabb as the group approached him. "Oops, sorry," he added, seeing the little girl. Craig made the introductions.

"Got a surprise for ya," said Mal, tapping Craig on the shoulder.

"What? An all-in-one blender?" asked Craig, looking mockingly hopeful. "I always wanted one."

"No, you bloody chicken-lipped fuck-eye," said Mal. "Oops, sorry," he added with a grimace, casting a glance in Jade's direction.

He slapped Craig on the back. "No, mate. Come this way; I want to show you something."

The pair walked away, Craig casting a glance at Tanya and shrugging. As they walked closer to the ATH, a small group of medics rounded a corner and stopped. They were staring at the pair and it took Craig a moment to recognise the man that stood between them. His head was half shaved, the other half sporting black, scraggly hair reaching the nape of his neck.

"Matty!" shouted Craig, running forward.

He slammed into his comrade and pulled him into a powerful hug.

"Oi, steady on, mate," said Matty, grinning. "Good to see ya, bro."

Craig stepped away and stared at his fellow soldier. A long scar decorated his scalp where his hair had been shaved back to the skin. He stepped forward and ruffled Matty's hair.

"Nice haircut, dickhead. Where'd you go, Budget Cuts?" grinned Craig.

"Yeah, it's the new in thing," replied Matty, passing a hand through his hair.

"Fuck, it's good to see ya, mate," said Craig. "Come on." He slapped Matty's shoulder. "There's some people I want you to meet."

Stopping, as if he'd forgotten something, he turned back to the medics who had been chuckling at the exchange between the two men. "Sorry, I forgot. Thank you, guys, you saved my mate's life."

"Yeah, they did a good job," Mal said, walking beside the pair, occasionally popping bubble wrap held securely in his pocket. "But it was the medics on board the Ronald Reagan who saved Matty. You scared the living shit out of the sailor guarding the theatre room by the way." Mal looked at Craig.

Matty glanced at his mate quizzically.

Craig shrugged. "I'll tell ya later."

A soldier came running towards Mal. "Sir!" he called, his eyes glinting with fear.

"Oh fuck me, what now dip shit?" Mal said grinning, slapping the young man on the shoulder.

The soldier spoke quietly into the officer's ear, Mal's eyes losing their comedic glint to be replaced with genuine concern and worry. "For fuck sake," he said softly, shaking his head and looking out to sea.

"What's up?" asked Craig.

"There's an entire Australian platoon still out there. They called for dust off and some arse-clown on the Ronald Reagan denied them; told them it was too dangerous to fly. Fuck, I wish I'd know about this earlier!" snapped Mal, punching a fist into an open palm.

"Where are they located?" asked Craig shooting an eager glance across at the still, silent Blackhawks. Although attached to the USS Ronald Reagan and technically coming under the carrier's command element, the aircrew were afforded some freedom of movement operating from the mainland.

"Roughly about twenty clicks from where they picked you guys up," replied Mal.

The trio looked west. They couldn't see the forests or mountains for thousands of houses populating the suburbs of Redcliffe , Kippa-Ring, and North Lakes. They weren't able to hear the bombs exploding either. But the thick, black pall ascending into the sky, looking foreign and sinister against the innocent, gentle clouds, was obvious. The blanket of dark smoke smeared the sky from one end of the horizon to the other, seeming to grow thicker by the second.

"It'll all be over by now," said Craig, placing hands on hips.

"Yeah, mate," replied Mal quietly. "Too late." He swore again and turned away, shaking his head.

"You never know, they might have pulled through," said Craig.

Mal looked at him doubtfully. "You've got to be shitting me, Linacre?"

Craig shrugged. "You never know, mate." But he knew himself there was no hope. It was his way of trying to cheer Mal up.

* * * * *

"Holy shit!" Matty shouted when he saw the group to whom Craig intended to introduce him.

"How the bloody hell did you end up back with old Mick?" Matty looked at Craig.

The soldier burst out laughing and explained, introducing Finn as he did so. Jade ran to Matty and jumped into his arms.

"Your head looks funny," she giggled, gently touching the half of his scalp shaved bare.

"My head always looked funny, remember?"

Jade burst out laughing and snuggled into his chest.

* * * * *

Craig pulled Tanya to him and kissed her. Hand in hand, they walked away from the group towards the eastern perimetre of the showgrounds and looked out to sea.

"Good to have you back," she said, hugging and kissing him again.

"Good to be back," he said as he smiled.

They held one another, looking out at Moreton Island. They hoped and dreamed while they stood holding one another, silently basked in each other's warmth, not knowing what the future held other than the fact it included one another.

The distant, quiet thunder rolled across the area, constant and growing in volume by the moment. The couple looked up, still holding each other close. The huge formation of B-52s screeched high above them, heading North West and preparing to commence a fresh bombing run.

Chapter 17

"Mass bombing raids have commenced in Queensland, Australia. On the first day of bombing, reports suggest more than 3.5 million pounds of ordnance fell on and around The Great Dividing Range. Conservative estimates suggest nearly two thousand Indonesian soldiers killed." – *Adirondack Daily Enterprise (US)*

"What is it, love?" Chris Hollen asked his wife, Therese.

Therese stood, staring out a window of their Narangba home, a western suburb of Brisbane.

"Soldiers," she murmured.

The first wave of bombers had been relentless, the dull thuds of distant explosions continuing ceaselessly for almost half an hour. The entire western sky was black, thick smoke drawing ever closer. Soon the sun would disappear; for how long was anyone's guess. Just prior to the bombings, Chris' neighbour, an old man not long from a retirement home, mentioned the bombing runs would likely drive the entrenched Indonesian soldiers eastward. If that were the case, they would come streaming out of the forest by the hundreds; possibly thousands.

Fear filled Chris as he reached for the weapon he'd taken off a dead Indonesian soldier long before. He pushed in beside her and stared out the window.

At first, he didn't see them. Pulling the curtain back farther, he squinted and raked the forest surrounding their home, finally catching movement to the west. Focusing on the men, he relaxed and leaned the weapon against the wall nearby.

They were Australian soldiers. Their uniforms were grubby, in some cases tattered. Some of them sported bandages covering wounds to arms, legs, or face, but he'd know that uniform anywhere.

"Aussies," he said, smiling and feeling Therese relax beside him.

In the middle of the group strode two soldiers. One of whom was a burly man. The other was a smaller man of Aboriginal heritage. He was lean, wiry, walked with a spring in his step, and wore a large smile on his face. Between the pair, hands tied behind his back, a filthy sock wedged in his mouth, stumbled an Indonesian soldier.

"If you're reading this, you're one of the five hundred households for which we are currently able to cater. We're slowly getting back on our feet, and next month will have our main printing press back in operation. But for now, we have three important words to share with you:

'The invasion's over!'

…now let's pick up the pieces." – *The Brisbane Times (AU)*

Author's Note

Thank you for reading Aftermath, I hope you enjoyed it. If you've been following my journey so far, you'll know that some of my characters are based upon people I have the honour of knowing or have known. These men and women have had a positive, powerful impact upon my life in one way or another.

As a young soldier (a rifleman), straight out of grade 12 and with no life experience, I had a lot to learn. That was in 1996, which feels like a long time ago now. I learned most about soldiering from a lance corporal in another section of my platoon, a man by the name of Craig Linacre.

Craig was not only a smart arse, but he'd leave some of the most skilled singers for dead and was an incredibly good soldier. I lost contact with Craig when he passed selection and recruited into the Special Air Service. He was a great man and one of the finest soldiers beside whom I ever served.

As you might have gathered by now, the character 'Craig', in both The Reckoning and Aftermath, is based upon Lance Corporal Craig Linacre. A man larger than life.

Craig saw combat deployments to East Timor, Iraq and Afghanistan, where he earned the Commendation for Gallantry. Unfortunately, before I ever had the chance to reconnect with Craig, he was sadly killed in a car accident here in Australia, on April 9, 2007.

I'm not sure I can do Craig justice, so I'm passing the reigns over to Troy Simmonds, his best mate, and Taryn Linacre, Craig's wife.

Rest in peace, mate.

Keith.

Craig

One of the most significant things about Craig was his ability to be completely in the moment with people and connect with anyone-from the Prime Minister, to a man that lived in a village in PNG that didn't speak a lot of English. When he spoke to people, he was fully engaged and made everyone feel important. He had an amazing positive energy that everyone was drawn to and I always felt so proud to be his wife.

When he was away in Afghanistan, I always felt 100 percent supported even though he wasn't physically there. He was fun, very grounded and my rock. He was an amazing father to Asha and spent hours playing exciting games with her. He would draw up maps and hide things at the park and they would go on adventures together.

From what I've been told, he was the ultimate professional soldier at work but when he was home, I really never saw that side to him. He was very humble and the most loving, supportive husband and father.

He loved singing and playing the guitar. Most weekends were spent with friends and family having a few drinks, Craig playing guitar and singing with my dad or a friend.

The last time I saw him was two weeks before the accident, when he was flown home to receive his Commendation for Gallantry. It so happened it was on our first wedding anniversary. Craig had written a poem for me on a plane sick bag, which he read out in front of my family. After he died, two cards were found in his room, one addressed to me and the other to Asha, saying how much he loved and missed us and couldn't wait to see us.

Taryn.

Also by Keith McArdle

The Unforeseen Series

The Reckoning: The Day Australia Fell (Book 1)

Australia has been invaded.

While the outnumbered Australian Defence Force fights on the ground, in the air and at sea, this quickly becomes a war involving ordinary people. Ben, an IT consultant has never fought a day in his life. Will he survive? Grant, a security guard at Sydney's International Airport, finds himself captured and living in the filth and squalor of one of the concentration camps dotted around Australia.

Knowing death awaits him if he stays, he plans a daring escape. This is a dark day in Australia's history. This is terror, loneliness, starvation and adrenaline all mixed together in a sour cocktail.

This is the day Australia fell.

Stand Alone Novels

Tour To Midgard: The Forgotten Land

Tasked with a mission in Iraq, an Australian SAS patrol deploy deep behind enemy lines. But when they activate a time portal, the soldiers find themselves in 10th century Viking Denmark, a place far more dangerous and lawless than modern Iraq.

The soldiers have no way back. Join the SAS patrol on this action adventure and journey into the depths of a hostile land, far from the support of the Allied front line.

Step into another world…another time.